BY MADELEINE ROUX

Allison Hewitt Is Trapped
Sadie Walker Is Stranded
Salvaged
Reclaimed
The Book of Living Secrets
The Proposition
Much Ado About Margaret
A Girl Walks into the Forest
These Violet Delights

ASYLUM
Asylum
The Scarlets
Sanctum
The Bone Artists
Catacomb
The Warden
Escape from Asylum

HOUSE OF FURIES
House of Furies
Court of Shadows
Tomb of Ancients

WORLD OF WARCRAFT
Traveler: The Shining Blade
Shadowlands: Shadows Rising

DUNGEONS & DRAGONS
Dungeon Academy: No Humans Allowed!
Dungeon Academy: Tourney of Terror
Dungeon Academy: Last Best Hope

Critical Role: The Mighty Nein—The Nine Eyes of Lucien

Marvel: What If . . . Loki Was Worthy?

These Violet Delights

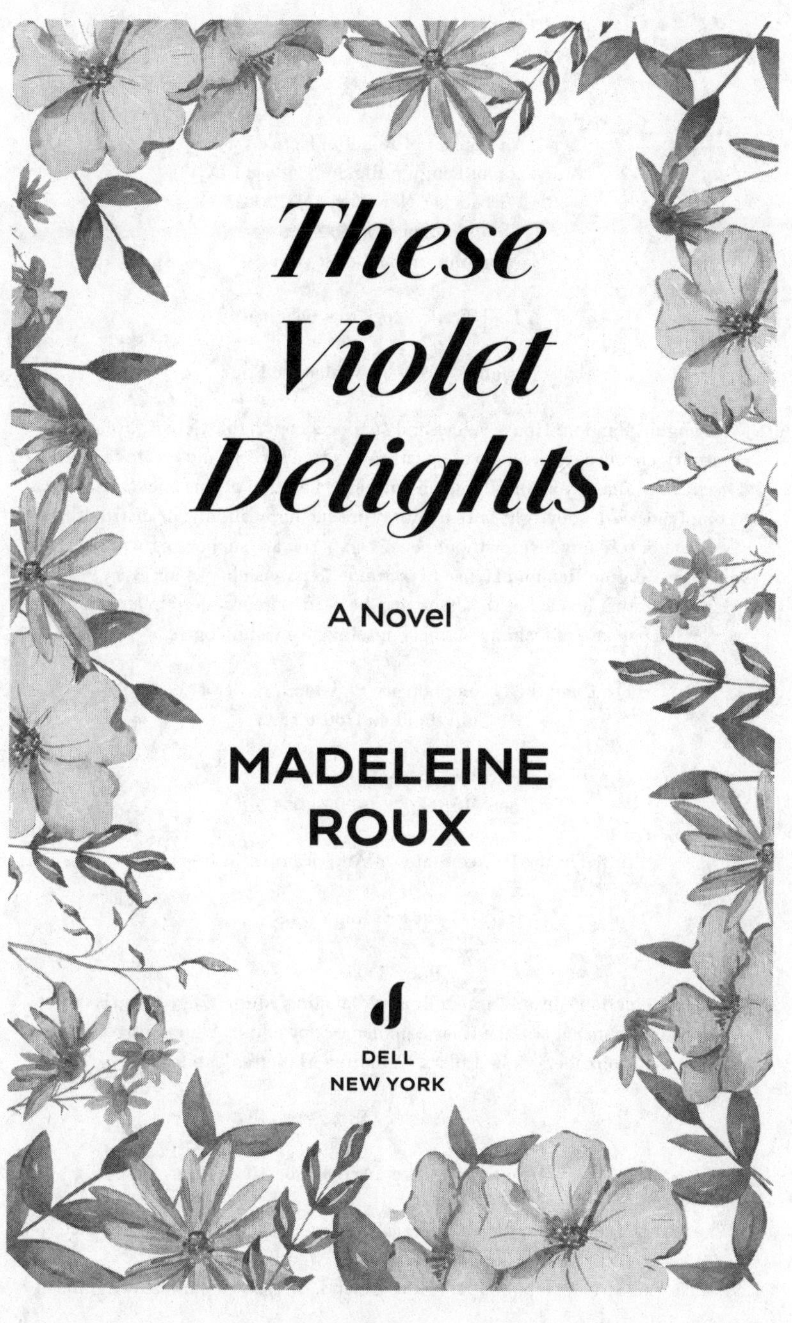

These Violet Delights

A Novel

MADELEINE ROUX

DELL
NEW YORK

Dell
An imprint of Random House
A division of Penguin Random House LLC
1745 Broadway, New York, NY 10019
randomhousebooks.com
penguinrandomhouse.com

A Dell Trade Paperback Original

ISBN 978-0-593-49941-2
Ebook ISBN 978-0-593-49942-9

Printed in the United States of America on acid-free paper

1st Printing

Book Team:
Production editor: Cara DuBois • Managing editor: Saige Francis
Production manager: Jane Haas Sankner • Copy editor: Laura Dragonette
Proofreaders: Julie Ehlers, Catherine Mallette, Jennifer Sale

Book design by Sara Bereta

Interior art: SvetaArt/Adobe Stock

The authorized representative in the EU for product safety and compliance is Penguin Random House Ireland, Morrison Chambers, 32 Nassau Street, Dublin D02 YH68, Ireland. https://eu-contact.penguin.ie

This book is dedicated to the painters
Anne Frances Byrne and Harriet Gouldsmith,
women of immense dedication and passion
who braved the sexism of the day
to share their paintings publicly.

And, as always, for Trevor, with love.

O, she doth teach the torches to burn bright!

Romeo and Juliet—Act 1, Scene 5

These Violet Delights

1

Love is a smoke made with the fume of sighs;
Being purged, a fire sparkling in lovers' eyes;
Being vexed, a sea nourished with loving tears.
Romeo and Juliet—Act 1, Scene 1

London
June 1818

Violet Arden, beautiful, exuberant, and strange, was never expected to amount to much. The second of three daughters in a family of no great fortune, she was supposed to use her looks to advance in the world. Though much was said of her fine features and elegant figure, she was known to her family, lovingly so, as a bit of a fringe case.

To Violet, it was the world that was odd; rules and expectations made the world smaller, duller, and she had always been one to see in colors so vivid they hurt.

"At first I thought it was a shocking disappointment," said Violet, standing in front of a painting that was meant to convince the ton of her emergent skill. Her aunt, Mrs. Eliza Burton, sighed and sharpened her glare. "But then I moved a few feet away from it and realized I might not have fribbled away my time after all. That's painting for you: horrible until it isn't."

"Please keep such observations to yourself," said her aunt, with the amount of exasperation she reserved just for Violet. She reached over and clasped Violet's hand in silken gloves, squeezing. "Remember, you are to pose nicely before your work, smile, and graciously accept whatever compliments arise, or you are to say nothing at all."

With that, Eliza drifted away to spend her evening among acquaintances who wouldn't give her a headache.

Violet rocked up onto her toes, nervous, feeling as if, alone for mere seconds, she were already collecting dust in her aunt's gleaming Mayfair ballroom. This was a home of great destiny, or so Violet believed, for it was not far from where she stood—just in the corridor around the corner, among some tall ferns—that her older sister, Margaret, had first met the man who would become her loving husband.

Violet hadn't known for certain whether she believed in destiny until she'd had a chance meeting with an artist, Renaud Moncelle. Renaud put everything in perspective, the first person outside the family to see Violet's scattered nature not as a weakness, but as an unutilized strength. For six months he had been showing her how the disorganized thoughts in her head could be ordered and transferred to canvas, and now her life was stretching out ahead of her, as real as the bright ivory-and-gold carpet soaring across the floor.

How freeing, how glorious, to be standing right in front of a dream one could wrap one's arms around and hold. Six chaotic, thrilling months had changed everything. *How utterly Violet,* those who knew her would say if, in fact, they knew about the passion that had grown between her and the Frenchman.

"There you are! You look marvelous, though that's to be expected." Here came her sister Margaret, usually called Maggie, golden ringlets suspended like champagne bubbles around her intelligent blue eyes. They took hands and stood at the edge of the mingling guests. "Is it not terribly warm?" Maggie tugged one hand away and flourished a small fan she pulled from a reticule around her wrist, ruffling the damp curls at her temples.

"I can't feel anything," said Violet, trying not to shake with every emotion at once. "Do I look happy or sad? Excited? Mad? Nauseous?"

"Sister, dear, you look . . ." Maggie smirked and shook her head. "I've barely seen you since Christmas, and you are only more radiant. Honing an art has done you a world of good."

Maggie would say as much. She had cultivated a lifelong love for literature and writing, and just the year before, she had anonymously published her novel, to growing acclaim. In doing so, she had met her husband, Bridger Darrow, a man who had risen in all their estimations the day he came to his senses, published Maggie's book, and married her. At the mention of Christmas, Violet flushed.

"Is something the matter?" Maggie asked, her fawn-colored brows tenting.

"What was it like?" Violet began, covering her unease with a question. "Surely you or Bridger have heard criticisms of *The Killbride*, and how did you manage it? I don't know if I'll be able to control myself if someone with no taste and less sense degrades my hard work . . ."

Maggie tilted her head to the side, fanning herself more slowly. "It stings, I admit, but then there is the praise, and you must train your eye to seek the sunlight, not the storm."

"But you *hated* Bridger when first you met! He couldn't breathe without insulting your book . . ."

"Well. It was a temporary hatred, and one I was happy to revise only after *he* revised his wrong opinion."

While they shared a laugh, Violet caught sight of their younger sister, Winny, weaving her way through the forest of varicolored gowns worn by Aunt Eliza's wealthy friends. For a moment, Violet nearly relaxed, but then Maggie took her by the arm and led her away from the wall, toward Winny, asking, "Our aunt has assembled these people to delight in you, Violet. It is a soft crowd easily won, and even if they do not fall in love with your paintings, they will adore the artist. Why sour an evening meant for merriment?"

It was true; they were not among the sharp-eyed and sharper-tongued set who would gleefully rip an artwork to pieces over a misplaced shadow or misshapen berry. Still, Violet had spotted a few strangers who were avoiding the refreshments and studying the art with alarming solemnity. Her mind fixed itself there, circling around all the nasty things they might say.

"Mm," Violet muttered. She wanted to listen to her sister, but it was hard. "Between the very strong punch and the number of cataracts, who could trust their assessment?"

"That's the spirit," replied Maggie, waving to their sister. "Besides, I've never known you to care about what anyone thinks. Why would that change now?"

She flinched. In the past, Violet couldn't give two figs about what anyone thought of her, but now . . . Something had shifted when she met Renaud. He had stuck out at the Christmas party where they met, a king striding among peasants. Their eyes had sparked over the pastillage cherub nestled in sugar flowers, and for the first time in her life, Violet Arden had been speechless. He was so ornate, so sharply defined, so *French.* She couldn't look away from his rumpled rakishness; the intensity of his black gaze made her heart beat wildly. After that—indeed, almost every moment after that until this very evening—

Renaud's eyes had remained pinned to Violet as if she were not a striking young woman of middling prospects and almost no dowry but a Greek muse.

Some would call this foreshadowing, but to Violet, it was that elusive thing she wanted so desperately: destiny. A path. And so, Violet's decision to take up painting in earnest was declared mere moments after she learned Renaud Moncelle was a visiting artist and teacher from Paris who would be spending the next year in England.

Quelle surprise.

That nobody had noticed their budding and, frankly, flagrant romance over the last six months was due in large part to her cousin, Lane Richmond, for his wife had struggled with a difficult pregnancy. All eyes, prayers, love, and care had gone to the young couple, and with mother and child now safe, only recently had anyone in their circle begun to question why Violet Arden, known to be theatrical but never diligent, had all but sprouted paintbrushes from her fingertips and devoted herself to practice.

"What chance!" cried Winny, arriving and greeting her sisters with her usual overflowing cheerfulness.

"Winny, dear, we were all invited," Maggie pointed out.

"Yet it is always to be enjoyed, is it not? And remarked upon—when a family can reunite in health and in joyful circumstances."

Winny, rosy-cheeked and cherubic as the sugar-paste baby that had hovered beneath Violet and Renaud's meeting, looked as well and ample as she always did. With all her might, Violet tried to hang on to that phrase she had just used: joyful circumstances. Yes. *Joyful.* This was meant to be Violet's first foray into being taken seriously as an artist, or as seriously as a female artist could be taken. Only, it was not her ascension alone; Renaud Moncelle of Mont-de-Marsan, then Veneto, then Paris, close personal companion of a close personal companion of Hortense Haudebourt-Lescot, was meant to share in Violet's triumph.

And, more notably, he was meant to arrive ages ago. The man of the hour was more than an hour late. More than two.

Violet knitted her hands together, nervously pressing the fabric of her gloves until the grooves between her fingers were wet with sweat. Renaud was no stranger to a saucy cup (or four) of wine before an evening's entertainment, but he also never resisted an opportunity to be adored.

So where was he?

"Oh, just look at your darling paintings," said Winny, drifting toward the art. One of Violet's watercolors of a basket of fruit on a sill was positioned to the right and slightly below Renaud's rendition of a nearly identical collection of apples. "I thought you preferred portraits, Violet."

"I do," she replied, stealing anxious glances at the archway behind them. "But Ren—Monsieur Moncelle insists that I am not ready, and it is better to master still lifes and landscapes first."

"And you listened?" Winny giggled and craned her neck, her nose perilously close to the canvas. "This bauble you painted here has real charm . . ."

Violet stared at her sister in disbelief. "Winny, that's a grape."

"Oh! I knew that! I was teasing." She was not, and rarely did. "'Tis . . . perfectly discernible, confidently a grape."

Violet snatched the fan out of Maggie's hands and attempted to cool herself. While Winny was swept away by the grapes, Maggie loomed over Violet's left shoulder. Aunt Eliza entered the salon with a retinue that included her short, maudlin husband, Mr. Burton, who had always reminded Violet of a perfectly round robin. His garish red cravat made the similarity all the more striking.

Their aunt, predominately neck and slender as a swan, luminous in her jewels, turned to address the smattering of well-dressed friends that she had gathered. "Oh, yes," she was saying to them, in answer to some unheard question. "Miss Violet is quite eligible. She is the great beauty of the family, and this brief detour into daubery will be forgotten once the right proposal comes along. This is merely an announcing of her many accomplishments!"

"Ignore her," said Maggie, bristling. "I think it's marvelous that we have all found our art—Winny has her stitching, of course, and I have my books, and you are becoming a more accomplished painter every day."

Violet barely heard her. The blood had risen to her ears and begun to pound, first distantly and now with the ferocity of a regiment passing through the parlor. It felt like her toes were vibrating in her shoes. She was aware of the guests moving around her, though all their faces had blurred away to nothingness.

"Mm," she murmured, feeling how hoarse she was becoming. A single bead of sweat traced the line from the damp black curls at her nape to the shallow hollow at the base of her spine. She shivered. "Yes, the Arden girls never could make it easy on themselves . . ."

This was unbearable. She had to confess. She had to tell someone, for Violet had never excelled at keeping her mouth shut and was even clumsier about keeping secrets. Maggie had been so distracted by writing her follow-up to *The Killbride* and so concerned about Ann Richmond's health that Violet's obsession with Renaud had escaped even her notice. And Winny . . .

Well. Winny never noticed much of anything, and they loved her for it.

"What are you talking about?" Maggie asked, coming around to face Violet. She was the littlest bit taller and used that to her advantage, staring down into Violet's periwinkle-blue eyes with sudden intensity, an edge known only to elder siblings. "Violet, you're turning green."

"But where is Monsieur Moncelle? You know I detest to wait upon a Frenchman." Aunt Eliza was sighing, casting her queenly gaze into every corner of the place.

"Come to think of it, haven't seen the man all evening," Mr. Burton added with a winded huff.

"I— We— Oh, Maggie, I've been so foolish," said Violet. It was all coming out in a rush. Every guest surged closer, as if they meant to pile on top of her.

"Will someone search throughout the house, please?" Aunt Eliza was trying to summon a footman for just this purpose. "These artists, so prone to wandering, utterly imprisoned by their whims. I should have chained him to the punch table!" Her hot beam of a gaze fell on Violet, unblinking, as if daring the young lady to move a muscle. *Stay right where you are.*

But Violet couldn't have fled, though she desperately wanted to.

"More foolish than usual, I mean," Violet stumbled on, avoiding Maggie's searching eyes. "I meant to tell you and Winny before this, and Renaud was going to be here with me. I was going to tell you everything, and if he was telling the truth, then he was going to d-declare . . . declare that he's seeking my hand—"

The footman had just started through the arch that led to the lofty front hall when a body collided with him, coming in haste from the opposite direction. The footman's wig flew off as he tumbled into one side of the arch, and a ripple of noise spread across the party, a rising tide of gasps and shrieks, as a young woman forced her way in.

"No! Oh! Corbyn, who is this person?" Mr. Burton was already on his way toward the stranger.

Somehow, Violet knew what this was before it even began. The widening pit in her stomach whispered with terrible prophecy. Two footmen stormed in from the front hall and tried to grab the young woman, but she wrenched her arms free.

"I will be heard! I will not be silenced! Where is he? Renaud! Renaud?" Her voice cracked. Even afraid, Violet felt a pang of sympathy; she recognized herself in this person, with her jittery eyes, her pallor, the tight, sideways purse of her lips, as if they were tired of holding back secrets. "But he should be here! I see, I see, it matters not!" She threw off the footmen again, strengthened by a desperation Violet also understood.

Maggie clutched her; Violet had begun to sway.

"You! It is you that fetched him away, stole his heart. You that made him false to a loving fiancée of three agonizing years!" Now the woman hurried toward them, toward Violet. She pointed an accusing finger; there were marks on her ungloved hands, and the hem of her dark green frock was torn. Even shabby as she was, there was no denying her good looks—an upturned, elfin nose, full lips, a pointed chin, and thick waves of black hair, all of it so like Violet's own appearance. "Look at my face!" she screamed, finally caught and held by the footmen, who gathered her close and tried to force her toward the archway. "Do not forget it! I hope it haunts you, you . . . you . . . thief of hearts! You will never have him, Miss Arden! Whatever his promises, whatever his lies, you will not have him. Let the whole world know your secret: that you are but liars in love! Renaud Moncelle belongs to me!" She tossed and bucked against the footmen. "Unhand me! That hurts, stop! Stop it this instant!"

But she was carried away, kicking and screaming, her final, broken shriek striking Violet like a well-aimed shot. The whispers thickened like portending clouds, her own name sizzling on a dozen tongues, flickers of lightning, Aunt Eliza's shocked gasp the sizzle before the total unleashing.

Now everyone knew her secret.

Not like this, she thought. *Not like this.*

Violet managed to stay upright, shielded by the bodies of her sisters as she retreated to the one place that felt safe—her favorite painting, the one of fruits that Winny had been so enamored with. Everything else in the vicinity turned—the wine in her own stomach churned violently, and the light from the chandeliers hanging overhead crackled, then dimmed.

"Vicious speculation! Who could take the word of a complete stranger? Well! Well! To think! That man will never be welcome in this house again!" She could hear Aunt Eliza's voice above the crowd. Already, she was trying to spin the evening into something less embarrassing. If Aunt Eliza could not save face, she would invent a new one out of whole cloth.

Maggie fanned her. "Can you hear us? Violet? Violet? Oh, Winny, get her some punch, she's faint!"

Violet perceived them just fine. Two men stood near them, insensible of or uninterested in the drama that had played out. Violet could see only the backs of their heads; the man closest to her, just behind Maggie, was tall and imposing, adjusting a pair of spectacles and inspecting her painting at various distances with the air of a person who lived to espouse an opinion.

"This is practically that," he muttered with utter disdain.

"Derivative and silly," he added in a cold undertone. "And for no one."

Then, he and his companion were gone, winding through the whispering and gossiping as if impervious, upright ships slicing through a gathering storm. Violet stared at the man, watching him go with laughter spilling out of her. And so what if her work was just like Renaud's? He had taught her to love art. He had taught her to *love* . . .

And wasn't that love? To be perfectly entangled. *Indistinguishable.*

"I loved him," Violet said, hiccupping. Maggie fanned her again and then held her.

"I know, sweetling."

"I should have told you . . ."

"You tried, didn't you? We should take you away from here, Violet."

"Yes, everyone is staring," Violet whispered. This was to be her debut. Her triumph. She and Renaud would show London their beautiful paintings and their love. Maggie lifted her up, and Winny appeared, and together Violet's sisters helped her toward the library and the stairs in the hall beyond, carrying her away from the erupting scandal. "If only I could speak to him; there must be some reason, some . . . *something.*"

Maggie and Winny brought her to the stairs, and Violet climbed them on all fours, realizing she couldn't feel her hands or feet.

"I don't think that will be possible," Maggie told her.

"No," said Violet, heartbroken, insulted, and ill. "No, I suspect I will never speak to Renaud Moncelle again."

2

Crowns in my purse I have and goods at home,
And so am come abroad to see the world.
The Taming of the Shrew—Act 1, Scene 2

September

Alasdair Kerr had been considering going home for years; he lacked only the necessary inducement to finally get on with it.

Ah, he thought. *And here it is, with the accuracy of Atalanta's bow.*

He watched the room fall to Julianna within heartbeats of her entrance. The late afternoon sun swarmed to her with almost religious fervor, cradling her and brightening her reddish-gold hair until it burned. A dozen or so others had gathered in Robert Daly's overthought hall, but they may as well have been phantoms beside her earthly beauty. Even slight, even delicate though she was, there was a weight to her steps that reminded him of a marble statue. With her pure simplicity, she made the room—grand enough for a prince but furnished by a festooning pretender—seem even more unpleasant.

Julianna was there for the same reason he was—a promise of hidden treasure.

Her eye for art was perhaps even more developed than his, which was why she noticed the small table and raced toward it before realizing Alasdair was already there, silently staking his claim.

"You're still in London," she said, her mouth rounding with genuine surprise.

"Hello again, Julianna."

She curtsied, and he bowed, though the drift of her hair and clothes through the air filled the space around them with her dizzying scent. His expression crusted with ice. Tucking his hands behind his back, he kept his attention firmly on the tiny painted table.

"I thought you would be in the country by now," she said, airy. Was that annoyance he detected or regret? Whatever it was, he felt it, too. All of it and more, pain and frustration and rage, though he wouldn't let her see it. The only satisfaction to be had now was in flatly denying her. His time. His attention.

His anger.

"And you in Vienna," he observed. "Yet, here you are."

"Here *we* are. Unless everything is to be my fault."

Alasdair's nostrils flared. Across the garish, terrible chamber, Robert Daly bayed with laughter. He was holding court, fiendish and smug about the gathering and what was on offer; Daly, no doubt leveraging his friendship with the Duke of Kent, had managed to commission George Dawe. That painting wasn't for auction today, but it was becoming clear this whole affair was really meant to be about everyone congratulating him over the piece. Alasdair fussed with his spectacles and fumed over the table, pretending not to be jealous; Dawe was about to go abroad, and nobody knew when he would return to England and make himself available.

"Here we are," he echoed, ignoring the needling other bit. "For the table."

"The table," Julianna agreed with a wistful sigh.

It was a darling object. The artist who had decorated it was obscure, but there was no denying their command of light and shadow. Clusters of purplish-blue bilberries hid in the enameled corners, so ripe and fresh, the details so expertly plucked out with hints of carmine and grayish green that they looked real enough to pick up and eat. Curling sprigs of forget-me-nots and violets flirted along the edges. It was a relief to have found it; he had been all over various auctions and private exhibitions that summer, but none of them produced. He had very nearly been tempted by a few amateur studies, but then the evening had taken a strange turn, and his view of the work had soured. But this table! A relief. And it was just the sort of furniture his mother would adore having in her piano room—their piano room—when the family home was rebuilt and all was back in its right place.

He had always wondered what his mother might make of Julianna, his sometime paramour, but now it was clear he would never find out. Perhaps it was for the best; Lady Edith Kerr preferred demure, pious women, as evidenced by the many she had placed in front of Alasdair in the hope he would marry one.

Out of the corner of his eye, he noticed Julianna arch a fine brow in his direction.

"You really want it, don't you?" she asked, drawing out the word *want* in such a manner that Alasdair almost flinched at the indecency. When they were still courting, that sort of thing would have driven him mad. "You can just say it, you know. I wish you would say it. In fact, if you do, I won't fight you for it."

"I'll outbid you," Alasdair told her flatly, his face maintaining its cold mask.

He chanced looking at her and found the sight of her luminosity unexpectedly sickening, like a cream puff crammed in the mouth after one was already stuffed from dinner. She was too much now that he had diminished to so little. *Withered. I've withered. And yes, it's all your bloody fault.*

Her golden eyes sparkled with emotion, sadness or pity that came too late. When she frothed up like this, her Bavarian accent thickened her words. "But you wouldn't have to. You could have the table for a song. Nobody else is interested; they just want to see the Dawe, of course. I am your sole competition, but not if you simply tell me how much you want to have it."

Julianna stared at him for a long moment, silently imploring. He would have the table. When he desired a thing, he got it.

Well, except Julianna.

Even after destroying his hopes, here she stood, demanding things he couldn't give.

His mouth became a fissure in the frosted stone of his face. "No."

Julianna stepped away from him, her right hand fluttering nervously over her exposed neck. All of her was ethereally pretty, but her neck was perhaps her most alluring feature. He could have just let her have the table, but now pride was involved. Julianna blinked once, very slowly, then let her hands fall together in a soft loop.

"I don't know why I expected anything else," she said, then drifted away from him and back toward her brother, Elias, with whom she had arrived. The pair approached Robert Daly, probably to discuss the table. Behind him, centered between two tall windows, was the Dawe portrait everyone was whispering about. It was an enviably adroit painting of Robert's wife, the reds so bold they looked like smears of blood over Robert's shoulder.

Alasdair had met Robert at Cambridge; Robert was affable if domineering then, but a social lighthouse to Alasdair's floundering skiff. He had even been the connection that gave Alasdair entry into the Tenebris Circle, an outrageously exclusive club of art afficionados who sold rare pieces only to one another. Now, between the noise and the boastful Dawe, he was just domineering. Had they been similar once? Perhaps. But now their differences couldn't be more evident; Robert needed all eyes on him whenever possible, while Alasdair vastly preferred solitude. Alasdair liked a good, solid home; Robert wanted to live inside Parisian mille-feuille.

Even the rising portraitist Sir Thomas Lawrence was there that day, dowdy and balding but doing his best, suffering through Robert's speeches with a pained expression, one that Alasdair was certain matched his own. Alasdair looked around the hall with glacial impassivity, discovering he felt nothing for anyone in the room, including—increasingly—himself.

Then, he glanced down at the charming painted table, itself a sort of beacon.

I must go home. I must rebuild Clafton.

He waited until Julianna and her brother had concluded their conversation with Robert; she gestured back toward the table, spoke more to Robert, then made a hasty exit afterward. The room seemed lighter after she had gone, though less lively. Other women, wives mostly, had sacrificed their afternoons to come. They hovered by the windows farthest from the Dawe melee, dreaming of places other than Robert Daly's raffish hall. He approached Robert as one might an aggravated hornet's nest: slow steps, vigilant eyes, waiting for the crucial moment when the man stopped to draw breath.

Alasdair politely intervened, offering his respects to Sir Thomas before pulling Robert aside.

"That table in the corner . . ."

"I knew you would want it," said Robert, smirking. He had immense hair, copiously piled, and was sharply dressed, as any true Brummell devotee. When they had both taken up river swimming at Cambridge, it had slimmed Robert down fashionably but managed to somehow make Alasdair bigger and broader. Robert's watery blue eyes flashed. "Your lady wants it also. What am I to do?"

"Please. She isn't mine," Alasdair replied, gruff. "But I will have the table."

"Miss Holzer has already named a price, though you'll have no trouble matching it."

"I thought she would stay longer," said Alasdair, frowning.

"Thought or hoped? She isn't some uncivilized beast, Alasdair. She wouldn't dare be seen aggressively bidding, nor aggressively doing anything. She made a polite bid, feel free to recklessly exceed it. Afterward, gift the table to Miss Holzer. That ought to impress her."

Maybe Julianna ought to do more things passionately, and perhaps that was the bridge that was missing between them. "I told you—she isn't mine."

Robert lowered his head and clucked his tongue, uncannily like Alasdair's own mother. "My good fellow, you ought to have both. A pretty wife to stand beside a pretty table, isn't that just what every man requires?"

"Two hundred," said Alasdair.

Robert's eyes widened. "Pounds?"

Too loud. The guests swarming the portrait of Robert's wife recoiled while Alasdair flinched.

"Just wrap it carefully, it must survive the trip to Clafton in one piece."

He turned to go, and Robert called after him, laughing playfully. Mocking him, maybe. Alasdair stiffened, plunged inside himself, and lengthened his already lengthy stride. "Is that where you're off to, then? To brood across the countryside?"

"Home," Alasdair told him shortly. "I'm going home."

—

The road to Warwickshire was long and muddy, but Alasdair had always been a confident rider invigorated by exercise and country views. Going home was perhaps easier said than done; back in the county of his origin, he passed the little church at Cray Arches and the inn, taking the northerly road that sliced through a forest of silver birch. There was a small path that ran alongside and eventually veered west, which met up with a lane that led to the Richmond property. Trotting through the birch, he came upon a narrow little bridge, one that had featured prominently in his childhood adventures. He smiled at the memories of two boys spending forever afternoons on that bridge, kicking off their shoes to let their toes cool in the water, then popping up onto the boards and demanding tolls from passersby, who humored the lads with a farthing or two.

He urged his horse faster down the road. The bridge of his nose itched, sweat gathering there beneath his spectacles. The birch gave way to yet denser forest, a woodland sprawl thickened with beech and hawthorn. He didn't look too hard, knowing that somewhere beyond that beauty lay a wound etched into the landscape. Another mile along and the road split, the left fork leading to Sampson Park, a place that was his but that he only ever considered as belonging to his mother.

Some distant farm had been burning its leaves, for a gust of smoky wind traveled down the road at him, enfolding him, making his eyes water until he shook it off. He turned his shoulder against the watchful west, the site of his last joyful days. Clafton had once risen like a gray spike from the hillside, towering above the wood, but now, destroyed, it was no more than a suggestion of what had once been.

He'd left one day for Cambridge, a tender and cheerful nineteen, and returned to a smoldering ruin and the burden of burying his father. The fire might have killed him, too, had he been at home, for it chewed most ferociously through the west wing, where his father's libraries and study were, and where Alasdair had slept as a boy. The smoke-tipped wind came again, insistent, and, succumbing, Alasdair breathed it in, letting it cover him like a shroud.

And so, he came to Sampson Park, while only ever thinking of his true home, Clafton, and the fire that claimed it.

The two buildings couldn't be more dissimilar. The road carried on west across the hills just as the forest dropped away. Alasdair urged his horse down a pebbly path that curled east, guarded by iron gates with a scrolled top, and those firmly shut. There was nobody there minding the entrance to Sampson Park, so Alasdair slid down and opened the gates himself, then led his horse on foot, shaking out the cramp of so long a ride. Red, papery wild cherry trees had been planted at intervals along the well-manicured drive. Looking at them now, he could all but taste the bursting cherry brandy their cook would make with the summer crop, and he wondered if there was any left for him in the kitchen.

With his inebriate little brother, Freddie, at home, likely not.

Ahead, Sampson announced itself with all the subtlety of a peacock flouncing in a pleasure garden. It was a pale, Palladian confection built a hundred years ago by a successful London merchant who had been all too eager to sell it on after nearly bankrupting himself constructing the thing. The gardens were luxurious, though nobody ever seemed to use them. The drive split to circle a grass lawn, a lonely wind scattering leaves across the façade. It seemed a place that ought to be lively, filled with the laughing Robert Dalys of the world, but instead it was quiet, withdrawn, a great stone lady in hiding.

Or in mourning.

Maybe the quiet would soothe him, wipe the smell of smoke from his nose and mouth, bring him back to a necessary calm. He could imagine inviting the builder to Sampson, where they could sit together in the cold light and sip cherry brandy. They would nod over the plans while his mother was tucked away in another part of the house. Sampson Park was so spacious that they need not stumble over each other. He had just come around to the idea of all that heavenly peace when he heard the raised voices inside. They spilled out as a footman met him at the door, louder as the disagreement echoed through the cavernous front hall.

Alasdair handed over his hat and gloves, marching through the house to the sitting room that overlooked the back gardens. The doors there were propped open, the bonfire wind from the road blowing inside, and his brother, Freddie, was there mid-step. Or at least he was until a book of sermons sailed by his head, thunking off a statuary with one arm.

"There is certainly no need for that!" Freddie was whimpering, shielding his head against further projectiles. His younger brother was almost Alasdair in miniature—several inches shorter, but with the same golden eyes and thick, waving brown hair. Freddie favored their mother more, mirroring her slight proportions and narrow chin.

"On the contrary!" Their mother was not in robust health and hadn't been since the fire. The physicians they brought to the house said she had taken on too much smoke, permanently damaging her body and imbuing her with visible frailty. She still sat by the overbearing carved Stanton fireplace, the book of sermons she had thrown taken from a stack on a table beside her chair. "We must always guard ourselves against deceit, is that not so, Mr. Danforth?"

Lady Edith hoisted another book, preparing to throw it, but Mr. Danforth, her constant companion and ever-consulted clergyman, deftly tugged it out of her grasp.

"Alasdair!" Freddie shouted, bounding into the house and racing over to him with a growing smile. "Thank God, you're here."

He could tell from the flurry of staff on the periphery of his vision that they were alarmed by both Lady Edith's outburst and Alasdair's arrival. His mother's eyes widened below the frilly edges of her cap. "But were you expected?" she seemed to ask herself first, then Mr. Danforth. "Are we expecting him?"

"I wrote," said Alasdair.

"He did," Mr. Danforth confirmed. He was of a similar age to Alasdair, dressed in neat and sober black, and by far the comeliest clergyman in the county. There was a decided slipperiness to Danforth's smile that never settled well with Alasdair. "Remember, Lady Edith, his room was to be made ready, and his wardrobe aired out. You gave the instruction yourself just last week."

Lady Edith frowned, puzzled, then relaxed into a grin and beckoned Alasdair forward. "Then, it is a blessing. There was joy in the learning it from your letter, and joy now in the remembering! You must forgive an old woman's memory . . ."

"There is nothing to forgive," Alasdair assured her. He went to her and received her greeting, which was a light pat on his hand while he bowed. They had never been an affectionate bunch. "I do wonder, however, what I have stumbled upon." He swiveled toward his brother, who seemed poised to run back outside if necessary. "Would anyone care to provide an explanation?"

"Frederick has always been defiant and unruly, but now he has simply gone too far," said Lady Edith. She took another book from the pile, and this time Alasdair intervened to take it. "No! He should be punished."

Beside him, Mr. Danforth made a soft, strangled sound.

"For what, exactly?" Alasdair asked.

"For a passing comment. I said only that Miss Emilia Graddock looks well these days," Freddie supplied, eyes fixed to the carpet.

"*And* that you had been to Pressmore to see her!" Lady Edith croaked, receding into a mound of heavy blankets. "She is a Richmond in everything but name! You have been coming and going, coming and going, and now I know it was to skulk away and see *that girl* in secret." She craned her neck to look up at Alasdair, then reached for his hand, her papery skin hot from the blazing fire at their backs. "You are home. Oh, thank God, thank God, you are home. Will you speak to him? He is profligate, I say, profligate when you are gone, son, and you are gone all the time."

Gone because you begged me to go.

Alasdair tucked her featherlight hand back onto the chair's arm, then went to his brother, nodding toward the front of the house. "Come, we will have this all untangled straightaway."

"It was only a passing comment," Freddie mumbled, allowing himself to be led away. They returned to the front hall, then took the wide staircase carpeted in deep blue, ascending to the landing while doors and windows were opened and closed hastily, a soft drumming in distant rooms. "It is a blessing you've returned, brother. I say, I am not the wild one at all. It is Mother who has lost her senses, emboldened by that cunning little rat, Danforth."

"Mother relies on his constancy," said Alasdair. "We could have been better sons in Father's absence, provided more comfort."

"How could we?" Freddie squeaked. "You'd need a broadsword to sever them. Besides, neither of us shares her convictions. She may have just tried to cave my head in with *A Discourse on Pain*, but soon she will be engrossed in it again. She isn't strong enough to attend church, so it must come to her, and thus, Danforth. We cannot give her what he can."

"And maybe that is our failing, too."

Freddie shook his head. "You are not the failure here. You have always done exactly as she asked."

"What's this about a Richmond girl?" Alasdair asked. It was just like Freddie to try to worm his way out of confrontation by throwing someone else out onto the road. There was a frenzy of activity in the hall outside Alasdair's rooms. He watched a stream of sheepish staff hurry by with crates laden with books, folded cloths, and diaries.

"Danforth's things," Freddie said with a sigh. They waited until the rooms were quiet and empty, and Alasdair went inside. It smelled wrong somehow. "He was using your chambers, you know. Mother allowed it. *Insisted* upon it."

"I suppose nothing has been done to prepare for Gordon's arrival, then."

Alasdair crossed to the tall window beside his four-poster bed and urged the casement open; immediately the fire-tipped air blustered inside, and he thought better of it, shutting the window with a *thump*. Even the cloying ambergris ghost of Danforth's presence was better than smelling smoke.

"Gordon?" Freddie shifted out of the doorway, a footman returning with the small number of items Alasdair had packed in his saddlebags.

"The builder. Does anyone at Sampson speak to one another? I warned of his imminent arrival. The east pavilion was to be made ready for his ease and comfort while Clafton is rebuilt."

Freddie's golden eyes burst with stars. In a few eager steps, he was at Alasdair's elbow, mouth open, quietly mystified. "You're really doing it. You're resurrecting the old beast."

Alasdair flinched at his choice of words. "I haven't been running all over the continent hunting furnishings for the place only to let them rot in a London warehouse. Mother has sent me after enough statuary and art to fill Clafton six times over."

"How marvelous! How utterly marvelous! And, of course, I am at your disposal."

"Yes, I imagine you are keen to make yourself useful." Alasdair took advantage of his proximity, grabbing Freddie by the forearm and bringing them nose to nose. "So. The Richmond girl. What has made Mother this agitated? Surely, it was more than a *passing comment*."

The blood drained from his brother's face. Even through his sleeve, he could feel Freddie go cold. Just as swiftly, red pinpoints gathered in his cheeks. "There is some truth to what she says."

"Some?" Alasdair's grip tightened.

Freddie winced. "More . . . m-more than some."

"Christ, Freddie, the years march on, yet here you remain, an utter fool."

"What!" His brother retreated, hugging his arm to his stomach and perching on the sill. In the early evening light, his brother looked perfectly angelic. Freddie was anything but; the man had left a string of broken hearts across the county, seducing anything with long lashes and a coy smile. Alasdair went to find the brandy he knew would be hidden in the globe near his writing desk. The compartment, however, was empty, filmed with dust, and he groaned.

"If you only saw her, you would understand."

Alasdair snarled, turning and leaning against his desk. "If I saw her, I would ignore her and choose quite literally any other woman in England. Use your head, brother; where the Richmonds are concerned, there is but one rival for Mother's hatred, and that's the devil himself."

"I know," Freddie whined, dragging out the words. He continued gazing out the window, though now Alasdair knew it to be deep and pathetic pining.

"Cut her out of your thoughts," Alasdair told him, sharp. "What is forbidden is always tempting, but you were given a mind to temper your heart."

"Cut her out of my thoughts? I would sooner cut off a limb! Can you not at least try to take my side against Mother's? She is so dour now, so unhappy; a wedding would cheer us all."

"You will please leave your arms and legs where they are and forget this misguided obsession. In time, you will see it for the distraction it is. What's more, Mother will not be swayed; nothing nourishes a sick mind quite like a grudge."

There was one other place Alasdair kept a hidden bottle: a retracting drawer on the top of his desk. He flicked the handle open, hoping for luck, but was confronted with scarcity. Scraps of paper had been left behind there, the beginnings of a Sunday sermon. Alasdair rammed the drawer closed and punched his hands, knuckles down, into the worn surface of the desk.

"Bloody Danforth," he spat.

"And what, pray tell, makes you so qualified to dispense this advice, brother?" Freddie sneered, though there was no malice in it, just desperation. Could it be? Did little Freddie actually care genuinely for a woman? No, it didn't matter. Anyone associated with the Richmonds was out of the question. "Is a wife soon to follow you here? Has love come for you at last?"

"No." An image of Julianna flashed across his mind unbidden. He ground his teeth together until the muscles in his jaw ached. "No, I have returned to rebuild our home. For me, there is Clafton and nothing else."

3

Our wills and fates do so contrary run
That our devices still are overthrown;
Our thoughts are ours, their ends none of our own.
Hamlet—Act 3, Scene 2

The women ventured out early on a brisk, bright autumn day. Violet and Emilia left Pressmore by the rear doors that spilled out onto a stone path that wound down to a broad, still pond. The water was sapphire glass, unmoving, sluggish from the bracing cold. Near a cluster of climbing wisteria along the back wall of the house, Ann's scraggly gray goat, Puck, munched along the verge. One of the Richmond tenants had tried to get rid of the creature, but Ann, with her too-big heart, had taken pity on the thing and let it come to Pressmore. Everyone regretted it and came around to the farmer's view, for Puck lived up to his name, mischievous and wayward, and prone to putting his horns to unexpecting backsides.

Violet, who also had a too-big heart but didn't know it, likewise chided Ann for taking in the impish goat; lately she had been hardened against many things, specifically romantic love, men with spectacles, the color green, and the French. She had been at her cousin's estate in the country for months undergoing this darksome transformation, and though most of the household remained consumed with the arrival of Ann and Lane's first child, care had been taken where Violet was concerned.

Unspoken yet felt was the fear that, now sullied, Violet would be tempted to slide further into ignominy; she had damaged her reputation by dallying with the Frenchman, and she could not afford even the specter of misbehavior.

By and by, her good humor returned, but not, unfortunately, her appreciation of spectacles and love. Once more, to the rich and meddlesome Aunt Eliza and Aunt Mildred, it had become clear that the Arden women could not be trusted with the safekeeping of their own destinies.

Violet and Emilia were two footsteps outside when Cristabel Bilbury appeared, yawning and wrapping a knit shawl tightly around herself. Cristabel was Ann's doing. Ann Richmond, pretty, fashionable, connected, knew everyone who was worth knowing in London and, concerned that Violet would give up her painting just as she had been forced to give up Monsieur Moncelle and her tolerance in general for the French, had arranged for a new painting teacher. Cristabel, decidedly English, had arrived at the estate just after Violet.

"Forgetting something?" Cristabel asked.

"Oh!" Violet blushed and scrambled. "We thought it would be rude to bother you so early in the day . . ."

"And we weren't going far!" Emilia added, helpful.

Violet fidgeted with the foldable easel under her left arm. Cristabel went where Violet did, part tutor, part chaperone.

Grinning at Emilia, Cristabel shook her head of lush, graying curls and shivered beneath her shawl, then stepped out to join them. "You are not so quiet or so sly, and you are fortunate only I heard your giggling . . ."

Violet narrowed her eyes. "Then you will tell no one that we tried to sneak away?"

"That depends entirely on the quality of your painting today." And with a gleeful cackle, Cristabel took her by the arm, leading Violet away from the house. The older woman's grip was strong; Miss Bilbury possessed a tall, broad frame, hale and reliable, her every word and gesture precise, utilitarian. In short, she was nothing like the Frenchman.

That was what he had become: the Frenchman. Her sisters forbade her from speaking his name, and in their insistence and intensity, Violet detected embarrassment. Maggie in particular seemed angry at herself that she had let Violet fall under his spell; she was also relieved that Violet had, for the moment, put aside men to focus on herself.

"How will I improve if I am always to be observed?" Violet muttered.

"A true artist will persevere under any circumstances," said Cristabel. "Whether on top of a mountain or under the sea, watched or alone, it should make no difference. Do you want to paint, or do you want to complain?"

Emilia, who had graciously volunteered to carry the canvases and supply case, didn't seem too disappointed in having a tagalong, and she started down the hill. Puck bleated at her as she went. "Well!" she called over her shoulder. "She is right! We will have a jolly day no matter what, won't we? Come! Paint me in those old ruins across the water. It will be terribly romantic." And she raced ahead, practically floating over the grass, her burgundy skirts and the little dagger points on her spencer jacket trailing.

Violet paused briefly to tilt her head up toward the sky,

taking in the quality of the light and the delicious freshness in the air. Then she stuck out her tongue at Emilia's suggestion that the painting would be at all romantic. Moody? Perhaps. Atmospheric? Certainly. But romantic? *Never.*

"Hm," said Cristabel, standing beside her. "It is a lovely day to be tolerated."

"You know we don't mean anything by it," Violet replied. "We are used to ruling this little fairy kingdom of Pressmore. No chaperones, no watchers . . ."

"I've no interest in hindering you. You will come to see painting as the freedom it is and succeed, or chafe against a prison of your own making, stagnate, and fail. I know which I would prefer to see." The painter shrugged and picked her way down the hill, Violet following.

The Arden girls had been allowed to do as they pleased as children, encouraged and enabled by their doting father. He had never scolded Violet when she stood on the dining room chairs to recite (or shriek) a monologue from Helena or Titania. Mrs. Arden found Violet's obsession with acting out Shakespeare's heroines concerning, but not Mr. Arden, who would kneel and listen and clap or gasp where appropriate. Whenever little Violet did something truly objectionable (hiding one of Maggie's books in a fit of pique, stealing Winny's ribbons before a ball, chasing the chickens too energetically in the yard), he would come roaring into the room with a mighty "Full of vexation come I, with complaint against my child, my daughter Violet!"

Instead of frightening her, it made her dissolve into giggles.

They were nearly to the water, where they would veer right along the still, blue edge until they reached the bridge that crossed the stream in the forest.

"Where did you go?" Cristabel asked, observing Violet with her alert gray eyes. She was always observing, sometimes so fiercely it made people freeze. But ever since taking up the paintbrush, Violet understood what her teacher was doing. She was studying the light, deciding if a shape on the face was gray or blue or dark brown, watching the way a wallpaper or coat changed the colors that bounced along the cheek and chin.

"I was thinking about my father," said Violet.

"Have you ever painted him?"

"No." Violet pressed her lips together firmly. "I don't think I could. I would cry and spoil the whole thing."

"Which is precisely why you should do it."

Violet shook her head. "I've sworn off painting men."

"That will somewhat narrow your available commissions," said Miss Bilbury, laughing.

They crossed the bridge, where Emilia was waiting for them on the other side. Leaves scattered around them, blown across the path by a wind rich with the smoke of far-off burning leaves, a scent that somehow reminded Violet of being home in the fall no matter where she happened to encounter it.

"There!" Emilia pointed up a hill that rolled into another one, and at the top, a broken crown of gray stone. "The grass is wet. Watch your feet, please."

The journey took them nearly a mile from Pressmore and painted roses on the ladies' cheeks. By the time they climbed the slope to the ruins, Cristabel was huffing and puffing, leaning a little against Violet.

Emilia trotted into the ruins with no compunction whatsoever. Violet, however, paused at what had once been the back façade of Clafton, chilled by an imagined breeze. Yet again, Cristabel studied her.

"Should we fear the spirits that linger here?" her tutor asked.

"No . . . I don't know. I haven't been here since the fire destroyed the house. Maybe it's pity I feel and nothing more, pity that they lost their father in the blaze. He was said to be a great and generous man, and I know what it is to lose such a person suddenly." Violet scrunched up her face, confused. "And that will be the first and last time I feel pity for a Kerr."

"That stupid feud," Emilia spat bitterly, waiting in a long shard of light that speared through a missing window.

Violet grimaced at her. "It isn't stupid. Besides, you should revel in it. 'Tis like something from one of your beloved novels."

Emilia seemed only put out by the suggestion. Cristabel released Violet's arm and surveyed the patchy ground and various places where one might pose a sitter, interrupting them to say, "Set up your easel, Violet. The light will slip away faster than you expect. Hurry now. Did you pack a picnic? We will starve."

While Cristabel continued to criticize every aspect of this ill-planned adventure, Violet set out her things and began to work. Emilia posed in a pretty pool of light on a thick fallen column as Violet opened her jar of water and lined up her brushes. No sooner had she touched her pencil to the canvas to begin sketching than Cristabel had thoughts to share.

"Why do you attack the canvas so? Did it give offense? Relax your hand. Do you want to be Moncelle?" Looming over her, Cristabel pinched the knobby bone on the outer edge of Violet's wrist.

"Certainly not," Violet muttered. She shared a pained look with Emilia.

"We aren't supposed to say his name," Emilia whispered. Cristabel ignored her.

"Then stop sketching like him! Light strokes. *Light.* Decisive only when you have begun to understand the face!" She picked up Violet's empty palette and whacked her lightly on the back of the head. Violet persevered, determined, her brow drawn low over her eyes in concentration. She had finished blocking out the column and Emilia's skirts when Cristabel piped up again. "Is that what you *think* her skirts look like, or is it the truth before your eyes?"

Violet rubbed out her error, quietly fuming, annoyed that the eminent Miss Bilbury, who had joined and withdrawn from the Royal Watercolour Society several times, whose rendition of hydrangeas and grapes had been widely lauded until it was discovered to have been painted by a woman, was right.

"Observe more," said Cristabel, stern. "Think slower."

"I only think one speed," Violet replied miserably. "At a gallop."

That made her tutor laugh in earnest. "Too clever, Violet, that is what you are, imprisoned by that cleverness. A painter is not smart, they are patient and receptive."

After a while, they were both satisfied with her sketch, and Violet began to mix her pigments.

"So," Cristabel drawled, standing behind her with a hand tucked under her chin. "You can paint something besides the woman in green."

Violet blanched. In truth, she had become fixated on the woman who had burst into her aunt's exhibition and accused Violet of stealing the Frenchman. Lately, she had done nothing but try to capture the lady's exact expression of outrage and sadness. With every iteration, Violet noticed a troubling slippage, a transference between their faces; after a while, she was painting herself in that green dress, horrified and imploring, her broken heart on display for all the world.

"I couldn't get her quite right," Violet replied softly.

"Ah. Yes. That's because this fool Frenchman has made you a mimic, not an artist in your own right. No matter. We will tear him out by the root until we find the violets hidden among these weeds."

On the tumbled stone, Emilia whimpered. "That's quite harsh."

Cristabel glared until Emilia went silent. "The sitter will say nothing and squirm even less, thank you."

With nothing but the waxwings at the edge of the wood to fill the cold, quiet air, Violet began to paint, and Emilia, for those hours, became her sole concern and obsession. The young women had much in common—they were both two and twenty, both younger sisters to boldly energetic ladies who had married and settled, and they shared a love of art, literature, and theater. Emilia, however, hailed from a wealthy family; she was the daughter of a colonel who had made his fortune in the West Indies, found love there, and sent his two lovely daughters back to England. Violet, therefore, did not protest the chance to paint the lady, luminous in the autumn light, but rather, she found the ruins of Clafton unsettling and could not understand why Emilia insisted upon it.

"Can we not speak at all?" Emilia asked, jutting out her lip.

Cristabel leaned over Violet's shoulder. "You have captured her mouth, I suppose, and that is where the likeness of a person lives. What could possibly be more urgent than art?"

Emilia visibly relaxed. "Why, finding Violet a husband, of course." And before Violet could protest or point out that she had written off love, Emilia clobbered her way through a list of bachelors. "What about Mr. Delridge? He is tall, although I find his very small eyes disconcerting. Or Mr. Prandle? Did you meet him over the summer?" Emilia asked.

Violet's brush moved swiftly but gently over the paper as she began to carve out the slender shadows beneath Emilia's chin. "How can you think of romance in a place like this?"

The black curls framing Emilia's face bounced as she shrugged, then returned to her careful pose. "Are lovers not often trotting off to ruins in the novels you like?"

"Certainly," said Violet, glancing up at the broken walls hemming them in on three sides. Though Emilia sat in an advantageous wedge of sunlight, Violet herself was enfolded in the unforgiving shadows cast by what remained of the estate. Only her hand, creating more and more of Emilia, felt a touch of warmth from the sun. "It all seems far more romantic when it's in a book. A terrible fire destroyed this place, but that was well before you and Ann came to Pressmore. We were visiting Lane the summer it happened; I can still remember the great clouds of black smoke. There was a haze in the air for a whole week . . ."

"How awful," Emilia murmured. She looked forlorn; perhaps she felt the same chill that crept across Violet's back and up her neck.

"The Kerrs have given up on it, I think," said Violet, turning to the little folding table they had carried along. Upon it, she mixed her pigments, eager to capture that slight melancholy in Emilia's expression.

"More color," she heard Cristabel mutter. "In her eyes, do you see the hint of carmine? Do not paint vacancy where there is life."

And Emilia was full of life. Young. Vibrant. So, it wasn't surprising that her sadness converted seamlessly into joy. "Oh, no, there you are wrong, Violet. Have you not heard the news? It is all over Cray Arches. The gossips at Gray and Simon are beside themselves!" Gray and Simon, a shop for hats and accoutrements, was where Violet and the other young ladies of the village spent an inordinate amount of time agonizing over ribbons and buttons; Winny practically lived there. "Mr. Kerr has returned from abroad, and it's said he has been seen spending money from here to Lighthorne Heath on the best stone and timber."

Another tickle of frost raced up Violet's spine at the words *Mr. Kerr*, for the only Mr. Kerr she knew about had died in this doomed and dilapidated place. Although now that she thought on it, he had been *Sir* Kerr, which meant . . .

A dreadful image flashed before her: the back of a head, sandy brown, the silhouette of a towering man with a devastating manner about him. *Derivative and silly*, he had sneered directly at her art. *And for no one.*

She was thinking too much again. Cristabel drew close.

Put it—him—and his scornful opinions from your mind.

"I never pay attention to what the Kerrs do," Violet sniffed.

"But why should that be so?" Emilia pressed. "There are two eligible men in the family, are there not? Yet nobody will tell me the first thing about them, all because of some ridiculous feud . . ."

Violet's head snapped up. "I love you like a sister, Emilia, and you have not lived here long, so I will not tell Lane of this." Emilia's sister, Ann, had married Violet's cousin Lane just two years earlier at Pressmore. Thus, she could not expect Ann and Emilia to feel the kind of loathing decades of enmity engendered. "You will notice none of the Kerrs attended Ann and Lane's wedding, and there is good reason for it—"

"Well, yes, they were not invited," Emilia interrupted. It was her turn to sniff.

Shaking her head impatiently, Violet slashed her brush across the canvas, applying the lightest piece of the sky visible above the ruins. It was gray there, and getting grayer, thicker clouds gathering. She did not appreciate Emilia's skeptical eyebrows. This was family lore, and family lore was sacred. "You mustn't make light of it, especially in front of my aunt. You see, it began long ago when Lady Edith Kerr, then unmarried, thought she had well and truly won Mr. Richmond. Of course, she was wrong, and he was besotted with Aunt Mildred. Drinking vinegar would have made Lady Edith less sour, and she spread vile rumors about Mildred and the family. Then, there was the hedge maze disaster—"

"What could possibly be serious about a hedge maze?" asked Emilia.

"It does sound frivolous," Cristabel added, which won her a scathing glare from Violet, aimed over her shoulder.

As her words became more heated, her brush swished faster. "Aunt Mildred now has the finest hedges in the county, which did not sit right with the Kerrs, who had boasted to anyone with ears to listen that their gardens would never be outdone and Clafton never outshone. I think we both know how that turned out." She paused to gesture vaguely around herself with the brush, then dunked it in water. "I heard Lady Edith nearly fainted when your sister, Ann, had the Grecian temple built . . ." Here, Violet paused, and Emilia raised an eyebrow. "And Sir Kerr, who was always excessively proud of his well-stocked pond, never extended an invitation to fish to our uncle or to Cousin Lane."

This list did not seem to move Emilia even a little. "These hardly seem like meaningful trespasses."

Violet painted faster and faster. Now came the very tops of the broken walls, glazed with buttery light; now the faintest cool red of the leaves that tried to infringe upon what had once been a soaring room fit for dinners and balls; now the halo of blue signifying the top of Emilia's head . . . "And the fire that ruined them. Everyone knows it was done by the youngest boy, Francis—"

"Freddie," Emilia corrected, breathless. After all their talk, she had finally gone still.

"Yes, thank you, Freddie. He's feral, that one. You mustn't think him eligible, not for me, not for you, not for anyone. He isn't fit for the Vauxhall cages, let alone polite society. He's lamed two horses racing through Anselm and Cray Arches, and we all know his antics will kill Lady Edith any day now."

"Violet," Emilia whispered, this time more urgently. At last, Violet careened to a stop, looking up from her work. She peered between Emilia and the portrait—there was a frantic life to the painting so far, an instinctual, loose movement to this first layer of watercolors that she had never achieved before.

As if reading her thoughts, Cristabel Bilbury gave a mild "Hm" that sounded terrifyingly like approval. "Perhaps I should let you chat away after all," she said.

"Ha! Maybe you should. I haven't even mentioned the eldest son," said Violet, more deliberate, more managed. She mixed another set of paints, impatient to continue.

"You shouldn't. It seems wrong to speak ill of the family in the ruins of their home."

"It was your idea to come here." Violet set down her brush, letting the first layer of thin paint dry. It occurred to her that she had been painting Emilia but not *seeing* her. She studied the young woman, the slight purse of her full lips, the downward slump to her shoulders, her strained grip on the book in her lap . . . What was she missing? "Why did you insist on this place?"

Another sound from Cristabel, this one musical with curiosity.

"I . . . thought it would be exciting, but now I see my error," said Emilia after a moment's pause to think. Her eyelashes fluttered, and the faintest roses bloomed dark across her brown cheeks. "I didn't know your family hated the Kerrs so much."

"It's your family, too," Violet pointed out. "Your sister is a Richmond now, and Pressmore is your home. I may not be all that fond of Aunt Mildred, but I can at least take her side in this."

Aunt Mildred, a Richmond by marriage, had most recently taken up the crusade for Violet's older sister, Maggie, who defied Mildred's wishes and married a man who had scarcely a penny to his name. It had caused something of a rift in the family until things turned around for Maggie and Bridger Darrow, who together, by and by, earned money from his publishing of her book. Aunt Mildred was quiet on the subject now, but only because her doomsaying had come to nothing.

"I always knew clever Margaret would find her way," Aunt Mildred had said to Emilia and Violet just the previous afternoon while discussing the family during a stroll through the gardens. Emilia and Violet had suppressed their skeptical laughter; Aunt Mildred loved to be right, and the girls knew better than to argue with a widow who had nothing better to do than take constant accounting of the family's fortunes, past, present, and future.

A harsh, rattling wind rustled the trees encroaching on the ruins. Violet looked up, her attention taken, that gale tugging at her hair and her gown, demanding something she couldn't interpret. She often felt herself drawn to similar vague portents and tried never to resist them. *The world around us is constantly trying to teach us things*, Miss Bilbury had told her when they first began their relationship, and Violet agreed. The silvery music of a sudden rain shower, the kitchen door creaking early on a late summer morning, the protective scream of a crow guarding its nest, they all felt like messages from an unseen world.

Maybe that was why she had devoted herself to painting when she had never devoted herself to anything but her sisters—it was a chance to capture the secrets hidden in what others considered the mundane.

She let the wind tug her. Violet turned away from her easel, looking out the gap where a window had once been. Clafton sat on a hill twin to the one that lay across the water. There, whole and happy and teeming with life, sat the wonderfully lush bouquet that was Pressmore Estate. Beadle Cottage, where Violet lived with Maggie and Winny, their mother, and Bridger, was not a mile from it, yet Pressmore seemed a nation of its own. The extensive gardens and woods made Pressmore feel like a fairy land, or perhaps that was simply the imposition of memory and nostalgia; Violet and her family had passed so many pleasant summers there, having picnics, playing pirates and highwaymen, every milestone of girlhood to womanhood marked by the plain magic of the place.

"The Kerr boys would play with us when we were children," Violet heard herself say. The memories emerged as if from a dream, blurred, simplified to shockingly bright colors. "The younger one, Freddie, and Alasdair. They used to take a little rowboat across the water from here to there. Freddie always had frogs in his pockets, and it frightened Winny. We didn't know anything about the feud then, and if we had, we probably would have laughed at it. What fun! I've always enjoyed doing what I shouldn't . . ." She trailed off, softly wistful.

"What were they like?" Emilia asked, and it sounded like she was smiling.

"Loud. Wild. Lane is shy now and he was shy as a boy, so

we would have to stand up for him," Violet replied with a laugh. "Alasdair was big for his age. I remember he always wanted to be in charge. That did not sit well with me."

"Shocking," said Emilia, wry.

"Indeed. The last day they ran off to play with us, he pulled my hair so hard that I chased him down the hill to thump him, and we ended up rolling and rolling . . . We were both covered in filth and grass, but it was so silly we forgot to be angry at each other once we landed by the water." Violet hadn't thought of little big Alasdair Kerr for ages. Unbidden, the memory took on a hard edge of bitterness. She sighed. "They came back the next day only to tell us we were disgusting creatures, unladylike, unfit for their company. And that was that."

"Surely their parents filled their heads with that nonsense."

"Surely. But I was only little, and all I knew was that I had lost a friend."

Violet returned to the painting, memory's hold on her releasing. To Emilia, she must have looked very serious, consumed by her work, but inside it was all racing thoughts and tumult. Whatever happened to those boys? How did Freddie become so wild? There were nasty rumors about him, not just that he had caused the fire that destroyed Clafton, but that he had broken hearts across the county, gaining a reputation that disappointed his pious mother. And the other one, the older brother, Alasdair, had seemingly vanished. One day he was covered in grass and mud, playing pirates with her in the endless days of summer, the next he was gone. Violet herself had never worked with oil paints, but she had spent hours watching Cristabel do so, struck by how a swipe of solvent across the picture could remove the color, leaving behind just an impression, a faded ghost of once-bright shapes.

Hours slipped by. Morning gave way to afternoon, and the

light changed into something warmer while the air shimmered with a chill. "I don't know," began Violet, standing back to judge her work. "You were right, Emilia. There is something romantic about this place, feud and all. Yet I know something is missing. Never mind, stay back—it isn't any good at all."

Emilia ignored her, smelling lightly of lilacs as she rushed to Violet's side. Emilia stretched her stiff limbs, then her eyes widened. She hugged herself, glancing down at her shoes, then back, shyly, at the painting. "How can you disparage it so? It's lovely, Violet. Truly." She turned toward Violet's tutor with a searching look.

"Better than what came before" was all Cristabel would grant. Derivative and silly it was not. She touched Violet's shoulder lightly, and there was approval in it. Violet didn't move, seeing only the flaws. "Better and better, that is all a teacher can ask." Turning back the way they had come, Cristabel sighed. "But now, as I knew I would be, I am very hungry. We should return to the house before the weather turns."

Emilia twirled, delighted still by her portrait. Then her stomach gurgled with hunger, and she laughed. "Miss Bilbury has the right idea—we've earned a nice, long tea in the gardens, or in the temple! It sounds lovely in there when the rain comes."

"You two go ahead," said Violet. She nodded toward the easel. "Just once, I want to paint something and feel like I've triumphed."

"I cannot even tempt you with Martha's scones?" Emilia pouted. "I could smell her baking them fresh this morning before we ventured out."

"No, we will go," said Cristabel. She stared into Violet's eyes, recognizing the impulse that told Violet to go again. While Emilia embraced Violet and hurried toward the archway leading out from the ruins, Cristabel patted her shoulder again with quiet, flinty approval. Violet's heart swelled; it felt more validating than all of the Frenchman's effusive, flowery praise, which he heaped on Violet whenever she made so much as a slightly thoughtful brushstroke. And it felt good, hopeful, to discover she could want this, want to keep going, without him.

"Anything but the lady in green, mm?" Cristabel asked, squinting.

Violet gestured to the small hand mirror she had tucked into the supply case. "A self-portrait, I think. Finally. I like the clouds today, the shadows . . . it suits my mood."

"Just be mindful of the rain," said Cristabel as she left. "It will ruin today's work."

Then, alone, Violet picked up the mirror and started sketching what she saw. The hours passed, the clouds clumped while the shadows stretched and thickened, but she saw her own image, resilient even in that encroaching darkness. By and by, she appeared on the canvas. The sketch must be perfect, a skeleton for the paint to be draped across. A delicate figure peered out at her, and as she mixed her pigments and painted her own eyes—large, prying, periwinkle—the power and awe of the ruins appeared in the reflection.

She hadn't quite finished, but, standing back, she was overcome with what she had managed, and happiness, so fleeting in those days of first heartbreak, fluttered in her breast. Maybe it wasn't hopelessly terrible.

But that was short-lived. It was getting dark, and those clouds, once simply moody and inspiring, had become genuinely threatening. Violet hurried to put away her things, realizing with a start that thunder was rolling across the hillside toward her. No, she thought, stopping, hands frozen into claws, thunder was felt first in the chest, not in the ground. A horse was approaching, storming into the ruins, hooves drumming hard.

Violet shoved her wooden case of supplies closed, latching it, though she knew she had left many things behind. She felt suddenly guilty and knew she shouldn't be caught there. This was a serious place, draped in sad memories, not to be made light of or defiled. Yet there she was, caught out as the rider burst through the break between two crumbling walls. It was not yet evening, but the iron sky melted one ghoulish shadow into another, and the man and his horse seemed a punishment, a haunting. The man was as immense as the horse, with a hat and dark coat, the whites of his eyes as vivid as two dashes of vigorously struck paint.

She was at once familiar with the stranger, drawn to him, and repelled by the shrieking cry of his horse as it reared and then crashed back down, upsetting her easel. Violet's heart raced; her self-portrait was nearly trampled beneath the beast's hooves. With a gasp, she stumbled away, clutching her packed paints and brushes.

"Do you know where you stand?" the rider demanded, shouting at her.

"I'm . . ." There was a small archway through which the comforting promise of Pressmore Estate could be seen. Violet threw herself that way, realizing the horse and rider couldn't possibly follow through the narrow opening. "I didn't mean any harm. I didn't mean . . . I wasn't . . . I merely wished to paint—"

"Leave," he commanded. "Leave this place!"

Violet swallowed a scream of fright. The rider calmed his horse, backing away, and the last gracious splendor of sunlight withdrew from the ruins, falling across the man's face for one instant. The light flickered strangely over his eyes, reflecting off spectacles. Familiarity turned to recognition, and recognition turned to disgust. It was the man from her aunt's exhibition in London, the one who had sneeringly insulted her work even while she wallowed inches away, shattered and at her lowest.

Derivative and silly. And for no one.

"You! *You.*" She paused in the archway, her eyes widening. An image of him resolved, like a portrait painted in a heartbeat. The sandy brown hair and honey-gold eyes, the size, the posture. It appeared the village gossips had been right about Clafton Hall rising again. So, the oafish little boy had matured into a monster; that made perfect sense. He was, after all, a Kerr. He drew up his shoulders, expanding impossibly, as if he were no man at all but an apparition.

Violet wouldn't give him the satisfaction of running; she raised her chin and strode toward the lip of the hill, hoping he saw the challenge in her eyes.

4

What Fates impose, that men must needs abide;
It boots not to resist both wind and tide.
Henry VI, Part 3—Act 4, Scene 3

The ruins were meant to be empty.

It was meant to be a graveyard, not occupied by the living.

Tomorrow, the first wagons would clatter up the hill to bring timber and stone, and the builders would fill the place to assess what of the remaining hall could be repurposed or folded into the restoration. Alasdair had wanted one moment alone with Clafton before it became overrun with strangers. He had not expected the woman to be there, or for her arresting eyes to fill with anger at the sight of him.

He hadn't expected his heart to stop either, but some faces demanded stillness.

Yet he had chased her off. Her face, her beauty, was known to him. Had they met before? Perhaps he had been too eager to shout, but then, nobody was meant to be there. This was solemn ground, a monument to grief, and he would suffer no trespassers. He looked around, realizing he was in the shambling remains of the west wing; his father had perished there, and if he listened too closely to the hollow, rising wind, he heard his faint whisper.

There you are, Cub. You've been away too long.

Alasdair slid from the saddle, tucking his crop under one arm and striding to the scattered easel and canvases on the ground. The offense he had taken at the woman's presence remained lodged in his throat as he knelt to flip over one of the paintings. That arresting face stared up at him with the same impertinent mouth, not open in surprise as he had just seen it, but the lips slightly parted in dawning realization. It was a self-portrait of the lady, and a good one.

"Incredible," he whispered.

And you screamed at her like a lunatic.

He glanced up at the broken towers that seemed to stand in judgment of his every move. Julianna considered him an emotionless hunk of stone, no different from the pillars surrounding him, but here the protective membrane of his stoicism thinned, and his chest tightened until he could hardly breathe. Looking again at the canvas in his hands, he was struck by the idea of a lady coming here to make new life in what he regarded as a tomb. Art, after all, was an act of creation. It was something he longed to sit with longer, but a fat raindrop slapped against his cheek. Alasdair swore under his breath and gathered up the other painting that had been beside the fallen easel, then ripped off his coat and wrapped it around the canvases. They were watercolors, and the smallest bit of moisture could destroy them utterly. Why he felt desperate to preserve them was a question to be interrogated later, preferably beside a fire.

The ride back to Sampson Park was a race against the clouds. Hilary, a groom who had served the family since the days when Clafton stood proudly on the hill, met him in the drive. Before ducking into the front hall, Alasdair directed him to send someone back to the ruins for the easel and anything else the woman had left behind. She was no doubt local to the area, and returning her possessions was the gentlemanly thing to do.

Returning the painting, however, was less attractive.

Alasdair found the house in a state of practiced bustle; the dinner chime would sound soon, but he had an hour or so to change before sitting through a tense meal with Danforth, Freddie, and his mother. He wasn't looking forward to it; if the evening before was any indication, he was staring down many strained, uncomfortable dinners in his future. Freddie, hotheaded and opinionated, could not possibly contain his dislike of Danforth while the clergyman extolled the virtues of sobriety, piety, and propriety. All of the *-iety*s, really, none of which Freddie embodied. It was little better for Alasdair, who had heard similar speeches from his mother since boyhood and was far more interested in discussing the Clafton rebuild.

As requested, the staff had placed a bottle of last year's cherry brandy in the hidden globe compartment in his chambers. It was perhaps not so hidden anymore, but needs must. He unwrapped the paintings covered by his coat and placed them against his desk, cheered to see that they had survived the rain. Discarding his wet shirt and damp breeches, he fetched out a dressing gown and sipped brandy while positioning the watercolor self-portrait on a short bookcase to the left of the door and across from an obliging window. He wiped the lenses of his round spectacles on his sleeve, finding them stained with dried raindrops.

"Thank God for those silly spectacles," Julianna once told him, laughing. "Without them you'd be too, too menacing."

It was true that he had his late father's hulking size. Sir Kerr had always insisted that came from the Scottish blood in their line, that one boy in the generation always inherited the Highlander strength. Alasdair had hated it as a boy, finding that others assumed him to be a bully, but now, nearing thirty years of age, he didn't mind it so much. Strangers tended to give him a wide berth, and that suited him just fine.

The world blurred around him, dimmed by myopia until he perched the lenses back on his nose. He scrunched his face, adjusting the spectacles higher, standing several paces away from the bookcase. With the knuckles of his right hand tucked under his chin, he studied the self-portrait. The artist had achieved an inarguable likeness, which was always preferable, but there was more to it. Her lips were shaped into a question, her shockingly cornflower-blue eyes fixed forward, staring directly into him, *skewering* him. He felt his own lips part in the same breathless expression, as if compelled by the subtle magic of the piece. Chuckling to himself, he realized his error; those intriguing eyes weren't meant for him but reflected the intensity of the artist's self-study. She was questioning herself, lost in her own image, yet somehow the painter had avoided all the usual maudlin pitfalls of self-portraiture. It was the insistent use of blues, he decided, that made the painting truly special. There was nothing coquettish about it, which was an achievement, he thought, given that he knew the creator was a woman. No, this was forthright, candid, almost brazen.

What do you see in me? the figure asked. *What do I see in myself?*

Something thumped against the wall to his right. Alasdair noticed he was still holding his brandy, half-sipped, then heard that infuriating noise again. Then a voice, and as it sharpened, he realized someone had been knocking and calling his name for a good long while. Alasdair leapt forward, opening the door to his brother.

At once, Freddie's eyes landed on the brandy and sparkled. "Good God, man, are you besotted?" He wrenched the glass out of Alasdair's grasp and drank what was left. "Give that here. I thought all the drink was removed from the house . . ."

"Cook found half a bottle of last year's brandy," he said, words coming to him slowly.

"Lucky, that. Danforth prevailed upon Mother, of course, and now it is rare even to have wine with dinner." Freddie marched to the globe to refill the glass. He paused with the bottle's neck in the air, his eye landing first on the portrait of one young lady, and then on the other propped on the bookcase. The sun had almost vanished, leaving them in the bruised gloom of twilight. "Why is it so bloody dark in here? And where did these come from?"

Alasdair retrieved the glass as Freddie hurried by. If the brandy was almost gone, then he wasn't about to let Freddie have it all.

"But this is Miss Emilia Graddock!" his brother half shouted. He snatched up the other painting Alasdair had rescued from the rain and marveled at it with the dazed abstraction of a man in love. "Wait a moment, how did you come to have this?" Freddie tore himself from the amorous brink and noticed the self-portrait again, squawking with laughter. "That is Violet Arden! God help us all if Mother sees either of these . . ."

The brandy soured on Alasdair's tongue.

"Violet Arden?" he repeated. A memory, some fifteen years old, slammed into him from behind, and he surged up onto his toes. "Didn't we play with her and some other children at Pressmore a hundred years ago?"

"Exactly so," Freddie said, still gazing at his apparent lady love. She *was* beautiful, he'd give Freddie that. "I used to chase the Arden girls with muddy fingers and a legion of frogs. They hated it! It was a lot of laughs until Mother put an end to it. Do you remember? She had our little boat dragged from the pond and chucked in the back garden to be filled with chrysanthemums." Freddie managed to look away from Emilia Graddock, squinting at Alasdair. "Were you just now standing in the dark gawking at Miss Arden?"

Alasdair rolled his shoulders, trying to ward off the cold feeling slithering into his stomach. "It can't be her."

"Well." Freddie snorted. "It is."

He lifted the brandy to his lips and downed it in one. The burn was clarifying. And cauterizing. Lord. He would never give Freddie the satisfaction of a confession, but indeed, he had just lost himself standing in the dark and gawking at Miss Arden. Yet every memory of her that remained from childhood was vexing. She was a whirlwind of stentorian opinions and instructions, proposing increasingly demented schemes for who would play what sort of pirate in the forest, perching on any available rock to perform monologues with her grass-stained chin pointed to the heavens.

It occurred to Alasdair that he had been away most of his life and that Freddie, with his penchant for seduction, might know Violet Arden better than most. He didn't like the shiver of disgust that ran through him at the thought.

"One of your conquests?" he asked, hoisting a brow.

"Her?" Freddie nearly dropped the painting. "God, no. She would eat me alive."

Alasdair glanced back at the self-portrait of Violet. Now

she appeared to be smirking at him. "Enjoy that while you can," he said, nodding toward the painting in Freddie's hands. "It goes back to Pressmore tomorrow."

"Can't I keep it?" he whined. "It's very good."

"It is very good, and no, you can't have it."

The dinner bell chimed, summoning them. To dine at Sampson was to chew and swallow beneath the weight of a hundred painted eyes. Since the day he was finished at Cambridge, Alasdair had been dispatched to hunt down and acquire art for his mother. The fruits of that effort, as many as could fit on the walls, now stared back at him. Lady Edith had a particular affinity for chubby, cheerful depictions of Jesus as an infant, and St. Paul painted in his signature crimson cloak. With a single chandelier suspended above the table and the candles in their holders burning low, one was left with the mere suggestion of these figures clustered along the walls, and the foreboding sense of being watched by eyes hidden in shadow.

Danforth spoke through most of the meal and glowered when Alasdair requested wine. And though Alasdair sat at the position of privilege as the man of the house, Danforth was unmistakably the preferred authority. Eating but not tasting his roasted pheasant, Alasdair leaned back and observed his mother hanging on the clergyman's every word.

It was clear to anyone with the eyes to notice, painted or otherwise, that he had been replaced.

Freddie fidgeted and moved his vegetables around his plate listlessly like a naughty child.

"To be sure, Bishop Jewel's homilies are not of a style fashionable for today's parishioners," Danforth was saying. He had been lecturing about *The Books of Homilies* since the soup course, ecstatic sounds of agreement floating up from Lady Edith at all the correct places. *I've been away too long.* Alasdair could imagine this exact same exchange playing out again and again, so practiced was the air. "I myself have championed the keeping of certain traditions, but we must also enliven the known sermons where appropriate, to excite even the most skeptical listener . . ."

At the other end of the table, across a field of candelabras, dishes, and plates, Lady Edith watched Danforth with a zeal that defied her seemingly weak constitution.

"The man I've hired for the build should arrive tomorrow or the day after, along with a shipment of furnishings from our warehouse in London," Alasdair declared. Lady Edith stared as if shocked to hear him speak. "The original plans for Clafton were lost in the blaze, but I've discovered a number of prints from a local artist that will aid him immensely in the re-creation. Assessments of the remaining walls will be completed within a fortnight."

"O-oh," Lady Edith murmured. "That reminds me, Mr. Danforth and I wanted to suggest some changes to the east wing. He will need a permanent chamber there."

"And I have drawn up a design for an enviable little chapel to be added to the grounds," said Danforth with a broad smile. "To be sure, my artistic skills are modest, but I think the general shape and size is well communicated."

"To be sure," Freddie mocked in a singsong voice.

"I have no intention of changing a thing about Clafton," Alasdair replied.

Lady Edith and Mr. Danforth exchanged an uneasy look.

"Perhaps because of your many absences, Alasdair, you are unaware of your mother's changing desires," the clergyman told him.

"My *many* absences were at the behest of the lady you claim to speak for. And you will please address me as Mr. Kerr." He stood, wiped his mouth, then dropped his napkin. "There will be no changes to Clafton. Regrettably, I've lost my appetite. Good evening."

He didn't bother listening to Danforth's stammering apologies. As he returned to his rooms, Freddie chased after him.

"You can't leave me alone with them," Freddie cried. "It's too dreadful."

"Go to bed," he commanded, wishing to do the same.

"Why? So you can be alone with your pretty little painting?"

Yes.

"Damn you, so that I might enjoy some peace and quiet."

Freddie trailed after him for a while, then lost interest and fell behind. In fact, Alasdair did want to be alone with Miss Arden's self-portrait. There was far more to understand of it. He'd hoped that upon returning to his room and upon returning to the painting, it would have lost some of its bewitching magic. Alas. If anything, it had only grown in power. When the valet was summoned to undress him and he was naked before the painting, he felt the urge to stand very tall and straight, then scolded himself silently.

Violet Arden would never behold him this way, nor would he ever see beneath the thin muslin of her gown, however much the idea increasingly intrigued him. It was just a bit of paint and pencil, it ought to hold no sway over him.

And yet.

Exhausted, Alasdair climbed into bed, finding that even with all the lamps extinguished, Violet's eyes found his in the dark. It would be painful to part with it, he thought, so perhaps the answer was simply not to.

He woke early, pulled from a dream of gray storms to discover someone creeping into his bedroom. Roaring out from beneath the blankets, he accosted the intruder in his nightshirt. Freddie.

"Mercy! Mercy!" his brother shrieked, caught by the collar of his jacket and jerked down to his knees. Alasdair breathed hard, looming over him. "I just wanted Emilia! I had a mind to return it to her, you know, an excuse to call! And . . . and . . ."

"And?" Alasdair shook him. "Out with it."

Freddie squeezed his eyes shut, going limp as an old rag in Alasdair's grasp. "And to make my intentions known. That I love her. That I mean to marry her."

With one powerful yank of his arm, Alasdair dragged his brother to his feet, then glared down into his eyes. "With what money?"

"Why, she has more than enough!"

"Indeed." He clamped his hand around the base of Freddie's neck, pinching. "And what does the lady's father have to say about all of this?"

"Colonel Graddock is a-abroad," Freddie whispered. "How should I know?"

"Fortunately, I'm here to speak sense for the both of us. You've no income of your own, no employment, nothing besides your eagerness and charm, and you're mad if you think that is enough to recommend you for marriage."

"Not mad, no, just in love. Can't you understand that?" He let Freddie go and his brother spun away, his eyes filling with tears. "In all your wanderings, were you never sick with love?"

No. Yes. I don't know.

Freddie charged on, his voice rising with every word. "Did you not write to me of a Georgiana or some such? And do you think our mother would approve of her? An Austrian, if memory serves, your lady, yes? And that would never do! Never! Miss Graddock is half-English, her mother from the Indies, and you should have heard the way our mother and Danforth spoke of it!"

His brother could go on and on, but it did not matter; Alasdair was beyond reach. He rubbed the sleep out of his eyes with the heel of his right hand and sighed. There was nothing for it. Freddie would continue on this impossible path until it was swept out from under him or he lost his feet entirely. It would be admirable, his determination, if it weren't exasperating. "Take the painting of your so-called lady love and wait for me to dress. Then, we depart for Pressmore—this foolishness ends today."

5

O, when she is angry, she is keen and shrewd.
She was a vixen when she went to school,
And though she be but little, she is fierce.
A Midsummer Night's Dream—Act 3, Scene 2

The affliction that prevented Violet Arden from ever starting a thing was the exact same condition that kept her from finishing: perfectionism.

"You're too hard on yourself," Maggie had warned her a thousand times, but Violet never listened. For most of her two and twenty years, she had failed to devote herself to any cause or passion for fear that her drawing or dancing or stitching would fail to live up to her own standards. Or, even ghastlier, that the lofty standard would be met, and then it would change, and the whole mortifying ordeal would begin again.

She had started and abandoned several sketches that morning. The proof of her failure was mounting in accusatory piles at her feet. Perfectionism. It was poison. Yet there was a face lodged in her mind, or the idea of one, and her want of perfection was in direct conflict with this surge of inspiration.

She outright refused to paint the whole face, for it would break the new laws she had established for herself. No, she would not paint the horrible man who had screamed at her in the ruins, but she might draw an eye, an ear, a certain corner of the mouth . . .

Violet grumbled and stepped back from the easel, appalled yet again at her inability to get it right or even to honor her own vows. She shouldn't be drawing him at all, not even bits. Her gaze wandered to the balcony and the wan hand of morning light stretching its fingers across the plummet to the pond. Beadle Cottage, a half mile down the hill from Pressmore, waited somewhere in the chilly embrace where the light had yet to spread. She thought of her sister Maggie, who was no doubt awake at that early hour and scribbling away, hard at work on her next novel.

"I'm not like you, Maggie," Violet said softly to that view out the balcony doors. "There is no inspiration in an insult for me, only doubt and shame."

Derivative and silly. And for no one.

Now Violet could put a face to the discourtesy, and that made the sting of it doubly powerful. She thought of young Violet in the Pressmore fields playing pirates with her friends on an endless summer's day, of Alasdair Kerr, who had seemed a friend then, laughing at her jokes and racing her along the water's edge to the bridge. Bigger, faster, he always won those races but never boasted of it to the others.

"Who are you speaking to? My easel? I should hope so! I hope you are the best of friends, for that might justify your thieving of it!" Cristabel Bilbury stood at the door, hair wild and tangled, fists perched on her waist. There was a vastness of carpet between them, for Ann always let Violet take one of the grander bedrooms in the estate when she spent the night, and with Maggie deep in her second novel, those stays were becoming more and more frequent.

"You went to bed so early last night," said Violet, putting down her pencil. "I didn't think you would need it until this afternoon."

"But where is yours?" Cristabel demanded, marching over to her. At once, she scrutinized the light marks, the bare beginnings of a face, not quite anyone, as if Violet had been sketching *around* the subject, afraid of the direct approach.

"I left it in the ruins. The rain caught me out." Cristabel had left her easel in the drawing room, and she was nowhere to be found when Violet returned from the ruins. At dinner, she learned from her aunt, Mrs. Mildred Richmond, that Cristabel had complained of a headache and had gone up to bed early. These abrupt comings and goings were referred to as "her little episodes."

Cristabel's eyes flared. "And your paintings?"

"Gone, I'm afraid," Violet replied quietly, her shoulders collapsing inward. They were both looking at the sketch now. There was no use lying. "A man startled me, chased me off. It's his land, and he had every right to do it, I suppose, but there was no need to be so . . . so . . ." She huffed and waved her hand at nothing. "Anyway, I will have to ask Lane to send someone to Sampson Park for my things."

"You cannot retrieve them?"

"Certainly not! I hope never to see that wretched man again."

Her tutor poked the paper so hard it creased. "Yet here something of a man emerges."

Violet plucked the sketch from the easel and tore it down the middle, staring back at Cristabel defiantly. "There. Gone. He plagued my mind because of the things he said about my paintings in London, but no more."

"Ah. *Derivative and silly*? *For no one*? That man?"

Even repeated in Cristabel's voice, the insult made Violet feel sick.

"Don't worry," Violet said, forcing a cheerful tone. "I know the paper is costly, I'll use the scraps. And I'll ask Bloom to have the easel brought back to the north drawing room."

But her teacher wasn't moving, was simply watching her with the strangest half smile. "Why should you feel doubt and shame for what someone else perceives in your work?"

Violet flushed to the tips of her ears, her face growing hot. "You heard me . . ."

"I was told many of the same things, and by my father, no less. It was my brother who saw the potential in me. We all helped with the family engraving, but Nicholas urged me to paint." She looked at the scraps of paper dangling from Violet's hands. "My father promised nobody would want my rubbish. But do you know how much my watercolor of hollyhocks fetched last winter? Seven hundred and thirty pounds. Perhaps you will not need a Frenchman, or a Mr. Derivative. Perhaps you will need no one at all."

Violet softly gasped. It was a bewildering sum.

"That was my aim," she whispered. "Could it really be possible?"

"Freedom, my pupil. Freedom. Use the easel until yours is returned," said Cristabel. "But for now, come down to breakfast. One can hardly be expected to create on an empty stomach."

They found Ann and Emilia in the very drawing room from which Violet had poached the easel. The two ladies (Ann in a dotted white muslin and Emilia in green) sat in conversation beside an airy wall of windows, the curtains ruffled from the ornate doors that were opened onto the back terrace. Ann and Lane had hosted their wedding breakfast in this room years earlier; Violet couldn't help but marvel at how much had changed since then. Ann, taking a brioche from a tiered platter, had good color in her cheeks, and she had lost the gaunt air of sickness that had followed her in the wake of her hard pregnancy. Letters had been brought in, and Emilia was perusing some correspondence, the fine handwriting upon it causing Violet to wonder if it was from her cousin Ruby, who had been returned to Lakhnau.

"Ladies!" Ann cried, waving them over. "Come! Come! You must forgive Lane's absence, for he is with Mrs. Kelly and the baby. He spends every moment he can with the boy, and I confess to only loving him more after finding him such a devoted father."

They all agreed it was a favorable quality in a man, though Miss Bilbury swore she would never have children, feeling they were too inclined to bring disease and chaos into the house. How was one to paint with all the sticky, prying fingers and crying? That was sensible for an artist, Ann allowed, but insisted the sticky fingers and crying were all forgotten once her little boy smiled at her. She did lament that caring for the infant chewed into the time she usually allotted for her many charitable pursuits. Indeed, Ann had only just established her next venture, the Ladies' Society for the Lonely, Abandoned, and Infirm, when her challenging pregnancy forced her to set it aside. Everyone present assured Ann that now, with her healthy once more, the Society would flourish.

Thoroughly distracted, Emilia summarized Ruby's letter for them but paused often to gaze longingly out the window.

"Are you expecting a caller?" Violet finally asked over her hot chocolate.

"Oh!" Emilia blushed. "Probably not. Puck is making mischief in the wisteria again; it is hard not to watch."

"Hmph," muttered Cristabel.

"Emilia has had her head in the sky for weeks," Ann teased, placing a plum cake on her sister's plate. Emilia had hardly eaten a crumb all morning.

"Winter will be here soon," said Emilia, unconvincingly, and still stealing glances beyond the billowing curtain. "It fills me with melancholy." Her gaze narrowed, then she sat up straighter, nearly upsetting her plate and plum cake. "Do you see? Someone is coming down the hill . . ."

All four ladies hurried to the window and, standing in a row, shoulder to shoulder, surveyed the distance.

"But that is the gentleman who lives at Sampson Park," cried Ann. "Mr. Kerr. But who is with him? Upon my word, have you ever seen a larger fellow?"

"That is the other Mr. Kerr, didi," added Emilia, her voice breathy and strained. She clasped her hands together, holding them over her heart.

"There are two?" asked Ann.

"Not good," muttered Cristabel.

"Oh, yes," Emilia said with a laugh. "The eldest son has returned to the country to oversee the rebuilding of Clafton."

The men veered toward the woods and the bridge that crossed the narrow stream. The smaller one appeared to be carrying a painting under one arm. Violet blanched and spun away from the window, crossing her arms over herself.

"Who cares why they have come? If they are coming here, then we should turn them away!"

"Violet," Ann chided, going to her. "That would be terribly discourteous—"

"Discourteous?" She knew she sounded hysterical, but the words tumbled out before she could stop them. "Discourteous! He nearly trampled me to death yesterday!" Everyone was looking at her now with varying degrees of surprise and interest. Emilia appeared like she might faint but had not abandoned her place at the window. "It's true! Oh, do not receive him, Ann, I beg you."

"On the contrary, do let him in. I should like to see what happens," said Cristabel, standing back and chuckling. "She's done nothing but pretend not to sketch him all morning."

Ann's black brows raised in shock. Tearing herself away, Violet paced in an anxious circle, her thumbnail between her lips. "That is because . . . because . . . you see—he was like a demon! An apparition! Immense! And with these eyes like hell's own embers. Oh, it was horrible. And the way he spoke to me! Who could possibly address a lady with such . . . such . . ."

"Violet, you were in the ruins of his old home," said Ann mildly. "That would make anyone uneasy."

"Certainly, certainly, were I an opportunistic looter, perhaps, and not a lady swishing about with a few paints!" Violet threw up her hands, addressing a staring, unsympathetic audience.

Ann cleared her throat gently and took Violet by the arm, leading her to a cozy chair away from the windows. "Mm. And if your families were friendlier or better acquainted, then you might expect an apology, but as it stands . . ."

"He should do it anyway, the scoundrel," Violet muttered, flopping bonelessly into the chair.

"And . . . you want this scoundrel to appear so he might apologize, yes? Not so that you might see his immensity and ember eyes again, but properly this time, and in daylight?" Ann smirked, gesturing to the north lawn. "You may just get your chance."

Violet soared out of the chair, turning on Ann with open-mouthed fury. "The suggestion! Ann!"

She shrugged. "I have not seen you this impassioned, dear cousin, since we took up Maggie's cause in London. Given your clear offense, I must be mistaken."

"Absolutely so, Ann. I should rather kiss Puck on his disgusting, demented old goat mouth than flutter my lashes at Alasdair Kerr." She was running out of breath. Ann watched with bemusement as Violet worked herself up into a state again. "As if he would ever say a kind word to me! I am some insipid pretender to him. He probably took my paintings and danced on them until they were muddy shreds! Insipid, uninspired, that's what he thinks of me. And, oh! I shall never see that self-portrait again, and I quite liked it, too. It was almost something."

Cristabel had returned to the breakfast table. She snorted at Violet's distress over saffron honey cake.

"Calm yourself, cousin, please." Ann looped her arm lightly around Violet's shoulders, leading her to the open doors where they could both have some air. Beyond the veranda, near the pebbly path winding down to the pond, not far from the back step, Puck tore mouthfuls of grass up, chewing lazily. "It sounds to me like you are writing fiction now."

Violet sagged against her cousin, her voice diminishing. "Not at all. He was at Aunt Eliza's exhibition in London, and he said the most dreadful things about my work. That was after . . . well, you know, the incident, and I was at my lowest, but he just had to get in one nasty little kick . . ."

"Enough! Enough!" Emilia shrieked, storming up to them.

"Sister, what has offended you—"

"This irrational feud! That's what offends me!" Emilia tore off her own shawl, balled it up, and tossed it onto the ground, stamping her feet. "Freddie Kerr is a kind, spirited, wonderful man! And he loves me, do you understand? He loves me, and I love him, and I hope that very soon we shall be engaged."

Emilia's voice seemed to echo in the cavernous drawing room for an eternity.

"My, um, my word," croaked Ann, looking at her sister with new eyes. None of them moved. Lane's mother, Violet's aunt, Mrs. Richmond, bustled into the room from the back garden, having clipped a few fading late summer blossoms. She arrived with a smile but absorbed the glacial atmosphere at once. Her small, keen blue eyes flicked from lady to lady.

"What could possibly inspire four young ladies to stand about in total silence?" she wondered aloud. As if to answer, the butler, Bloom, sashayed into the room from the front hall, bowing with a flourish. "A Mr. Frederick Kerr to see Miss Emilia, ma'am."

"But I must have misheard you," Mrs. Richmond replied, clutching the flowers to her breast. "Mr. *Kerr*? It isn't possible!"

"*And*," Bloom said, drawing out the word impatiently, "Mr. Alasdair Kerr to see Miss Arden."

Mrs. Richmond's lace cap was in danger of flying off of her head as she whipped her attention between Emilia and Violet. "Have I returned to the correct house? Not one but two Kerrs on my doorstep! And here it seemed such a lovely day . . . Well! I suppose we cannot leave them waiting outside, though I dearly wish propriety deemed we could. No, no, I shall not give that dubious family one more reason to speak ill of us." She turned to Emilia, then Violet. "Go! For heaven's sake, go!"

With her heart lodged in her throat, Violet drifted to the drawing room on the other side of the house. It was warmer there, the windows shut against the cold, the rich, dark swirl of the wallpaper and the ponderous purplish curtains giving one the sense one was safely enfolded in the belly of some giant, slumbering beast. She had no desire to come face-to-face with the man who had made such a tumult of her spirit, but at least she might receive a deserved apology and accept the return of her possessions. It did gladden her to imagine that she might see that self-portrait again.

She had just positioned herself near a small statue of Orpheus on a white plinth when Bloom returned to announce Mr. Kerr. The polite thing to do was turn and face him, which she did, but slowly, dread spinning her stomach into a nauseating vortex.

Mr. Kerr encompassed nearly the entire doorframe; as he swept off his hat, his head grazed the bottom edge of the trim. The light pouring in from the front hall made him wholly shadow until he bowed and took a step inside. She heard other voices in the house, but that did nothing to assuage the sense that she was being gradually trapped against that plinth.

"Miss Arden."

Glacial.

"Mr. Kerr."

Indifferent.

He tucked his hands behind his back, lowering his shoulders, though the shift did little to address his immensity. An unexpected pang of sympathy attacked her as she wondered if he often felt the need to diminish himself. Cristabel had taught her to be a better observer; she studied his demeanor, his face, finding there were but traces of the boy she remembered flapping around in the pond, sunburned and joyful as he splashed and played. It was evident he still spent ample time out of doors, and an appreciation for exercise must be maintaining his great size. Such proof made his breeches fit so snugly she could see the competing swells of muscle over his thighs.

Her eyes snapped to his before further study of his legs could be made.

Either she was imagining the keen glint in his eyes or he was making a similar analysis of her body. Violet raised her chin. She would pluck his horrible eyes out of his horrible face if he tried that again.

"I am ready to hear your apology, sir."

Mr. Kerr stared as if she had said nothing at all, and Violet did not flinch beneath his gaze. *I drew in his nose too thin and his chin too short. He is prone to squinting, and it's worn grooves into his forehead.*

At last, he cleared his throat, his brow lowering and retracting swiftly. "Forgive my ignorance. Apologize? To you?"

"Yes."

"For what offense, madam?"

Violet gasped with silent laughter, stepping away from the statue. "Yesterday you nearly frightened me to death, sir! Have you forgotten?"

"No, Miss Arden, I have not forgotten. It has been at the very forefront of my mind. It explains my presence before you now." His shoulders returned to their correct form, his hands bunching at his sides as he moved toward her. The scent of late summer came with him, full of sedge and sun-warmed hillsides, reminding her of a longing for innocence nobody kept forever. Violet shrank away from him, and his expression softened. He stopped in place, exhaling a long breath. "I came only to return what is yours. A man from Sampson Park will arrive soon with the easel, and my brother is bringing the portrait of Miss Graddock to the lady herself now."

No apology. No contrition. Violet pressed her lips together. "I hope he has not stained it with his gloves."

"Because he is a Kerr?" His mouth mirrored hers, taut with fury.

"Your words, not mine."

"Indeed. Your disdain is clear enough, madam." Another step. She noted the instant his orbit intersected with hers, and the light charge of nervousness that skittered up her forearms at his approach. Violet straightened up, craning her head back to maintain eye contact. "And so, I will disgust you no longer, and go; my errand is complete, my message given, your things returned."

Mr. Kerr huffed quietly and turned to go. Violet chased after him.

"Is that all, sir?"

"Absolutely," he growled, showing her his back. "I will not stay to withstand further insult." He had reached the open doors with Violet almost on his heels.

"Insults!" she cried. "It is *you* who bandies those about with thoughtless abandon!"

Mr. Kerr drew up short, whirling on her. A shock of real fear lanced through her, but Violet mastered herself and did not retreat. What a bully! An oaf! He could be six feet taller and still not frighten her in earnest. She declared it loudly in her mind until her body believed it to be so. His arm was still outstretched, his black hat poised there, a single tremor passing through his hand. There was a flicker of recognition in his golden eyes, his lips parting gradually.

"Mrs. Burton's watercolor exhibition in June, do you recall it?" she asked.

"I do."

He was likely remembering the outburst, the scandal, Violet's public humiliation at the hands of the Frenchman's fiancée. There was ugliness in his eyes now, judgment, and it spurred her on.

"You were free with your opinions there, with no regard for who might be listening, who might care! *Derivative and silly . . .*"

Her voice was rising; his eyes blackened.

"*And for no one,*" Violet finished, wrinkling her nose. "Those were your words, were they not?"

"I will not demean myself with a lie."

Violet wanted to scream; she had never met anyone so cold, so constructed. He seemed to stare through her, as if she were no more than a pane of thin glass. Where was that silly, laughing boy rolling in the grass? Was he a summer's dream?

"Then it must be a relief to be rid of my portrait. I'm sure it pains you to even be near it. But I wonder, why save it from the rain at all if the work was so objectionable?" she asked, fighting the urge to rise onto tiptoes to make herself larger. "What became of the self-portrait?"

Mr. Kerr's top lip twitched exactly once on the right side, and then he shook his head, snorted, and ducked through the doorway. Slamming his hat on and tugging impatiently at each wrist edge of his gloves, he did not wait for Bloom or anyone else before charging out of Pressmore and back into the chill morning air. There was no hesitation from Violet, who stormed out after him. They were well beyond propriety now, and who could care? It was a wonder the whole world wasn't locked in a feud with this odious family . . .

"And there are the manners I should have expected!" she shouted, struggling to match his stride, resorting to a trot to keep up. He didn't seem to know where to go, since his brother was still inside the house. "Where, sir, is my painting? Did you throw it on a bonfire? Save it for a round of darts? Or is it already on the road to London so that you and your friends may titter over my deficiencies forevermore?"

Veering off the drive and toward the hedge maze, Mr. Kerr stopped abruptly beneath a willow. The draping branches wept yellow tears, a carpet of tiny golden leaves gathering before the trunk. "No, nothing of the sort. I simply will not stand to be interrogated in this manner. God, a wall of mortared stone would balk at the task. Desist, madam, and draw breath."

She answered him with steely silence, waiting with crossed arms.

"It . . . was spoiled by the rain," he told her. He added something in such a quiet undertone she couldn't tell if it was "regrettably" or "predictably."

Violet shrank. "Oh." It was a harsh disappointment. "That's a shame, I almost liked it."

He seemed ready to say something else when his brother burst from the house. Clutching his hat with both hands, he ran toward them with his head bowed as if he might need to duck or dodge at any moment. His face was red, his blue jacket rumpled as if he had slept in it; unspent tears shined in his eyes.

"Well?" was Mr. Kerr's sneering inquiry.

"It's done," Freddie murmured. An agonized scream erupted from the house behind them. By and by, it flattened out into a wail. "Badly. It went badly." Mr. Kerr reached out and slapped Freddie hard on the shoulder, jostling him. "Please, can we go? I'd sooner be lashed to a rock and torn apart like Prometheus than stay and hear her cries . . ."

Mr. Kerr pulled his brother away from the willow and toward the road. With one stiff jerk of his head in Violet's direction, he started toward the gates up the drive. "Good day, Miss Arden."

Whatever urge Violet felt to follow was immediately quashed by the sound of Emilia continuing to suffer. She made a nasty face at the backs of the retreating men and hurried back to Pressmore, following the sounds of gulping sobs to the same drawing room where they had just eaten breakfast, finding that a distraught Emilia had flung herself across a low sofa to endure her breaking heart. It might have made a pretty picture if Emilia weren't her dear friend and in such obvious, harrowing pain.

Ann knelt at her sister's side, stroking the wet hair from Emilia's tearstained cheeks. And Violet joined them, wedging herself in beside Emilia and taking her by the waist, holding her tightly. Not so long ago, Violet had been the subject of just such a scene, though Winny and Maggie had been the women there to comfort and soothe.

"There now, my darling, it will be all right," Violet assured her, catching a droplet as it cascaded down to the edge of Emilia's delicate chin.

"H-he said we cannot be! That he does not love me! It is a lie—I know it is a l-lie!" Emilia got out between heaves.

"Freddie has given you a gift, Emilia. You will see, I promise, you will see just how much better off you are without him. There are a thousand better suitors in the world more deserving of your love." Violet caught Emilia as she tipped forward into her grasp and resumed sobbing. She shared a look with Ann over her sister's shoulder, and they both rubbed the young lady's back and let her pour it out. A calmness settled over her, one she hoped would pass to the woman in her arms. The image of Mr. Kerr's burning gold eyes turning black with rage flashed across her vision. "You were never meant to be with a Kerr. None of us were. Think of how they behaved today!" Golden eyes. A sneering mouth. The towering form of a fiend angelical.

Yet I behaved badly, too, allowed his coldness to provoke me.

That was a thought for another time; Emilia needed her.

"Violet is right, choṭī bahan," said Ann, soothing her sister in the Hindi language they shared. "There will be others."

Emilia fussed and shook her head. "I don't want others. I want him!"

Elsewhere in the house, Mrs. Richmond shut and re-shut doors as if the action could seal the house against another incursion of unwanted visitors.

"Disarray!" she could be heard shrieking. "Crying and wailing and whatever else! Never again, I tell you! How is my hospitality rewarded, Bloom? We are left all out of sorts with a screaming young lady! Well! *Well.* That is what courtesy affords you with the Kerrs."

6

Are you more stubborn-hard than hammered iron?

King John—Act 4, Scene 1

"I need to get drunk immediately."

The men made it as far as the outer gates of Pressmore before their paths diverged. The edge of Freddie's hat was mangled where he had been squeezing it like a wet rag. He gazed off toward the village below, Cray Arches, no doubt envisioning all the cups he would drain in his misery. Straight ahead, a wild row of low, shapely trees formed a reddish-gold wall, lining the road.

"Wallowing in self-pity will not make this easier," Alasdair insisted.

"You don't know that. Join me, we can find out together."

He almost accepted the offer, then remembered he was trying to nudge Freddie toward his better nature, if for no other reason than to appease their mother. "Come home with me instead."

"Nothing about that place is reassuring. Go, run back to Mother, one of us should."

"Don't do anything rash." Alasdair watched him float away, as if pulled toward the brandy and wine on an invisible string. A wave of melancholy hit him then that almost knocked him off his feet. He often felt panicked at goodbyes, haunted by the leave-taking with his father that had been their last. *Be wise and good, Cub, the other boys won't have your sense.* Foolishly, Alasdair had been eager to get on his way, to be at Cambridge, a man on his own, brimming with half-cocked ideas about what his life would look like. If he had known his father would die in the Clafton fire a few months later, he would have never left.

Freddie stormed off; regret locked Alasdair in place.

"I haven't been the best brother to you, have I?" he wondered aloud.

"Did you say something?"

Alasdair shook his head, and Freddie turned away. He watched his brother turn left down the road toward Cray Arches, hearing the last words he had spoken to his father bleed into the present. *You worry over me too much, Father; the carriage is here, and I must depart.*

How impatient he had been, how arrogant.

The sun was high by the time he returned to Sampson Park, and he ducked into the house drenched in the prickly sweat of a chill day made over-warm by a cloudless sky. He had considered a swim on his walk back, but there were too many people out about their business, and he had no interest in returning to the county only to set tongues wagging about his habits. He discovered Mr. Danforth rocking from heel to toe outside his room.

"Your mother is within," said the clergyman, smirking. "To be sure, she's eager to know everything is taken care of where your brother is concerned."

Alasdair frowned. "Lady Edith rarely leaves the comfort of her chair. How did she—"

"I took the liberty of carrying her with Hilary's assistance."

Odd. All of it was odd. His mother was a known snooper, but on conversations, never intruding physically on their private spaces like this. Alasdair said nothing and pushed by Danforth, closing the door resolutely behind him. His mother leaned on her cane in the middle of the chamber, shivering beneath her shawl, squinting at the self-portrait of Violet Arden on the bookcase.

"Good afternoon, Mother, I trust—"

"Since your father's death, you have always been a reliable child," she said, cutting him off. She had been an incomparable in her youth, but the fire had robbed them all differently. Her rare smiles became something only remembered, her appetite withering and her body along with it, her trust and kindness reserved for God and Danforth and whatever quiet counsel she kept with herself. Without looking at Alasdair, she continued, "You have always given me the gift of obedience, and I am grateful for it. Where is your brother?"

"He's off to the inn, I suspect, to drown his disappointments."

"That is all he gives me of late, disappointments," she said with a sigh, and seemed to become yet smaller. "But there will be no more discussion of any engagement."

"None," said Alasdair.

That brought the wintriest hint of a smile to her face.

"Mr. Danforth has tried to encourage him toward better things—study, modesty, sobriety—but he has concluded it a fruitless endeavor."

"And what do you think?" he asked, afraid to step closer and come into the powerful gaze of the painting.

"I don't, Alasdair," she told him sadly. "I pray. How did you come to have this . . . this thing?" She risked taking one hand from the cane and waved it toward the portrait.

"Not intentionally, I assure you," he replied, refusing to look at Violet, who was not a thing, though he could not yet decide what exactly she was. "It was left behind in the Clafton ruins, I simply removed it here to keep it from the rain."

Lady Edith sniffed and shrugged and began struggling toward the door. Alasdair leapt to help her, supporting her with his left forearm. The fingers she draped across his wrist were like a dusting of feathers. Then, her grip tightened, startling him. "Get rid of it," she commanded when they reached the door. Danforth was waiting outside, grinning and at attention.

"Of course," said Alasdair.

When he was alone, he took the self-portrait and covered it in a cloth from his wardrobe, briefly considered feeding it to the fire, then, with a sizzle of shame, slid it beneath his four-poster bed, the symbolism of which was greatly annoying. He could part with it, he *ought* to. Why had he lied about it?

Why did he want so badly to keep it for himself?

Returning the portrait cured two ills—it would please his mother and Miss Arden. Yet other symptoms remained unaddressed, and the painting was not moved.

Clark Gordon arrived bright and early the next day. His coming was a welcome distraction, significantly reducing the number of times Alasdair felt the urge to check under his bed and verify that Danforth hadn't crept in like a thief and discovered his secret. There was absolutely no additional benefit to these little spikes of suspicion, and he did not experience a shudder of emotion at each glimpse of Violet's questioning gaze.

Or that was what he insisted to himself whenever he was gripped by self-recrimination.

He liked Clark Gordon right away; he was a stocky badger of a man, all beard and chin, reddened and callused from head to foot.

"It'll be a monstrous undertaking," said Gordon when presented with the hollowed-out shell of Clafton. It took mere moments for the man to win the builder's confidence and awe. "Monstrous," he growled again through the ungroomed mustache of his unfashionably huge beard. "But this hill ought to have a crown. It's missing something, don't you think? And we'll provide it. Ha-ha!" He often laughed explosively at his own declarations, whether they were humorous or otherwise. Alasdair liked that, too; Gordon seemed a man utterly unburdened.

Alasdair insisted that, when able, Mr. Gordon dine with them at Sampson, an honor the man took in stride. But each night the party remained four, with always a place laid for the youngest Kerr, who never appeared. Danforth claimed he was unperturbed, but Alasdair couldn't help but worry; it had been four busy days since they had last seen Freddie.

7

I know not how to tell thee who I am.
My name, dear saint, is hateful to myself
Because it is an enemy to thee.
Had I it written, I would tear the word.
Romeo and Juliet—Act 2, Scene 2

Violet dreamed of smoke and screams.

She woke with a gasp, tasting ash, and turned to shake her friend awake. Emilia's heartbreak had not abated, and she had taken to sleeping in Violet's room, too despondent to be left alone. It eased the minds of Ann and Lane to know that Emilia had someone with her, though Miss Bilbury complained that it was too great a distraction for Violet, whose diligence had tapered off.

Emilia groaned and flopped one arm over her eyes. "It's late," she mumbled.

"Can you smell that?" Violet tumbled out of bed, reaching for her dressing gown and pulling it on as she hurried to the balcony doors. Her easel, returned, was set up nearby, holding an unfinished study of lilacs in a tall vase. *Are all my paintings to be destroyed by acts of God? First the rain, now fire . . .*

Throwing open the balcony doors ushered the smell inside. She coughed and batted at the air, pulling up a fistful of dressing gown to shield her mouth and nose while she went to the railing. Curling plumes of black smoke swirled against the pinkish curtain of dawn draped over the horizon. Emilia had gained her senses and joined Violet outside, then clutched her friend's arm.

"The trees have caught there!" she shouted, pointing.

"And the pavilion," Violet added, watching as one of the white canvas tents collapsed against the back portico, showering the house with sparks, the wooden frame of the pavilion burning steadily. "My God, we have to wake the house!"

The restlessness of the night fell away, the last vestiges of drowsiness swept off by the fear running hot through her veins. Violet took Emilia by the hand and dragged her to the door until they were both running together.

"Go to Ann and Lane, I'll find Bloom," Violet shouted, frantic, pushing Emilia toward the opposite wing of the large estate. Such grandeur worked against them now, as it was a long journey to the landing overlooking the foyer and then down two flights of curving stairs to the front hall. The house was locked in the silence of sleep, though now, above, she heard the first stirrings of the family as Emilia reached Ann and Lane. They had to be warned first, for the safety of their child was paramount.

That same noise must have alerted Bloom, for she nearly collided with him as he emerged from the dining room. Hot wax from the candelabra he was carrying splashed them both as he jolted to a stop.

Violet ignored the slight sting of the wax as it plopped against her neck. "Fire, Bloom! Just below my balcony—I think the house is about to catch!"

Bloom, bless him, snapped into immediate action. His expression hardened as readily as the wax cooling on Violet's collarbone, and with a tidy pivot, he rushed back into the dining room, calling for the rest of the staff as he did so.

"Come, Miss Arden, you will please show me to the issue," he said, resolute and efficient.

Violet led him out the back doors, onto the marble slab beneath the portico, but there was no need for her to point or say more, for the flames were rising higher on the burning tent. A footman rushed past her carrying a bucket, and Violet, realizing she was only in the way, scrambled down the steps of the veranda and into the cold, wet grass. The freezing bite of it against her feet momentarily dulled the panic. She cast her gaze upward, seeing that more windows were aglow, and soon familiar faces were pouring out of the same doors through which she had fled. Ann appeared with her son wrapped tightly in a bundle of blankets, Lane at her side. Then came Mrs. Richmond, Emilia, and several of the staff, including Ann's maid, Fanny. They spread out across the lawn, watching as men rushed by with buckets, calling to one another as they put out the blaze.

It was a disaster narrowly avoided, and Violet couldn't help but wonder what—or who—could have caused it. There had been sporadic rain, and the blaze seemed to have begun outside the house, not as the consequence of an errant candle left too near a curtain. And so, seeing that everyone was away from the flames and the crisis well in hand, Violet went to Emilia, who stood some distance from the house, hugging herself and shivering. She was nearly beside her friend when she noticed a dark shape moving across the lawn, just down the gentle slope of the hill that ended at the pond. A bloat of gray mist rose from the water like steam from a basin.

"Violet?" Emilia asked, noticing her sharpening gaze.

"Stay here," she murmured.

"Wait, Violet—"

The fleeing shape was suspiciously human-shaped, the cloak covering them twisting this way and that. She had hoped it was just Puck escaping his loft again, but this creature neither moved like a goat nor shared one's interest in fresh, dewy grass. It was decidedly a person running away from what was very nearly a deadly blaze.

What could have caused it, indeed.

Violet picked up the hem of her nightgown and began her pursuit, the curling cloths tied in her hair bouncing against her head as she trotted and then broke into a sprint. Dawn's luminous pink beginning burned orange at the edges; if she could just get close enough to the stranger to ascertain their identity, if the sun could play conspirator and rise a bit more, light the lawn and disperse the veil of mystery . . .

She breathed hard, chest tingling, legs churning, allowing the momentum of the hill to carry her faster and faster. There was no muting the sound of her pounding footsteps, and the stranger took one glance over their shoulder, their face cruelly obscured by their hood as they did so. They were not expecting to be chased and redoubled their speed to evade her. There was little to remember about the person; in Violet's opinion, they ran more like a man might, with a robust if clumsy stride, but the particulars of their garments were obscured by the cloak. With one hand, they clasped the hood to their head, cleverly concealing even the color of their hair.

But Violet refused to give up.

"Ho there!" she called, gulping down her breaths. "Have you come from Pressmore this morning? Why such haste, sir? Why the haste?"

She did not expect an answer and was given none. The hill flattened out somewhat as they reached the bottom of it, the serene pond lending the air a green, fishy scent. To their right, the forest carving the edge of the lawn reached thorny fingers toward the water's edge. The stranger tore through a gap between pond and wood, leading Violet to assume they were making for the bridge. Instead, when Violet followed through that narrow opening, she discovered they had struck out into the trees. She pursued them with a muttered curse, twigs and branches tearing at her as she picked up her feet to avoid the fallen logs and deep, descending clumps of mounded leaves. Here it was darker, and though she could hear the snap of wood marking the stranger's progress, it was difficult to discern them among the trunks. Everything blended together.

This slice of the forest was narrow, and as the sun rose, Violet realized she was being led to a small clearing. It occurred to her only then that she was in danger; if this stranger was indeed intent on starting a fire on Pressmore's grounds, then they were capable of other sorts of violence. She paused midstep, peering into the clearing, listening to the crunch of twigs and leaves and the fluttering wing-startle of birds scattering overhead. A chorus of shrieks from the birds surprised her, and she gasped, reaching for a branch to steady herself before moving more carefully through the densely packed wood. Then, in the gloom of the clearing ahead, a jangle like a pocket full of coins—no, reins. A horse. The beast, chestnut brown, whickered and tossed its head, then accepted its rider and eased through a gap in the trees. Eventually, there would be a path that cut through the forest and led to Cray Arches, a narrow lane used by the Pressmore staff to easily ferry goods from market to house.

She made it to the clearing in time to see the horse and

rider disappear for good. Slumping, she accepted her defeat, deciding she might be able to send a rider from Pressmore to intercept the stranger in the village. She plucked up her nerve and left the clearing, though she went but ten or so paces before also accepting she was turned around and quite lost.

Damp and tired, she turned herself toward the brightening sky, orienting herself to the east. If she pushed forward that way, eventually she would meet the edge of the forest where the road from town ran along the stream. Once she found water, the rest would take care of itself. She trudged forward, colder by the minute, the fear receding and leaving behind an empty feeling. By the time she reached where the trees were thinnest and the trickling of the stream could be heard over her heartbeat, she must have seemed a foundling raised by fairies, her feet so caked in mud and leaves they looked like ungainly shoes, her nightgown and robe torn and dragging.

She broke free of the forest just east of the bridge, stumbling down a steep embankment toward the mist blanketing the water. She plunged her feet into the shallows, gasping from the snap of the freezing water, bending over to rub the muck from her ankles. Her hem was mangled, and she shook her head; she had to laugh at the absurdity of it all. Yet Violet turned from the stream quickly, knowing she shouldn't dawdle. She had to get back to the house and send someone after the rider, even if their lead was significant and the search hopeless.

Her laughter drew a noise from the wider part of the stream, well beyond the bridge and the banks, and she stood straighter, watching a large shape cut across the water, slicing through it with almost eerie precision. Several deranged thoughts crossed her mind, including that she could be witnessing the first shark to ever reach the placid waters of

Warwickshire. The shape reached the clump of reeds poking up from the waterline across the bridge from her, and through the mist, she watched it rise up and resolve into the shape of a man. The mist held him briefly in a gauzy tousle of ivory streamers, maintaining his modesty for the amount of time it took Violet to realize she was gawking at a naked person.

And not just any naked person, but Mr. Alasdair Kerr.

My God, she thought, covering her mouth with one hand and her eyes with the other. *What a structure.*

She heard an intake of breath, then his snorted laugh, and finally the rustle of clothing. Peering between two fingers, she discovered that he had managed to tug on his breeches. *Thank God.*

And yet, a twinge of regret.

The obliging little beads left behind after his swim drew her eye to every bulging contour of his chest, every dark hair, every angle chiseled into his sides.

"Miss Arden," he called, taking a few steps toward her until his toes were back in the water. He had found his spectacles and perched them back on his nose, squinting. "Are you quite well?"

"No!" she squawked. "I . . ." She wiped both palms down her face and went to stand on the other side of the stream from him. Her cheeks burned until they hurt. It pained her to think he could draw this kind of reaction from her. "There's been a fire at Pressmore," she stammered. "I went after the culprit but lost him in the woods just there." Turning, she pointed.

"A fire?" Mr. Kerr hurried back to his pile of clothes and grabbed his shirt, tugging it over his head in one efficient movement. Though it eased the heat in her cheeks, Violet couldn't help but feel a bit sorry at the loss of such a sight. "Is everyone accounted for? Is anyone harmed?"

Of course he would deeply feel the gravity of such a thing.

"N-no," she answered, moving toward the bridge. "But I must return there right away and tell the family what I saw." In her haste, her steps were bungling, and she slid, then slipped, tumbling down the shallow embankment until she caught herself awkwardly on her right foot. The surge of pain flickered up her leg, and as soon as she put weight on the foot again, she found it too tender to bear her.

"Ooh!" she exclaimed, hissing. She hopped forward, then grabbed the post of the bridge for support. "Never mind that, I mustn't be delayed."

"If there is a criminal lurking in the woods, then I insist that you allow me to escort you home."

Violet's hackles raised at his tone: commanding, certain, leaving absolutely no room for argument. Yet when he appeared again through the mist, marching across the bridge, there was genuine concern written across his face. He pulled on his boots and jacket, then nodded toward the silhouette of the estate in the distance.

"Please," he added, seeing her expression. "Set your distaste for me aside. You should not be alone. More than that, you appear injured, Miss Arden."

"It's nothing," she assured him, then risked a look at her right ankle, which had rapidly begun to swell. To prove her capability, Violet began limping and then jumping on her good foot across the road and away from him. *Ow, ow, ow.*

"Am I to stand and watch you hop and hobble clear across two fields?" he asked, stifling a laugh. "Madam, I cannot allow it."

The pain made a similarly compelling argument.

Violet sighed and stalled, gesturing him forward with a souring expression. How odd—he had been devoid of emotion during their last encounter, and so the sound of his laughter now came as if from someone else entirely. It dragged her back to the past, to this same bridge but sunnier days and rosier smiles. Her chest throbbed at a loss she could not tally or define, and it worsened as Mr. Kerr came to her, coughed nervously into his ham hock of a fist, and bowed his head.

"With your permission?"

Violet nodded, unable to meet his gaze.

"If you can forgive the state of me, that is," he added, a bit red in the cheeks himself.

"The state of *us.*"

"Indeed, I thought a spirit of the forest had come upon me; I did consider swimming away and abandoning my clothes altogether."

"Oh, no, sir," said Violet, grinning and indicating her swollen leg. "You were never in any danger. I had only come to wash away my mud boots. I don't know how you stand to be in the water this time of year. You should be a block of ice!"

She flinched as he reached toward her, but it was just to carefully pry away a glob of wax that had dried to her throat. The quick, crisp release of the hardened wax was almost pleasurable.

"Wax," he told her, seeming to lose his train of thought before gathering it up again. His eyes had changed color, his breaths coming faster, rasping his voice. The air sizzled around them, charged, as if a tempest gathered just for them on this otherwise clear day; Violet felt it through her entire body. "I weathered all manner of far more dire dares swimming the River Cam. My contemporaries at Cambridge were determined to give the waterman the challenge of a lifetime." He shook his head and stared away from her at a distant memory along the stream, a thought hidden in the lightening fog. Coming back to himself, he glanced down and plucked a leafy twig from her hair, flicked it away, then carefully stooped to scoop her into his arms. He did as much with no trouble, for she seemed to be merely the burden of a single folded blanket. "This look rather suits you."

"Does it?" Violet wanted to roll her eyes but couldn't decide if he was having fun at her expense.

"Yes. It's more how I remember you," he said, his voice softening. "A Peaseblossom among the hollyhocks. Certainly, the shrieking from the other day was familiar—"

"Shrieking?" Violet tensed in his arms.

"—and how you and I were the most hardheaded of the bunch. How you loved endlessly quoting speeches at us . . ." he went on, frowning, looking at her askance as he carried her into the swirling mist. "'She is but little, but she is fierce.'"

They broke away from the water's edge, angling toward the charming stone path that picked its way up to the house proper. "So much for a Cambridge education, Mr. Kerr. The line is: 'And though she be but little, she is fierce.' I can shriek it if that will help you remember it better."

He was silent for a moment, then laughed. "Exactly so."

"Ha! Is that what you think of me?" she asked, finding that his golden eyes had not veered from her face. And the intensity of it . . . She was suddenly grateful for the cold, worrying she might melt like a candle left in the sun under the scrutiny of those eyes, and that was to say nothing of the heat radiating from his chest. Renaud—no, the Frenchman, as he must now be known—was all sharp angles. They had never embraced to this extent. *Don't think of the word* embrace, *you idiot, this is purely functional.* But how could one not feel the alluring texture of the man through his sodden, sticking clothes, the unexpected cushioning softness of his chest and arms? Violet's eyelashes dipped, and she scolded herself, demanding her body reject the urges that flooded through her at his touch.

Remember who he is, the things he said.

"I don't know quite what to think of you, Miss Arden," he replied, shrugging her.

It was becoming very hard to remember. Violet quickly changed the subject. "Do you ever wonder if we're still in these fields somehow? Catching frogs, and playing, and not a care in the world . . . Still there, but we just can't see it."

In her desperation to change the subject, she hadn't considered most genteel company would find such an observation incredibly bizarre. Mr. Kerr only frowned, drawing his heavy brows down as if giving the question real merit.

"Like an underpainting."

Terrible. She had wanted to like him less, not more. How bothersome to entertain that her first conceptions of him were incomplete. Well. They couldn't make the rest of the journey in silence, not when her head had begun blasting out so many questions. "How did you come to know so much about art?"

"A friend at Cambridge ran in the right circles. He brought me around to the right exhibitions, made the right introductions, and then I had some success discerning nascent talents in London. Lady Edith enjoyed the idea of me filling the house with art of the apostles and so on, so I was sent to Madrid, Florence, Vienna . . ."

Florence! Violet almost moaned with jealousy. "Yet you never considered learning the art yourself?"

"Maybe I did, briefly, but I doubt anyone would take interest in how I observe the world."

"That's very sad. I find it a relief," she said, wearing a private smile. "Like a . . . confirmation, you see, proof that the world is as I see it. I'm so often stuck in my head, held captive in it; sometimes painting is the only thing that can pull me out of it." She shook her head and closed her eyes tightly. "My aunts tell me I am a strange person, and that the men must never find out or I will die a spinster. But Miss Bilbury supports herself with her paintings and teaching, and I could do the same. Lord, Mrs. Richmond would scream if she knew that I had just admitted all of that in front of you. *Violet Arden, you strange, silly girl,*" she said, pitching her voice up, mimicking Mrs. Richmond. "*Close your mouth this instant!*"

"But there's little harm," he added for her. "Given our circumstances. Our families."

"Yes, exactly. Perhaps there is comfort in that."

There was comfort in his arms, too, though Violet at least knew better than to say that one aloud.

"We may speak freely, then, as other men and women cannot," he said, breathing out as if relieved, the rush of air ruffling the front of her nightgown.

"Yes. Besides the matter of our families, I have sworn off men entirely," Violet declared.

For some reason, that made him smirk.

"Oh? Any reason in particular?"

"You can imagine the inspiration well enough," she said quietly, coolly. "You were there for it. I will never be humiliated like that again."

"The woman who made a spectacle of herself in your aunt's home? I barely heard her. I was studying the art, and my attention remained fixed there."

It was her turn to smirk. "Studying the *bad* art."

"Monsieur Moncelle is not completely without talent."

Violet sat up straighter in his grasp, twisting.

"A jest, a jest," he assured her, chuckling, anticipating her while sneaking a look at her from the corner of his eye. "Moncelle's art is even more insipid than yours."

"Have you ever doled out a compliment without a knife

hidden behind your back?" she asked, laughing despite herself. She inhaled deeply through her nose. "Insipid. Oh, but I like when you call him that. Were it not for our families, perhaps we could be friends after all."

He cleared his throat.

"And there I go again, saying far too much. *Close your mouth this instant.*"

Mr. Kerr's head swiveled toward her, bringing them almost nose to nose. His breath skittered across her chin, alluring as a whispered secret. What was coming over her? She wouldn't allow herself to forget the terrible things he had said about her paintings. She wouldn't. "For whatever my opinion is worth—and I'm sure, being a Kerr, that is little indeed—I often feel the same. Imprisoned by my thoughts, never mastering them for long before the churning begins again."

Violet nodded fervently. "The churning, that's how I would describe it, too. I've always had it, but it became so much worse when Father died."

Mr. Kerr flinched and looked elsewhere, falling into a despair she recognized.

"I didn't mean to—"

"No, no," he said, gruff. "It is my own fault; I insisted we could speak freely."

A door was shutting. Violet didn't fight it, instead marking the distance he had carried her. The silence stretched on, though she wouldn't call it unpleasant. She expected to fall back into the mire of her thoughts but instead found herself remarkably at ease.

After a while, he said, "We are to be commended, Miss Arden."

"Oh? For what, I wonder?"

"For completing a pleasant exchange, and with not a single serious offense given. Impressive, mm?"

"You're teasing, Mr. Kerr." Violet swished her lips to the side. "Your celebration is premature—we have not yet reached the house, and I will not forget you complained of my so-called shrieking when it was only spirited debate."

"Mm, too true. I hope you will not debate me when I say that it is immensely relieving to know the fire did not claim any lives. From here, I can see that the damage is minimal."

"Yes," said Violet as they crested the second gentle hill, passing out of the mist completely. "We can abide no more excitement at the house. Emilia's melancholy was more than enough of a strain." She felt an icy curtain descend between them at once. It was a betrayal, she thought, to laugh with him when Freddie had treated Emilia cruelly. "She has taken it badly. He might have disappointed her gently, but his harshness has left a wound."

"Would it be better to let her cling to hope? Confusion is a greater unkindness."

"And how is your brother?"

Mr. Kerr wrinkled his nose and tilted his head to one side, a nervous gesture. "He has not been at Sampson Park for many days now."

"Curious," Violet murmured.

"Suspicious, you mean."

"Your words, not mine."

Mr. Kerr snorted and widened the distance between them. "And so, you were right. My celebration *was* premature. I will not apologize for what transpired between my brother and Miss Graddock; he has no future with her. The matter is closed."

Violet looked away, disgusted. Even if she agreed that Emilia could do better, it was ugly the way he said it. "You should put me down."

"Tolerate this but a moment longer, Miss Arden. We are nearly there."

At the top of the hill, they were now in perfect view of the house and those still mingling outside below the portico. Here, Mr. Kerr hesitated. Violet waved toward Pressmore as Cousin Lane and Emilia broke away from the others, hurrying to where Mr. Kerr still held her in his arms. "I must ask again that you put me down, Mr. Kerr. It was good of you to bring me, but there is no need for you to go any farther."

Before another word could be exchanged between them, Lane and Emilia arrived, both of them breathless. Lane, the left sleeve of his shirt flapping from lack of an arm, looked them up and down, his eyes finally falling on the strange way Violet was holding up her foot.

"I twisted my ankle badly by the water," she said, hurrying to assuage their fears. "Mr. Kerr was . . . out for a morning walk and was good enough to carry me here. The person I was chasing escaped on horseback, but I believe they were riding for the village. If we send someone now, we might be able to catch them."

Neither of them commented on his curiously damp state.

"I'll go at once." Lane bowed curtly to Mr. Kerr. "Can you make it to the house, cousin, or shall I call for Bloom?"

"I'll manage," said Violet.

"We can reconvene in the front hall, Violet, and you can tell me all about our quarry."

Mr. Kerr lowered Violet to the ground, yet there was no way to do so without also sliding her somewhat down the sticking front of his shirt and breeches. It would have been bad enough alone, but with Emilia standing there gawking, it was enough to make her feverish with embarrassment.

Backing away slowly, his gaze searching along the grass at

her feet, Mr. Kerr struggled through his goodbye. "I would ask that you extend my good wishes and condolences to Mrs. Richmond, but given . . . well . . ."

"Yes," Violet whispered. "Yes, given it all . . ."

"Precisely." Mr. Kerr made it three strides away from her before spinning back around. He looked between the women, though Emilia was stupefied, by either his implausible presence, his wetness, or both. Mr. Kerr lowered his voice, speaking exclusively to Violet. "Freddie didn't do this. I know . . . my brother is many things—unserious, selfish, lacking in both discipline and tact—but he is not the sort of man to retaliate in this manner. For all his faults, he did love Miss Graddock and would not put her life at risk."

Violet felt the cool air settle around her. She wanted to believe him, but Clafton had burned and now this, and it was hard to ignore the miasma of misfortune swirling around the Kerrs. His eyes were no longer burning along her cheek and jaw but imploring, gently seeking. A dozen versions of his sketched face hid behind scraps she had repurposed for plein air studies and paintings of fruit. She hadn't managed to capture him to her satisfaction, and now, seeing this new softness in his eyes, she wondered if she would ever be able to render such contradictions in paint.

"I have heard you," she said, plain. "Good morning, Mr. Kerr."

He went away, back down the hill toward the water, and Violet accepted Emilia's offered hand to go back into the house. They waited in the front hall for Lane only briefly, for he was soon dressed and with them, a look of hard determination etched across his normally boyish face. Lane was copper-haired and prone to wide grins, and Violet had a difficult time seeing her cousin as anything but an immovably jolly fellow.

Now, however, with Pressmore set aflame, he brooded and paced.

Violet offered a description of the horse and rider, Lane called for his own conveyance to Cray Arches, and the women idled in the front hall wearing twin expressions of exhausted confusion. It was still quite early. Violet's ankle seethed and throbbed with pain.

"I want to go home," she said, at last. "I want to be with my sisters."

Arrangements were made for a carriage to take her to Beadle Cottage. Miss Bilbury made it clear that such an absence from Pressmore would not keep her from Violet and promised, or maybe threatened, to visit frequently to watch her progress. And so, Violet's easel and paints were packed along with her garments, and a tearful Emilia saw her off. They would not be parted long, but Emilia still took it to heart.

Almost as soon as the carriage stopped at the end of the cottage path, Winny was there to greet her, and at once, Violet felt better about her life. In Winny's warm glow, it was nearly impossible to stay glum; even the burden of her ankle lightened. And how much more welcome was Violet when she brought with her a veritable feast of news to be shared with Winny, Maggie, and their mother!

Beadle Cottage was nothing extraordinary, small and compact, but was charmingly drowning in honeysuckles. A winsome little black fence and gate did not guard but rather outlined the property, sitting before the sloped, cobbled path that wandered to the green front door. Moss grew between every crack. The shutters were also painted green, and Mrs. Arden had taken great pains to bolster the garden with all the flowers that made her daughters sigh and smile. Violet liked to call it a "homey home," or, on the days it rained and the tiled roof sprung a leak, a "homely home." It was not situated very well among the hills that rose around it, and there were other quirks—a crooked chimney, an awkward layout, the aforementioned naughty roof—that Violet considered endearing but that those with grand tastes would find irritating and shabby.

It had two sitting rooms, one office, and three bedrooms, which was not enough for them all, but do was made because it must be.

"The house is terribly dirty," Winny warned her, watching as the carriage driver helped Violet down and across the path, then to the sitting room on the left side of the house. "Why did nobody send word you were coming?"

"It was all extremely sudden," Violet told her, and then additionally Maggie and Mamma as they appeared, roused by the noise. "There was a fire at Pressmore this morning," she added to a chorus of gasps. She told the whole long story but carefully excised the part where Mr. Kerr appeared like a soggy Adonis cloaked in mist on the water's edge.

That, she decided silently, was just for her.

Her older sister, Maggie, stood apart, absorbing everything from near the hearth, watching her with strangely bright eyes. Maggie, who had been unceremoniously bludgeoned by Love, and who was the wisest and most worldly of the sisters, seemed to have recognized something in Violet, and the thought of it made her quake.

8

I have shot my arrow o'er the house
And hurt my brother.
Hamlet—Act 5, Scene 2

Some hours later, Alasdair sat hunched over a pile of roasted pheasant at the Gull and Knave. The time had come to collect his brother, if for no other reason than to verify he had been nowhere near Pressmore when the fire occurred. He was mortified to discover that the builders at the Clafton ruins knew precisely where Freddie had been; his younger brother was racking up quite the bill and twice the reputation at the postal inn on the edge of Cray Arches.

From the front counter, the knotted old tree trunk of a proprietor and a boy with sandy blond hair peered at him. That happened a lot when he ate in public, which was why he rarely did it. After a swim and a long walk, he could eat two braces of game birds if he wanted to, for his was a furnace that required copious fuel. Alasdair ignored their peeping looks and stabbed his knife down into the meat; he didn't relish what came next, but hauling Freddie out of the perverse little nest he had made was hungry work, so Alasdair ate his fill, even if he found no pleasure in it.

The Gull and Knave was comfortable enough, as far as he could tell, a clean and relatively upstanding place for travelers to rest, exchange their carriage, and enjoy a hot meal. A staircase ran up the right side of the main room, and Alasdair had taken a table with a good view of it; if Freddie tried to scuttle away, Alasdair would see it. And he knew Freddie was upstairs. The black-haired, bristling bear of a proprietor had reluctantly admitted it after Alasdair offered to pay Freddie's alarmingly mounting bill.

It was an underhanded tactic, perhaps, but everyone got what they needed.

And soon, once he finished eating, Alasdair would have his brother back.

He glowered down at his plate, annoyed at himself for stalling. There was a storm brewing in his head, and if he wasn't careful, the force of it would be unleashed upon Freddie. *Maybe he deserves it, I don't know.* But it was more than Freddie's absence bothering him; something Miss Arden had mentioned earlier was encouraging that gale in his mind to swirl all the harder.

Painting, to her, was a confirmation that the world truly existed as she saw it. In all his many years of curating and purchasing art, he had never considered such a concept, and it bothered him. She was an amateur, hardly an apprentice of Bilbury's, yet her observations were sound. Insightful. The meat on his plate was vanishing, and he was becoming almost uncomfortably full. Alasdair shifted, circling around another discomfiting realization—that he knew exactly what she meant. Art pulled Violet Arden out of herself, but Alasdair had never found what could do the same for him. Some of his contemporaries at Cambridge who liked to swim with him and go to the club started calling him the Mute Brute. They didn't understand that he had gone inside himself to escape the noise, the shrieking banshees of grief that descended after his father's death. Robert Daly had taken his side, but weakly, and Alasdair had always gotten the impression that Robert chuckled about the name behind his back. The Mute Brute. It lasted until he soundly beat Frank Miles during a river race; Frank trotted out the nickname in retaliation, and Alasdair broke his arm in three places, finally having enough.

He shuddered at the memory of Frank's gasping howl of pain. Perhaps he hadn't gained the respect of his peers after that, but he did gain their firmly shut mouths.

The tables around him were half-full. The families there chatted merrily. Talking and talking. He stared down at his empty plate, the conversations winding into one another until they were just a blur of sound threading through the room. He closed his eyes tightly, trying to shut it out, knowing the heat spreading through his chest would worsen, grow thorns, and creep up his neck until it choked him . . . Was it a curse or a skill that he could somehow feel shatteringly alone in a mostly occupied space . . .

The churning, that's how I would describe it, too. I've always had it, but it became so much worse when Father died.

And there, he had not felt alone in that conversation. He had learned early not to identify the strangeness of his mind to others. His father had lost a cousin to what he described as "malingering thoughts." And in these recollections of "madness," Alasdair recognized himself. The rumination. The indecision. The desire to retreat from the world entirely when overwhelmed. Cousin Muriel, as she was called, had refused to marry, resorted to frequent outbursts, and disappeared for days on end, until at last the family decided she was incurable and sent her to Bethlem at Moorfields. Alasdair stopped hearing about Cousin Muriel after that, and though her story faded from their lives, the moral of it never did.

Loud laughter trickled down from upstairs. Freddie. He stood abruptly and fixed his coat, then crossed resolutely to the stairs. The big, burly proprietor stumbled out from behind his counter. Lowering his brow, he grunted out, "Keep it quiet, eh, Mr. Kerr? Civil?"

"Believe me, sir, I have no intention of causing a scene."

No, this was about avoiding just such an outcome, although he feared the damage had already been done. Freddie didn't think, didn't dwell; he acted. Alasdair turned and charged up the stairs, taking them three at a time. What must it be like, he wondered, to not be a dog chained to a master of worries? To simply be, simply do, unmoored by doubts . . .

He tracked the sound of Freddie's muted voice through the walls to a door at the end of the upstairs hall. There was a damp, musty scent hanging in the air that made his eyes water and his throat protest. His fist landed three times on the door, hard, and the giggling within ceased at once.

"Do you think—" began a high, pretty voice.

"Put something on, damnit. I'll go and have a look."

Freddie.

A moment later he heard footsteps approaching and a shoulder lightly bang against the other side. "Is that the wine we wanted, boy?"

Alasdair smiled and pressed his head close to the wood. "Something stronger."

He could all but feel Freddie withering behind the door.

"Sod it, Alasdair, what do you want?"

"Your fun is at an end, I'm afraid. Time to come home."

"According to who? You? Mother?"

"According to nothing but good, common sense. By God, Freddie, is there not an ounce of decorum left in your body? Open this door, now, or I will splinter it myself."

"Yes, yes, all right!" Freddie then murmured something to his companion and slowly tugged the door open, standing before Alasdair with the wide, glistening eyes of a child standing beside the vase they had shattered. A woman came flying past him immediately, head bowed, the back of her neck red with embarrassment. Alasdair paid her no attention; according to the proprietor, she was simply one among a legion of willing admirers.

Alasdair shoved himself into the room before Freddie could change his mind. His brother's shirt was loose and open, his eyes bloodshot, his skin sallow from drink and lack of sleep. Bounding away to the table by the hearth, he began doing up the five buttons on his shirt and straightening out the cuffs. A sour perfume of sweat, old wine, and body musk lingered.

"Don't look at me like that," Freddie said, hunting down his scattered garments. "It's a perfectly natural response to the disappointment I've suffered. Did Mother send you?"

"I sent myself. Everyone knows you're here."

Freddie at least had the good grace to wince at that. He went to a basin of water standing on a table by the window and splashed his face. "Do you suppose Emilia knows, too?"

"It would be better if she did; her heart might mend the faster. I understand that she—" He cut himself off quickly, realizing sympathy would only complicate matters.

"It's natural," Freddie repeated himself, pushing his wet hands through his hair before sniffing and striding to the door.

"Who are you to judge? You . . . you who would choose a cold, flat painting over a flesh-and-blood woman."

Alasdair pushed him lightly through the open door, grunting. "I've taken my share of lovers. That you don't know about it speaks to my discretion, not my inexperience. Any man who crows about his exploits is pathetic, lying, or both, a lesson you could well learn after this . . . display."

They made it as far as the top of the stairs before Freddie stiffened and refused to go farther.

"My bill . . ."

"I've seen to it."

His brother fell quiet then and remained so until they had left the establishment, enduring so many inquiring gazes from the other patrons that Alasdair could only hope it scarred Freddie for life. He couldn't trust that Freddie would find his way home without another indulgent detour and thus delivered him to Sampson with the stoicism of a jailor. They were just outside the front doors of the estate when Freddie perked up and cast his gaze across the lawn, inhaling deeply.

"You were right," he said, rocking back on his heels and appraising the sky, which was threatening rain. "I'm not good enough for Miss Graddock."

Alasdair was very tired, expecting more long hours at Clafton before supper. "It's nice to see you've joined us in the world as it is."

"But I *shall* be good enough. You'll be happy to know I've decided on a profession, and it will please Mother even more, for I'm to join the clergy. Why, today I will write to the chancellor for a recommendation. It will be merry indeed to take the living at Anselm, and it will mean we are always near as family."

Alasdair removed his spectacles and pinched the bridge of his nose. "When, may I ask, did you decide upon this?"

"Just now."

"I see. There is the small problem that Mr. Danforth already has the living, Freddie."

"Some . . . reason for his removal can be devised, and Mother will see to it." Freddie frowned and waved both hands around at nothing. "Surely, she would choose her son over that man!" he added, dissolving into nervous laughter. "Wouldn't she?"

Alasdair didn't have an answer for him. "Bathe," he said. "Before she realizes you've returned."

The subject of Freddie's future was tabled until supper, when Alasdair returned from the build on sore, aching feet. Gordon was not the sort of man to stand on ceremony and gladly let Alasdair pitch in as much as he wanted; for that span of time, he had done precisely as Gordon instructed and was put to hard work, so much so that he had been grateful for the way it obliterated any thoughts of his wayward brother and the even more bothersome thoughts of Violet Arden.

But the work concluded eventually, and it was suggested by Mr. Danforth that Lady Edith would fall into despair if her sons continued eschewing her company at dinner. Peace around the braised venison did not last long. Alasdair busied himself with eating as much as he could, starving once more after so much backbreaking effort at Clafton, noticing new calluses rasping against his cutlery while he tried to ignore the eyes of the paintings looming just beyond the tight halo of candlelight surrounding them.

"I've made some important decisions," Freddie began, puffing up and preparing to drop his news. "In fact, I—"

Lady Edith, practically in another parish due to the size of the table, squished around under her shawl and skewered an asparagus with her fork. "That reminds me. Danforth has some employment for you tomorrow."

"To be sure," Danforth murmured, smiling beatifically over his vegetables.

"Right. But just this afternoon I've written to—"

"It is very bad, very bad indeed that they will not hear advice from Mr. Danforth at the Florizel," Lady Edith continued, undaunted. Freddie might as well have been trying to speak to her from the bottom of a distant well. "But for their edification, and the edification of all who might require it, Mr. Danforth has produced a marvelous pamphlet."

Alasdair reached for his wine.

"It urges us to reconsider Commonwealth ideas regarding public theater, and what is fit to display," said Danforth, visibly satisfied. His smile widened as he beamed at Freddie, then Alasdair. "Lady Edith has suggested you would both enjoy the subject and aid me in seeing these pamphlets distributed among the townsfolk."

Sitting back, wine in hand, Alasdair snorted. "No. I won't be doing that."

"I beg your pardon?" Danforth shifted.

"I sincerely doubt our feelings about secular art and its merits align, Mr. Danforth," he continued, short.

"Even so, Lady Edith assures me that—"

"Your time would be better served with Freddie, who has decided to join the clergy," said Alasdair. He looked down the table toward his mother, whose mouth was hanging open. "He's written to the chancellor, and I intend to do the same."

Everyone was silent, barely stirring.

"You . . . y-you do?" Freddie burbled with hope to his right.

Anything to make Danforth shut up.

Danforth glared at Alasdair through a gap in the candelabra.

"What a wholly unexpected pivot, Mr. Kerr. Would to God we all in this house might consider such a renewed commitment!" His smile widened, his gaze upon Alasdair unflinching.

"Meaning?" Alasdair held his look.

"Meaning that the good people of this parish, however pure their hearts, are not immune to the contagion of filth and folly. No better demonstrated than by an unmarried man escorting a single lady without chaperone while both of them are, heaven forgive us, *woefully* underdressed."

So. Word had spread about more than just Freddie's reprobate activities.

Lady Edith coughed strangely behind her hand. "Of what does Mr. Danforth speak?"

It was questionable whether Lady Edith's delicate constitution could withstand the knowledge that a soaking wet Mr. Kerr had carried a forbidden Richmond relation for two entire fields while she was in her nightgown, without so much as a shawl or shoe. The scope of her life had narrowed so grievously; she had only the art he brought home, Danforth, and Alasdair's grasping attempts at obedience.

That brief tenderness between him and the lady seemed suddenly precious. The warm suggestion of her through the thin, torn nightdress, the tiny pink mark left by the wax on her neck just like the evidence of a passionate, sucking kiss, the scent of lavender clinging to the dark abundance of her hair . . . And the painting upstairs. The painting he really ought to return. Now it must go back to her. It would break his mother's heart to discover that he had lied. He chewed hard on air, then wrinkled his nose, his entire face tightening with consternation.

"Nothing, Mother, vicious rumor and nothing more." To this, Danforth opened his mouth to correct him, but Alasdair didn't give him the chance. "It would be my pleasure—and Freddie's—to go with Mr. Danforth and his pamphlets tomorrow. What manner of *filth* will we be protesting, sir?"

Mr. Danforth's lips curled higher. "The very worst sort. A call to misbehavior and immorality if ever one was penned—the lamentable tragedy of *Romeo and Juliet.*"

9

And seeing ignorance is the curse of God,
Knowledge the wing wherewith we fly to heaven.
Henry VI, Part 2—Act 4, Scene 7

The rain descended for three straight days, lifting its lugubrious shroud at last to the joy and relief of the Arden sisters. During those gray afternoons and while her ankle healed, Violet had decided to paint Maggie while she wrote, a risky exercise that, they all agreed, kept Violet quietly occupied. Violet painted, Maggie scribbled, and Winny sewed. The morning when the sunshine finally spread across the winking wet grass of the cottage lawn, Violet packed her paints and her case and followed Winny on foot to town.

"Go!" Maggie had chased them off, ink staining the fingertips she flashed in their vicinity. "This book will never be finished if you two buzz around my ears like silly bees all day."

The post had come, with all the letters addressed to Maggie and Mrs. Arden.

"You don't look wistfully at the post anymore," Winny

noted cheerfully, hooking her arm through Violet's as they started off on their walk. She carried a compact bundle of wrapped costumes, which she had offered to mend for the Florizel. The theater was a small enterprise, and grateful for any extra hands. Winny patched rips and adjusted hems for personal money, which was a pittance, though she prized it all the same.

"I can't imagine what you mean," Violet replied, perfectly aware.

"Did the Frenchman never write? Not even to explain himself or apologize?"

"It's for the best," she said with a sigh, and shook her head, drinking down the chill, rain-quenched air. "At least, that's what everyone insists."

"You smile more," said Winny. "I missed that. And your painting is better than ever, don't you agree?"

"Small improvements, I suppose. At least my grapes look like grapes."

Winny blushed and looked down at her shoes. "They always did." And a few steps later: "But they *are* improved, so lifelike you could eat them."

"Thank you, sister, but that's neither here nor there," Violet began, with the exasperation of a woman twice her age. "Miss Bilbury will see to it that my studies continue, and I will see to it that Emilia stays far away from Freddie Kerr."

Alasdair could plead for Freddie's innocence until he was blue in the face and his spectacles cracked, but Violet held fast to her suspicions. It was too convenient: he and Emilia leave each other brokenhearted, and shortly after, Pressmore is set aflame.

"The fire," breathed Winny, her lashes fluttering nervously. "Do you really think—"

"It doesn't matter what I think, what matters is that Emilia is safe from him. And she has the play to anticipate! I only hope the subject matter does not discombobulate her all over again . . ."

"Or she will be grateful she did not end up like poor, poor Juliet."

It was suggested cheerfully, and Violet tried to smile in agreement. Unhelpfully, her thoughts turned to Mr. Kerr and whether he would attend the play. The strangest thing kept happening—her mind would conjure his image, then again, each version of him marginally different until she couldn't help but want to see him in person to determine whether he really was as handsome as she remembered. And to put all the wondering to bed.

She mustn't think of Mr. Kerr and bed, for serious danger waited in that direction. The last time she had allowed a man to become her world, it had ended in nothing but humiliation.

Cray Arches had few features to distinguish it from other towns of its size. It boasted, however, a rather fine church and the Florizel. The theater, unusual for such a modest place, was the passion project of a local family and sat across the square from Winny's favorite place in the world, Gray and Simon.

If Cray Arches was a squat table laid for a large family, then the Florizel Theatre was its lovably slipshod centerpiece, with its faded white façade and six pillars valiantly holding up the drooping triangular front. The paint was peeling, and one pillar on the right looked in danger of collapse; the wooden filigrees decorating the entrance were also in desperate need of refurbishment, but the humble establishment still felt like a dash of grandeur on a dreary day. It seated seven hundred and had almost closed five different times, saved at each perilous juncture by the charity of Aunt Mildred and the rest of the

Richmonds, who were friends of the owner and devoted patrons of the arts.

According to Violet's father, in the decades before Violet's birth, the Florizel had been opened, closed, and reopened repeatedly in accordance with the tastes and laws of the country. It never failed to gall her that there were folk so afraid of the theater and its delights that they sought to shutter the Florizel for good.

"Who will you paint today?" Winny asked. They had nearly completed the thirty-minute walk to the heart of Cray Arches. It was good to stretch the limbs and work out the last aches in Violet's stiff ankle. Stringy, pale clouds sketched themselves across the horizon, a coy little wind blowing harmless cyclones of red leaves in their path. "Claribel Wefling is the beauty of the company, but I think Ginny Thorpe has a remarkable nose."

Violet and Winny were not so much welcomed into the Florizel as they were blended seamlessly into the maelstrom—Winny was immediately swept away to lend her expertise to more costume fittings; Mr. Lavin, the owner of the theater, took noisy meetings in his office, punctuated by visits from the actors to argue this or that about their lines; Mercutio and Tybalt practiced their duel in a narrow corridor outside the office; Violet was intercepted by Ginny Thorpe, who was playing Juliet and still wearing half of her costume.

"Mr. Lavin brought Philippe all the way from Paris to paint our scenery, but he fell painting last night and broke his arm," said Ginny, out of breath and flustered. "Oh, but it's only half done and looks a right shambles."

"Let me put my paints in Mr. Lavin's office," Violet replied, eager. "Have you sent word to Pressmore? Perhaps Miss Bilbury and I could be of assistance? We both paint, though she is the superior talent."

Ginny melted with relief. Mr. Lavin was notified of Violet's desire to pitch in, and a request was dispatched to Pressmore. She could imagine her aunts' faces when they discovered Violet had volunteered to assist a bunch of actors. "Practically prostitutes!" Aunt Eliza would say with a gasp, fainting away. Violet's aunt on her father's side had been an actress, shunned for it, and died recently in London, impoverished. Impoverished but not lonely, at least, for the Arden sisters had tried to care for her in the end. Beatrice Arden had been a strong woman, determined, leaving a lasting impression on Violet.

Let Aunt Eliza faint, she thought. *The Florizel needs us.*

Cristabel agreed. She considered the scenic challenge perfect for Violet, who was accustomed to painting at small scale. Each afternoon, Violet would meet Cristabel at the theater, and they would paint in companionable silence, bringing to life Juliet's balcony, the interior of a chapel, and a basic piazza in Verona. Winny came along, hemming skirts and sewing on buttons when such things were needed. Ginny Thorpe's beloved orange cat, Sailor, snoozed beside Violet while her brush swished, Cristabel gave her corrections, and the actors rehearsed their lines.

"Shall I hear more, or shall I speak at this?" asked Romeo, a few feet from where the ladies worked. The man playing him was hilariously old to be portraying a teen, but he gave the words the right feeling. Cristabel rolled her eyes at every romantic declaration in the play, and there were plenty.

Ginny, as Juliet, answered. "'Tis but thy name that is my enemy. Thou art thyself, though not a Montague. What's Montague? It is nor hand, nor foot, nor arm, nor face. O, be some other name belonging to a man!"

Romeo flubbed his next line, and the whole scene started over again.

"Perhaps Mr. Lavin is trying to tell you and the Kerrs something by choosing this production," said Cristabel one afternoon, as they continued painting and rehearsals progressed. Sailor, no matter what, slept on Violet's shawl.

"It's a popular play," Violet told her.

"Of course." Her teacher fell silent for a spell, but Violet could hear the thoughtful steam hissing from her ears. Cristabel proved her right moments later. "Have you sketched him again?"

Him. Violet growled and hunched her shoulders. "No. My paints haven't moved from Mr. Lavin's office since we agreed to help. I hope you haven't been pouring poison in Ann's ears. She is terribly suggestible."

"Why would I do that?" Cristabel laughed. "Romance is a distraction. Art is truest love. Even if you try to hide it, I can see all this cloying drivel moves you. You sigh and flutter your lashes whenever the confessions start. Ha! That ridiculous Romeo is old enough to be Juliet's father."

"My father loved this play, and so do I, that's all. Maybe it is drivel, but I still have a heart. Even so, do not worry yourself—I haven't painted or sketched *him*, and I never will."

Despite Miss Bilbury's teasing, each day ended with a deep sense of satisfaction. The ladies worked well together, and Mr. Lavin and the company were effusively grateful. But gradually, both women had noticed a strange phenomenon; it began with just the one irksome preacher standing outside, glaring at everyone who came and went from the Florizel, but by and by, a small army built up around him. The following morning, Emilia and Cristabel called at Beadle Cottage.

"Good morning," Cristabel greeted them with a strained smile. Emilia clung to her side. "I thought Emilia could use the air today and brought her along."

She could use more than air.

Violet found it hard to believe how much Emilia had shrunk in just a fortnight. The poor lady was wasting away, her usually luminous brown skin almost gray. She had seen widows with stronger color in their cheeks.

"It is so lonely without you at Pressmore," Emilia said, leaning against Violet as they left through the cottage gate. "Ann has her child and her society now, and I am an afterthought. Did you know, there are men working at Clafton every day? I can see them from my window. It only reminds me of . . ."

She trailed off into bitter silence. Violet shot a wretched look at the other women, who were no help at all.

"Perhaps you should take up painting," Violet suggested. "It has been a balm for me."

Though I fear in this state you would struggle to lift the brush . . .

"Miss Bilbury said the same, but I find it hard to care about anything at all." Emilia's thinness through her dress and coat made Violet tense with worry. "To be unlovable and rejected, there is no greater pain."

"Come, Emilia, I'm sure he loves you, but that does not change the material circumstances."

Violet flinched. It had just spilled out. But how could she let Emilia suffer so? A small, surprisingly strong hand latched onto her wrist, and suddenly Emilia's huge brown eyes were peering into hers with owlish intensity.

"Do you really think so? Oh, but you are just trying to content me . . ."

"Mr. Kerr himself said as much." Another flinch. "He didn't want me to think Freddie could be responsible for the fire at Pressmore."

Emilia gasped.

"Then . . . then there is hope . . ."

Perhaps Mr. Kerr was right; finality is more merciful.

"No, dear, I think there is only the truth—that you should not and cannot marry him, and that love, sadly, is simply not enough."

But Emilia wasn't listening. Her entire demeanor changed, a sparkle gathering in her once-dull eyes. Violet, by contrast, brooded, realizing her mistake. She had offered hope where there ought to be plain rationality. The ladies neared the Florizel only to find a dense crowd gathering outside its doors. The sisters joined the stragglers at the back. Winny, popular in town from her constant trips to the ribbon shop, pulled an older lady aside, eager for an explanation. Why such a crowd on a Saturday afternoon?

"It is all in this pamphlet," said Winny's acquaintance, handing them a folded collection of yellowed papers. Violet took the manual, reading through it with a knot tightening in her belly.

"Unbelievable," she murmured. "Here this Danforth fellow describes *Romeo and Juliet* as an 'inculcation to impropriety and sin.' He can hardly be serious! It's meant to be a warning, not encouragement. There are Cristabel and Emilia; stay with them, I'm going to get to the bottom of this."

She didn't hear Winny's response, already pushing through the throng of townsfolk with the ridiculous pamphlet tucked under her arm. Mr. Danforth had taken it upon himself to perch on the front steps of the Florizel, preaching to those who had assembled, while Mr. Lavin, the owner, attempted to reason with the man.

"We are all allowed our beliefs, sir," Lavin was huffing,

crimson with fluster. "And I believe you are out of line. Not since the Licensing Act has the Florizel been met with opposition of any sort!"

"That is about to change," said the vicar. He had thick, curling hair and a smug way about him that Violet disliked immediately. Worse, hovering just over his shoulder was a familiar face, and not one she expected to see on the side of censorship.

"Mr. Kerr!" she exclaimed, coming to stand beside Mr. Lavin and making her position clear. The clergyman's timing could not be worse; the play was set to debut in just two days. Violet searched among the faces of those Danforth had brought, most of them strangers, leading her to wonder if these weren't the good people of Cray Arches at all but folk he had assembled in neighboring Anselm.

"Good morning, Miss Arden." Mr. Kerr angled out and away from the preacher; as he bowed, he wore an uncharacteristically sheepish expression. "I trust that your leg is much improved?"

"My—oh. Yes, thank you, it's no trouble at all now. You are with this . . . person?" she asked, nodding toward Danforth and his horrid little basket heaped with pamphlets.

They stepped aside while the vicar continued arguing with Mr. Lavin. The actors were trickling out from the theater's front doors, which only inflamed matters.

"I am near him," Mr. Kerr replied, his lip curling somewhat with disdain. "I am not *with* him."

To Violet's continued dismay, Freddie Kerr peered out from behind his brother's broad, concealing back. He looked pale and like he had not been sleeping adequately. If he caught sight of Emilia, there was no telling how he might react.

"Is this what clergymen are meant to do?" Freddie mumbled.

"My brother has taken a sudden interest in the profession," Mr. Kerr explained.

"Harangue the populace over Shakespeare?" his brother continued.

Mr. Kerr clamped a heavy hand on his shoulder. "Having second thoughts?"

"And third and fourth. Does he really think this will fill his pews on Sundays?"

Violet held up the pamphlet, waving it in Mr. Kerr's face. "What I want to know is how he afforded all of this! There must be hundreds of them . . ."

"My mother, I'm afraid," Mr. Kerr replied, sullen. He stepped out of the shadow of the theater portico, and Violet followed. It was quieter there, and she could finally hear him clearly above the crowd and Danforth. "She's inexplicably devoted to the man."

"And she's started the Ladies' Society for Decency and Restoration," said Freddie, whom she had not noticed coming around the corner with them.

"What?" Mr. Kerr rounded on him. "When did she do that?"

"Only yesterday. Wonder of wonders, Danforth set it up for her." Freddie's eyes rolled so vehemently they might have made a grinding sound. "Really. It sounds like he established the ladies' society. When has our mother ever expressed interest in such a thing?"

"Since Mrs. Ann Richmond established her own charitable society, I imagine," Mr. Kerr muttered, removing his spectacles and pinching the top of his nose.

Freddie shook his head. "Rivals to the bitter end."

"I hardly care who established what," Violet cut in. "I care about this," she cried, gesturing to the agitated crowd. "And this." She shoved the pamphlet into Mr. Kerr's grasp. He held it as if it were a used handkerchief.

"I agree, Miss Arden, it is an astonishing use of free will."

"Then get him out of here," she growled. Her vision was clouding at the edges, a surge of dizzy anger making her nearly topple as she spun and marched back to the front of the theater. Winny was waiting for her there, and, eager to be away from the rising noise, she took her sister by the hand and dodged around Mr. Lavin. A large shape blocked her path, and Violet stumbled back, another swell of rage sweeping over her as she craned to look Mr. Danforth in the eye.

"Let me pass, sir," Violet said, seething.

"Miss Arden, you seem to be without a pamphlet," he said, holding up one of the leaflets between them. "It pains me to think a lady of your gentle breeding might need educating upon this subject, but even God's purest lambs can be led astray."

When she did not take the offered material, the preacher held up his hands, lightly touching Violet's shoulders.

"Is this where you belong, dear child?" he murmured, almost sad. "With the dregs and the prostitutes and those who would parade themselves before the public for vanity's sake?"

A shadow fell across them, and Violet blinked up and out of her anger to see Mr. Kerr had come. He had only to gaze down at Danforth in his direct, silent way and the clergyman removed himself, lowering his presumptuous little hands to clutch his basket with a half-mumbled apology.

"I would not advise touching the lady again," warned Mr. Kerr.

The words nested inside her, somehow both warm and cold.

"Maybe he could come every day to escort us," she heard Winny breathe to her right.

Mr. Kerr touched his hat and kept the solid bulwark of his body between Danforth and Violet until she and the others hurried safely inside the Florizel. Violet did not draw breath until she noticed the tightness in her chest. People flowed around her, hardly more than streaks of color whooshing by her head. Mr. Kerr's presence, his protectiveness, had made her less afraid and even momentarily grateful.

"Did Emilia sneak in before us?" Winny asked, bringing Violet back to herself.

"I don't know," she stammered. But a quick glance around the front hall and office did not produce Emilia. Cristabel had already gone ahead to the stage to begin mixing pigments, and Mr. Lavin could be heard ranting about Danforth in his office. Ginny's cat, Sailor, rubbed against Violet's ankles until she picked up the creature and absent-mindedly stroked its neck.

"Perhaps Mr. Lavin can have someone look for her outside," Winny suggested. "I've no interest in elbowing through that crowd again."

Cristabel summoned Violet, impatient to begin the work they were in danger of not finishing in time, and she went, and let Sailor go to chase mice or dream of fountains of milk or whatever cats fantasized about, and the morning rolled on. And in all of it, surprisingly or not, Emilia's absence was forgotten. For Violet's part, she could not forgive herself for feeling so much relief when Mr. Kerr leveled his mild threat at Danforth.

Nor could she stop imagining that look of his, all of that considerable strength and concern rallied just for her.

When the afternoon wore on and there was no more to be done, when Violet's hands were stained with paint and cramped from effort, she and Winny said their goodbyes at the front doors, walking outside to find it blissfully quiet. Violet found herself wishing Mr. Kerr were there waiting for them, a sentinel to protect them in case Danforth burst from the bushes or flew down from the roof.

But he wasn't there, and neither was Emilia, whom, it became evident, they had entirely forgotten.

"I did ask Mr. Lavin to send someone out to search for her," said Winny, her voice rising as the ladies descended into panic.

"Emilia is a smart woman. I'm sure she returned to Pressmore," added Cristabel, though her pallor told the fuller story. "Of course she would. Of course . . ."

Violet let them spin and speculate while she sifted through her thoughts for the answer. "No, oh no," she murmured, slapping her cheek and holding her hand there. "I shouldn't have said anything, but I may have mentioned that Freddie Kerr still loves her."

"What?" Cristabel rounded on her. "Why would you say such a thing?"

"Because it's likely true," Violet groaned, stamping her feet against the cold. "Mr. Kerr said as much as a sort of defense of Freddie, an explanation for why it couldn't be him who set the fire at Pressmore."

"It could have been anybody," Cristabel said with a sigh. "Your cousin never found hide nor hair of the cloaked person you described."

"I know, *I know*, and they probably found each other in the crowd when we were distracted, and . . ."

Cristabel reached for her, turning Violet until they faced each other. "Let us not fall to mischief with our minds when reason will better serve, yes? She might have returned to the house. She probably returned to the house."

Violet had never let reason stop or serve her before. "*Or* they are already halfway to Gretna Green," she cried, her head falling back loose on her shoulders. "And it is all my fault. Oh, God, Ann is going to kill me . . ."

"She will do no such thing," Cristabel assured them. "But Ann is our answer. We will hire a carriage at the inn, it will be faster than walking back to the estate. If Emilia is not at Pressmore, then we can decide our degree of frenzy."

Winny called it an excellent solution, and so it was. They returned to Pressmore Estate with all haste, the driver from the Gull and Knave understanding the urgency very well, subsequently conveying them at appropriate speed. The ladies flung themselves from the carriage and raced up the drive to the front hall, where Bloom met them with the sort of long-suffering look only a butler who had seen decades of youthful waggery could conjure. It was put to the family simply that Emilia had not come into the theater, and only Lane and Ann were told about the alarming Freddieness of it all.

"Oh dear," said Ann.

"*Blazes*," said Lane.

"She is not here," Ann continued, her mouth turning down with fear. "But we will search the grounds at once."

By now it was dark, and the grounds were searched with lanterns and calls of "Emiliaaaaaa," but Emilia was nowhere to be found.

"As much as it pains me to say it," said Lane, as the collective consternation grew, "we should send word to the Kerrs. This could have everything to do with them."

"Winny and I will return to the Florizel," Violet told him. "They will still have rehearsal, and we can ask if anyone saw the two of them in town."

The hired carriage had left long ago, but Lane gave the sisters one of Pressmore's to expedite the journey. Violet sat like a lit cannon fuse, a heartbeat away from screaming at the top of her lungs. Nobody had mentioned to the Richmonds that Violet was to blame for it, but she knew it. *She* knew.

"If anything happens to her," Violet murmured, pressing her nose to the freezing-cold window, "I'll never forgive myself."

"We *will* find her," Winny promised.

Violet wanted with every sinew in her body to believe her.

They were trundling down the hill sloping toward Cray Arches when Violet, squeezed tight against the door and window, saw a flash of orange on the horizon. Her heart seized. The light grew, spreading like the tail of a comet, arcing in a yellow crest over the center of town. The unmistakable scent of burning wood followed soon after. Smoke rose in hazy torrents, obscuring the first twinkle of stars.

"Something is on fire," Winny whispered, cramming herself alongside Violet to look out the window.

"It's the Florizel," said Violet, her mouth bone-dry. "It's gone up in a blaze."

10

It is held
That valor is the chiefest virtue and
Most dignifies the haver.
Coriolanus—Act 2, Scene 2

The last person Alasdair expected to find at Sampson Park at that time of night was Lane Richmond. Lane was rich, well-liked, and known to be a cheerful sort of man, always ready with a smile. There was no trace of that boyish grin now as he tripped over his words to explain the state of things.

"I fear, Mr. Kerr, I must ask if your brother, Freddie, is at home." Lane was pale with embarrassment. "Please forgive the impudence of the question, but it is a matter of some urgency."

Alasdair had been busy at Clafton all afternoon, but to his knowledge, Freddie had not returned for supper. It had been a sleepy evening in general at Sampson; his mother had not been at all well, and Alasdair dined alone. His stomach clenched with nerves; Freddie knew he was meant to be on a short leash after his dayslong self-mortification in Cray Arches, and to disappear again so soon was bold indeed. Bold and stupid. Alasdair allowed Lane inside to wait while he directed the staff to search the grounds quickly for Freddie. For his part, he made a swift loop through the upper floors, discovering Sampson as dark and silent as a grave.

When he returned to the front hall, it was to the scandalized gasping of his mother.

"A Richmond in my house? At this hour?" She turned to Alasdair, hiding behind a maid and clutching the collar of her robe to her throat.

Alasdair didn't want to trouble her, escorting Lane outside with a grumbled apology.

"I shouldn't have come," said Lane, fretting with his hat.

"No, no," Alasdair assured him. "He broke things off badly with Miss Graddock, and he is often swayed by lesser impulses. You were right to raise the alarm."

Lane bowed his head with relief, then gestured to his horse. "I'm glad you understand, sir."

"All too well." Alasdair called for his valet, already formulating a plan. "He frequents the Gull and Knave. I'll go there myself and inquire. If I learn anything of use, I'll send a man to Pressmore."

"I am glad to hear it; I'll return there and await your message."

While Lane Richmond departed, Alasdair went to inspect the stables. No carriages were missing, and all animals were accounted for, which meant either Freddie was still on foot, as he had been that afternoon, or he had hired conveyance elsewhere. Elsewhere like a postal inn popular with travelers. Alasdair left Sampson Park not long after Lane, riding hard for the Gull and Knave. The cold sliced his cheeks, and his heart raced, but he wasn't about to let Freddie slip out of town for an elopement; it would break their mother's heart, and she was their only parent with a heart to protect.

As he was nearing town, he noticed the rising smell of smoke on the wind. At first, he thought he imagined its sickly, acrid tinge, but then he saw the hellish black cloud gathering over the middle of Cray Arches. The shrieking of townsfolk, the neighing of panicked horses, the sounds of shattering glass and breaking wood were seared into him. He briefly considered continuing to the inn but diverted and rode deeper into town, finding a dozen or so men running through the square, buckets sloshing with water as they pelted toward the theater. The building was like a hearth without a chimney, stones glowing beneath a crown of fire.

He secured his horse to a post at the blacksmith's a cautious distance away and joined the queue of helpers running toward the danger. A group had gathered outside the theater, watching in horror, clutching one another, some frozen to the spot by the fear, others hurrying to save what they could.

"Back!" he thundered, pushing them away from the front steps. One woman in particular was inching far too close, putting herself in needless danger. Alasdair put himself between her and the fire, holding out his hands to keep her from going any farther, and caught his words before they came roaring out. Violet Arden stared up into his eyes, her face heavily smudged with soot. There was a pile of belongings beside her, a heap of things she had already saved from the fire.

"There's still time . . ." She dodged around him, evading the sweep of his arm, frustratingly nimble.

Alasdair turned toward her and away from the sea of faces gawking at the theater. "Is there anyone left inside?"

"Sailor!" cried Violet, running toward the front doors. A swell of explosive heat met her, and she stumbled back, shielding her eyes. Undaunted, she charged toward the front office, where the windows had been broken out. She hitched her skirts and started climbing inside.

"A sailor?" he asked, following. He reached for her, trying to pull her back.

Violet shrugged him off, slippery with sweat from the heat, and threw herself into the burning building. "No! Sailor! Ginny's cat!"

"Miss Arden, I insist you stay here. It's simply too dangerous—"

Her black hair had come loose from its pins, tumbling over one shoulder as she spared him a single determined look. "Damn your insistence, and damn you, too. I won't leave an innocent soul behind."

Smoke poured out of the broken window around her, and then, swallowed by the gritty haze, she vanished.

Panic and smoke and fear squeezed his throat like a fist, but Alasdair vowed not to lose her to the fire. Something could fall on her, or the heat could overwhelm her . . . An image of her, helpless and limp, curled up on the stage, came to him, a bleak omen, and he heeded it, reckless of his own safety, hauling himself through the window and into the office. It may as well have been a furnace, for though nothing inside had caught fire yet, he could sense the flames on the floor above, greedy and growing, turning candles to puddles and bubbling the wallpaper around him like blistered skin. He glimpsed the back of Violet's gown as she tried to leave the room, shrieking and snatching her hand back when the doorknob burned her palm. Alasdair put his head down and lunged toward her, yanking her back before aiming a single hard kick at the door. It swung open awkwardly on broken hinges, a tremendous surge of heat bellowing up the main hall toward them.

"Sailor! Sailor!" Violet called, and coughed, wiping moisture from her eyes as she tumbled into the hall. She turned in a circle, took a few halting steps toward the seats and stage, then thought better of it and returned to the office door. "Perhaps we're too late . . ."

"Your compassion is understandable, Miss Arden, but it will get us both killed if—"

Violet's eyes snapped open. A tiny, soft sound threaded its way through the numbing roar of the fire spreading across the floor above them. "There! Did you hear it?"

She hurled herself toward the sound, stopping outside another closed door. Carefully, she pressed her ear to the wood. "I hear her!"

"Then step aside, please." Alasdair didn't allow himself to consider they were endangering themselves for some mangy stray. Absurd or otherwise, Miss Arden seemed resolved to throw her life away for the creature, and he wouldn't allow that. This door was fussier than the last, and he at last had to tear his own coat off, wrap it around his gloved hands, and use the whole bulk of it to pull the door until the knob nearly came off in his grasp. He wedged himself into the gap his effort had created, then shouldered it open the rest of the way until the wood creaked and splintered. Miss Arden pushed herself into the coatroom beyond and exclaimed with triumph, then reappeared with a small orange cat clinging desperately to her gown, claws extended.

"Through the front doors," he called to her, breathing hard. "Run as fast as you can."

For once, Miss Arden offered no argument and did as he instructed. Men called to one another outside. Above the terrible din could be heard the ineffectual splashing of water against the exterior of the building. The floor shook, and above him, Alasdair felt the weight of the conflagration threatening to spill down upon them like a cauterizing flood. He trained his eyes on Miss Arden, threw his jacket over his mouth against the rising smoke, and raced outside to safety.

As the cool night air surrounded them, he felt the building yield and the fire win out, and heard the commotion as the beams holding the upper floors began to give. It was like a dragon of legend inhaling before the great burning outcry. Miss Arden was too close to it all for his liking, and he herded her down the steps and away from the flame and smoke. A young woman trailed along, sobbing, reaching for the cat in Violet's arms. The yowling thing took a chunk of the lace on her gown with its claws as it was returned to the actress.

Alasdair shook his head, gazing down at Violet in total disbelief. "That was a mad thing to do."

"That little cat has been my steadfast companion for many days," said Violet, wiping at the black marks on her face and neck. "I couldn't stand by and do nothing. And look how happy it has made Ginny!" She beamed. "We will need that. So much is lost . . . we all worked so hard . . ."

"We?"

"Mr. Lavin and the actors, of course, but Miss Bilbury and I had taken over painting the scenery. Perhaps it wasn't perfect, but we did what we could with limited time. I was . . . proud of it." Miss Arden's shoulders caved inward as her spirit diminished and another thought dawned. "My easel and paints were in Mr. Lavin's office." She lifted her head, gazing off toward the theater as it was consumed.

"Don't even consider it," Alasdair warned, easing himself in front of her view.

A fleeting smile. A shrug. "It is nothing to some, I'm sure. I've no money to replace it all."

"You were not paid for your work on the scenery?"

Her brows lifted. "Oh, no, Mr. Kerr. As my aunt would say: a lady of good breeding does not seek employment. It was all to better my painting, and it did, but now it will be enjoyed by no one but the fire." She frowned and seemed to wilt again. He quashed a sudden urge to wipe the soot from below the soft pout of her lips, but she looked so sad, and it felt unbearable. "I shouldn't have said that. I've gone and made myself seem very lacking in front of a gentleman."

"You don't need to correct yourself in that manner," Alasdair told her, shaking out his ruined coat. "It doesn't bother me, you know . . ."

Violet blinked up at him in astonishment. "It doesn't? Why not?"

"Our understanding," he reminded her, though gently. "Our families?"

"Oh, of course."

"And . . ." It was his turn to frown and lose himself somewhat. "And I find most people incomprehensible. They speak in polite riddles, but you—"

"Ha!" Miss Arden covered her mouth, then graced him with one more coy smile. "And I'm no great mystery."

The actress had rallied and approached to draw Miss Arden into an embrace and thank her repeatedly, which was why Alasdair's words were lost to the night and the wind as he said quietly, "I don't know if I would go that far . . ."

More and more of the town arrived to watch the Florizel burn. It was clear now that there was absolutely no saving it. Like Clafton before it, it would be a charred shell by morning. Alasdair's face hardened as he watched the blaze feast and glut itself on the charming little theater. He thought of Miss Arden's wooden case of paints and brushes somewhere inside and imagined the pigments bursting in their compartments like miniature fireworks.

Margaret Darrow and Mrs. Arden arrived on foot, Mrs. Darrow clasping her cloak in both fists as the fire was reflected in her light blue eyes. Hasty greetings were exchanged.

Violet went to them at once. "Emilia . . . but she . . . and . . ." She glanced nervously at Alasdair.

"There is no need for secrecy," Alasdair assured her. "I know that Miss Graddock and my brother are missing. Indeed, I rode to town to search for him."

"Too many disasters for one evening," Mrs. Darrow muttered.

"And Emilia is not at Beadle?" asked Violet, clasping her sister's wrist.

"She is not, and I fear we can do nothing now but pray she is safe. It will be easier to search in the morning. And the Florizel! What horror! Does Mr. Lavin know how the blaze began?" asked Mrs. Darrow.

It was a question meant for Violet, but the young lady was off in her own world. She searched the ground near Alasdair's feet, her eyes moving faster and faster until her mouth popped open in apparent revelation. "No. *No*, but . . . I've just had a thought. Brilliant, Maggie, you never fail to inspire!"

"I . . . do?"

Alasdair took a small step toward them. "Are you well, Miss Arden?"

"Yes. Yes! Oh, I know it now. I know! I've done nothing all summer long but regale Emilia with stories of our childhood adventures, the way we ruled Pressmore and ran roughshod over the whole of the property," said Violet, struggling to get her words out fast enough. She pulled herself away from her family and began almost floating toward the town square. Sharing a confused look with Mrs. Darrow, Alasdair decided to follow.

"Playing pirates on the bridge, chasing each other through the maze, and, long before Ann had the Grecian temple put in, there was a thicket of raspberry bushes. Mrs. Richmond was wild about cultivating raspberries for a time, and we would gather them all with sticky fingers and carry them in our skirts across the hidden lane to the wood and eat them by the fistful until we were sick in Morning-glory Hollow."

"Morning-glory Hollow," said Alasdair, arriving at the thought at the same time.

"Mrs. Richmond never knew to look for us there," said Mrs. Darrow, nodding.

Miss Arden turned most urgently to her sister and mother, whispering, "Tell Winny where we have gone to look. If they are there, we can find them before the scandal widens." With big, hopeful eyes and her smudged elfin face, she fidgeted in Alasdair's direction. "No more lives should be ruined this night."

It was deliberately said, and slowly, and with the weight of a question.

Alasdair gave a single nod and gestured toward the blacksmith's. "My horse is nearby," he offered, and off they went.

11

Stars, hide your fires;
Let not light see my black and deep desires.
Macbeth—Act 1, Scene 4

A hard rain had begun to fall, the slap of the droplets against the remaining forest leaves giving the impression a hundred creatures galloped alongside them as they rode to the hollow.

It was a stroke of fortune for the burning Florizel, but less ideal for two exhausted people unprepared for such weather. *Maybe this is what it's like to drown very fast,* thought Violet, scrunching her face down into her neck and closing her eyes against the rain. Sitting in the warm, awkward cradle of Alasdair's saddle and lap, she was reminded of their walk across the fields, of his arms holding her as if she weighed nothing at all, and the intriguing slide of his wet shirt against her back.

"We seem doomed to odd, moist arrangements," she muttered, flinching from the jostle of the horse and the unforgiving rain shower.

"What?" Alasdair called over the noise of the hooves and the storm.

Violet shook her head and fell silent. Surely they would be there soon; she wasn't sure how much longer she could take. The saddle dug into her thigh, but when she tried to hold on to the pommel, her left hand screamed with pain; the burn was worse than she wanted to admit. But if she relied on Alasdair's body to keep her in place, other considerations arose. *Don't think of anything rising, don't think about his body, or him, or what you saw coming out of that river. In fact, don't think at all.*

But that was easier said than done for one of Violet's makeup. She couldn't breathe or sneeze but think and wonder. There was no escaping the man partially wrapped around her, the insides of his arms rubbing up and down against her as he controlled the horse, the subtle but powerful way his legs flexed to urge the beast faster or slower . . . He seemed completely unaware of her, which somehow made her that much more aware of *him.* The rain soaked them both, strengthening the rich, dark scent from his soap, hair pomade, and sweat. It had been hours since she ate, but that was just partially to blame for her sudden lightheadedness.

Morning-glory Hollow sat in something of a no-man's-land between Pressmore and Clafton. Certainly, someone somewhere knew the exact boundaries of the estates, but as children, they thought the large assortment of tumbled stones and overgrown plants felt like a world between worlds. If the adults of either side knew about it, they never indicated as much. It was the perfect place to stash secret treasures, to hold silly contests, and it often featured as the bandit or pirate stronghold, as needed. None of them knew its true origin, though Violet suspected it had probably been a tiny medieval chapel that had fallen into disrepair, forgotten by humans to be reclaimed by the woods.

Somebody—Maggie, probably—had given it the name Morning-glory Hollow, for the bold purple trumpets hung like curtains over the warped, sloped entrance to the cave-like hollow.

"A lantern," Alasdair said close to her ear. "Do you see it?"

Violet shivered and caught herself before she could lean fully against him. She decided he did not need to keep his mouth so near to her face; why was he doing that? Why had he charged into the Florizel after her? He was confounding. There was the man who had insulted her paintings in London and the man cradling her gently on his horse now, and how could they be the same? To discard the one in favor of the other felt like an abandonment of self-respect she couldn't abide.

You must think of Emilia now and keep her from making a terrible mistake . . .

"I see it," Violet said, sighing with relief as he brought the horse to a walk. They stopped just in view of the dull glow emanating from the hollow. The rain eased a little, and Mr. Kerr slid down from the horse, reaching up for her. He handled her cautiously, careful not to graze her against his chest as he set her feet onto the spongy earth. With a furrowed, shy glance, he offered his arm.

"The way is uneven," he said. "Take care that you do not sink into the mud."

"That is all I need," she muttered. "Another twisted ankle."

They moved gradually, for the hollow was not far from the stream on their right, and the ground was sodden from both the storm and proximity to the water. A gradual hill loped down to the stream, a good number of trees protecting the place from the road behind them and to the left. She noticed a pair of footprints running parallel to theirs and pointed.

"Oh, Freddie," he grunted. "You damned fool."

"You don't think . . . He wouldn't . . ."

Mr. Kerr said nothing but went with greater haste, tugging her along. Violet struggled to match his stride, clinging to his arm to keep from slipping. The trees offered some shelter, and as the storm moved on, she saw the lantern and the reddish light pouring from the mouth of the hollow with greater clarity. There were sounds now, too, smacking and sighing, and the occasional giggle that she instantly knew belonged to Emilia.

"This may not be a sight fit for a delicate lady," Mr. Kerr warned, holding her back.

"Please." Violet withdrew her hand, marching toward the lantern. "There will be time for delicacy when Emilia is safely back at Pressmore." She ducked into the hollow, interrupting Freddie's exploration of Emilia's bare neck and shoulders. His hand shot out from under her skirts.

"Christ!" Freddie screamed, flying back against the stone and banging his head.

"Violet!" Emilia gasped and scrambled to cover herself as Mr. Kerr stepped into view at Violet's side. "Mr. Kerr! This is . . . We weren't . . . That is to say . . ."

"Say nothing and dress now," Violet huffed, turning around to give them some privacy. "Honestly, Emilia, everyone is in an uproar looking for you. Ann and Lane are beside themselves."

"That's a surprise," Emilia murmured. Fabric rustled. Freddie muttered to himself. Violet stared up at the slick stones of the hollow above, irritated. "They hardly notice anything about me these days. And it was you who told me Freddie still cared, Violet. Why say such a thing if you hate the idea of our love?"

She felt rather than saw Mr. Kerr's eyes swivel toward her.

Violet pursed her lips and crossed her arms. "You were so unbelievably miserable! I was just trying to keep you from harming yourself further!"

"Miss Arden . . ."

She shook her head, refusing to look up at Mr. Kerr. "What do we do?"

Mr. Kerr shifted. "Ordinarily, one would demand they marry given what they have likely accomplished here this evening . . ." He squeezed his face hard with one hand. "Yet that is precisely what they want, to be married, an outcome which could put our mother into an early grave. She would not withstand the disappointment."

"So," said Violet, softly, "it is our secret."

"We never saw them here," he added.

"They were independently lost, waylaid by the storm," Violet continued, nodding. "And we will return them home, the whole ugly business forgotten."

Freddie joined them, still shrugging on his rain-dampened jacket. "You can't do that! We should be forced to marry; I've gone and made love to—"

Mr. Kerr whirled on his brother, drawing up to his full size, his arm stiffening as if he meant to strike the words right out of Freddie's mouth. "You are in the presence of a lady," he said, seething, then paused, glanced toward Emilia, and drew a calming breath, lowering his shoulders somewhat. "You are in the presence of two ladies. Mind yourself. How many times must disaster be averted on your behalf?"

Eager to be somewhere dry, cozy, and close to a bed, Violet extended her hand toward Emilia. "Come, dearest. I will get you back to Pressmore."

"Yes," said Emilia miserably, dragging herself toward the

mouth of the cave. "And you will tell Ann what happened, and just like Ruby, I will be shipped back to Lakhnau."

"No, Mr. Kerr and I won't breathe a word of this to anyone," Violet replied. "And we will find you—*ouch!*" She hissed and shook out her hand, having forgotten its tender state. Emilia had grabbed it hard, and pain sizzled through Violet's entire body. Before she could explain herself, Mr. Kerr was there, holding her wrist, offering up the wounded palm to the light of the lantern for inspection.

"This is far worse than I assumed. You should be taken to a physician at once," he said, his solemn grimace perhaps giving away more than his measured words. Violet hazarded a close look at her palm, where the once-peachy skin had become violently red and wrinkled, the rain and her grip on the saddle aggravating the burn. It bubbled and oozed, and a thick curl of flesh came away, peeling back to reveal a glistening patch beneath.

"O-oh dear," said Mr. Kerr, sounding green. She had no idea if his face matched his tone, for all at once she could not see. Exhausted. Freezing. Damp. The shock of fear hit behind the nose, blurring her vision and tightening her guts before the hollow started to spin and Violet collapsed.

She had vague ideas about how she came to be in the cramped bed she shared with Winny in Beadle Cottage. The journey from Morning-glory Hollow to home returned to her in blurred bubbles of shaken memory; she had not remained unconscious the entire way, swimming in and out of reality, hearing the muted voices low with concern as the doctor arrived, then slipping into a dreamlike state after he asked her to drink something.

Her dreams were fitful. Tossing, twisting, she imagined herself in the cold, rainy hollow curtained with ivy and rain-slicked vines. Flowers bloomed impossibly in the chill. Everything around her was too bright, ice and splotches of wildflowers, and the hard stone wedged beneath her thighs. Nothing made sense until Mr. Kerr was there, and it was not Emilia draped across the flat bench of rock in the hollow but Violet herself, head thrown back, hair loose, her gown gaping open toward Alasdair as if in invitation. His big, warm hands slid across her, one up the extended length of her leg, bold and searching, his other taking hold of her sleeve and pulling until the fabric tore and her breasts were exposed to his gaze and then his lips. The kisses he placed along her neck and collarbone shivered through her, each a provocation, each widening the spread of her legs. He couldn't be close enough to satisfy her, touch and alignment a shallow imitation of what seemed achievable in dreams. If he could be in and without her, their lips sealed, their bodies one, then maybe, maybe . . .

Violet tore awake, gasping for breath. She was safe in her bed, the blankets heaped so high she was practically buried alive. The milky light of early morning made the bedroom glow, and she lifted her injured left hand to find it had been bandaged. And thank God for that; she couldn't stomach the idea of seeing her peeling, burned palm again so soon.

The dream lingered. Violet blushed and shook it off until she felt herself again. What was *that*? Perhaps she should not have allowed herself to see Emilia and Freddie in the hollow. It had planted seeds of thought she could not bear to water. Someone like Mr. Kerr would never have her, even if she wanted him; no, she would have to make her own difficult way in the world. Winny was curled up asleep beside her, Maggie half-awake with a book in her lap, seated in the rocking chair by the window. Violet's sudden movement alerted Maggie, and her sister sat up straighter, yawning and stretching both hands over her head.

"How did I get here?" Violet asked, looking around with a somewhat dazed expression.

"There was a great commotion at the front door," said Maggie, leaving her book on the chair to sit gently on the edge of the bed at Violet's side. She combed Violet's hair back from her forehead. "Mr. Kerr brought you back, with word that Emilia had been found and returned to Pressmore. What happened in the forest? Do you remember?"

Violet swallowed with difficulty and glanced away. Her feelings for Mr. Kerr were confusing and conflicting, but she knew it was wrong to lie to her sister. Still, Emilia's reputation had to be protected; she couldn't imagine letting another woman experience the sort of public humiliation she had suffered at her aunt's painting exhibition. Emilia was young, and one questionable decision should not alter her life forever.

"She was there with Freddie," Violet replied. "At the hollow. But we found them before any real mischief . . ."

"Violet." Maggie's hand stilled on her head. "Are you certain?"

"She seemed scared," Violet assured her. "I don't think she'll be inclined to run off with a man again."

"Well, that's a relief." Maggie sighed and returned to her rocking chair and book. "The rain somewhat slowed the fire at the Florizel, but the damage is significant. Though you mustn't worry about that now, simply rest and let your hand mend."

Violet held up the bandaged lump of her left hand. "At least it was this one," she murmured. "I can still paint."

"Rest, you mean, for that is all you are supposed to be doing."

"Yes, of course. Rest. That is what I shall do."

But rest was not a thing Violet had ever done well or willingly; her mind didn't allow it, and if she didn't keep it busy with books, and chatter, and art, then it would go places she did not want it to venture, like back to the hollow, where it felt somehow that Mr. Kerr was waiting for her, his eyes burning with questions she refused to entertain.

12

Love looks not with the eyes but with the mind;
And therefore is winged Cupid painted blind.
A Midsummer Night's Dream—Act 1, Scene 1

October

It was miserably wet and muddy at Clafton, but Alasdair insisted on visiting daily. There was real satisfaction in watching the progress: in seeing the stones change as they were shaped for placement, in listening as the mason and the bricklayers consulted one another beneath a drooping, damp tarpaulin. Gordon was growing confident that the manor could be finished by the start of February if they were lucky and the snow held. There was real momentum, and Alasdair could feel it. But that Saturday, everyone had been dismissed from the site around eleven in the morning, the rain simply too dogged, and the men were sent home to wait until sunshine brought reprieve. The weather had become Alasdair's grim nemesis, for it seemed to constantly interrupt progress.

Gordon found him before everyone cleared out, standing

beside Alasdair to survey the rain and rumbling with laughter. "It won't go up in a blink, no matter how hard ye wish it."

Alasdair said nothing and nodded.

"The lads in Anstey sent over two wagonloads we won't need," Gordon continued, flopping a cap over his snowy fall of hair. "I'll see to it that the bill gets adjusted, and the stone goes back."

"Could Mr. Lavin at the Florizel use it?" Alasdair asked, pivoting to watch the man gather his things.

Gordon answered with a red-faced, flustered look. "Well . . . I would have to assess the state of it. But 'tis possible, yes, possible."

"Make your assessments," he said, fetching his own hat and smoothing out his coat. "If it's useful to them, I'll see that they have it."

"Sir, that's hundreds of pounds worth of—"

"I'll see that they have it."

"Very good, sir. I hear ye."

His mood did not improve when he reached Sampson Park and discovered the customarily dark and empty sitting room east of the entryway was crowded with ladies. His mother sat surrounded by strangers, their quiet chatter like the sound of a swift-moving stream as he handed off his things to his valet and took in the gathering. Mr. Danforth surged from the crowd of ladies like a rooster strutting from a coop. He met Alasdair at the open doors onto the sitting room with a smile, a bow, and gently folded hands.

"What is this?" Alasdair asked absently. "And where is Freddie?"

"Your brother is handling some correspondence for me currently, part of his introduction to the profession," said Danforth. The preacher had preened with extra care that day, his dark curls waved back from his forehead, his black coat pressed and spotless. "And this is the inaugural meeting of the Ladies' Society for Decency and Restoration."

Lady Edith noticed them hovering and smiled with more vigor and intensity than she had displayed since Alasdair's return. Slowly, Alasdair allowed Mr. Danforth to guide him into the sea of lace and sofas to be introduced to the women, whose names he would certainly not remember. Most of the ladies present resembled his mother, though a few younger daughters had been dragged along. Those with offspring eyed him like a side of beef hanging in a butcher's window.

"Ladies," he said softly, inclining forward in a bow.

"How well-mannered," murmured one gray-haired beauty to his right, which was awfully magnanimous, given his one-word greeting. New pamphlets had been made and distributed for the occasion, and one was thrust into his hands.

"The conversation surrounding the Florizel has been incredibly animated," Danforth informed him, shoving him deeper into the room. "Mrs. Ellison has argued, persuasively, I think, that it could be only a miraculous intervention that kept the players from spreading their sinful gossip to the good people of Cray Arches."

Mrs. Ellison, presumably, perched on a sofa beside his mother, blushed and shied away.

"What do you think?" the woman who had praised his manners asked, gazing up at him. "Accident or intervention?" The daughter crumpled against her side looked like she craved to be absolutely anywhere else. *A feeling we undoubtedly share, madam.*

Alasdair cleared his throat, suddenly and terribly the center of much undivided attention. His eyes roamed the room for inspiration and fell on a small table near the doors he had just come through. It was the small, painted treasure he had won in London. It must have been delivered to Sampson at some point and nobody informed him, and afterward it was shoved unceremoniously into an already overdecorated span. Danforth had piled a number of his books on it, and the poor little table appeared in danger of collapse. Taken by the outrage of it, Alasdair dodged around the ladies until he reached the table, scooping up Danforth's copies of *The Folly, Infamy, and Misery of Unlawful Pleasure; Addresses to Young Men; A Discourse on Pain;* and others and placed them under his left arm, then he turned back to address the room.

"I think that a lot of people were in danger of losing their lives that night," he declared, avoiding his mother's gaze. Instead, he thought of Violet's hand and the burned skin peeling away from it like birch shavings. "And a lot of people did lose their livelihoods. And I think it will be very awkward for you to discover that I have offered the surplus stone from Clafton to Mr. Lavin, as a gesture of goodwill and charity."

He could see that this was going over about as well as a Montgolfier filled with burning refuse, so he picked up the painted table with his other hand, bowed, and made his exit. Danforth apologized trippingly to the ladies and followed him out.

"Did you really commit to this folly?" Danforth asked, making a strangled sound of discomfort as Alasdair heaped the books into the preacher's arms. He struggled under the weight of the heavy volumes. "I know you have never appreciated my overtures of friendship, Mr. Kerr, but I do hope that we are aligned where your mother's continued happiness is concerned. It would benefit her for us to find common ground, perhaps even gesture at something beyond civility."

Alasdair regarded him with total disinterest.

Danforth sighed, continuing, "Lady Edith has made her position on the theater and its chosen production known . . ."

"I was aware of your feelings, Mr. Danforth, not hers. And as we are neighbors to the Florizel, I hardly understand the objection. Charity is foremost in your heart, is it not, as a devoted man of faith? If there is to be a bridge between us, let it be built by a shared enthusiasm for philanthropy." Alasdair stared, feeling a twitch begin beneath his right eye. "We who have much must see to those who have less: a mandate given down to me by my father, and his father before him."

Mr. Danforth went pale at his invocation of Sir Kerr.

Alasdair lifted the table slightly. "This is mine. Don't overburden it with your things again."

"Of course, of course, to be sure," Danforth mumbled, chasing him to the foot of the stairs. "Can I not persuade you to stay for the sermon and discussion?"

"You cannot."

"But could I then—"

"I am a very busy man, Mr. Danforth."

"To be sure, to be sure, but one last question, before you retire . . ."

Alasdair paused, one foot on the first stair.

"Please."

"One question," Alasdair repeated.

"I only wished to inquire about a certain artist currently residing at Pressmore Estate," said Danforth, shifting the books in his arms again. "Miss Bilbury. Do you know her?"

"Know *of* her."

"To be sure." Danforth smiled through his obvious annoyance. "Are you aware of her education? Her people? From where does she hail?"

Alasdair squinted. "Why?"

"There's no harm in knowing the quality of an individual mingling with my parishioners, is there?"

Something about this line of questioning unnerved him. Since when was Danforth at all interested in artists? Other than to wag his finger at them, of course. Alasdair took a step down toward him. "We are little acquainted. I'm familiar with works she submitted to the Royal Watercolour Society, where she was a member until recently, when she withdrew. I haven't the faintest idea why she chose to leave London."

That was mostly true. There were rumors of angry debtors, commissions promised but not completed, and general questionable behavior, but Alasdair tried to avoid such ugly gossip if he could. Mr. Danforth seemed satisfied, at least, and thanked him, returning to the sitting room and his flock. Whatever was going on with this Ladies' Society for Decency and Restoration, Alasdair decided it wasn't his concern. He consoled himself with the thought that it was at least something to keep Lady Edith engaged with society. It was good for her to have friends.

This was the first time in a long time Sampson felt like something other than a mausoleum.

He passed Freddie's room and peered in through the open door, finding his brother slumped across his desk, asleep. Startling awake, Freddie muttered something, noticed Alasdair's presence, and snorted. "This? It's Danforth." There was ink smudged on Freddie's chin. He lifted a pen as if in explanation. "The man must correspond with every bored fool in Anselm."

"Still. It's a relief to see you working at something," Alasdair told him.

"Mm-hm," said Freddie. "Post came for you earlier; it was taken to your chambers."

"Are you—"

"Bit busy," he added, returning to the letters.

It felt like more ought to be said. The night they found Freddie and Emilia in flagrante delicto loomed around every conversation. When they returned to Sampson, Lady Edith had been waiting for them. Freddie had stood silently beside him while Alasdair concocted a story, covering for his brother by placing him as a helpful bystander at the fire. They had both been convinced to stay and help with the bucket brigade, Alasdair claimed. The heroism distracted their mother for only an instant, for she just as quickly turned to admonishing them for helping that "den of iniquity" with anything. Her flash of anger, however brief, had inspired Freddie toward silence; if she was that upset just about them helping at the Florizel, how would she react if she knew what Freddie was really doing?

And that silence had been encouraging until it stretched on between the brothers.

"You can't help but get in the way of everything, can you?" were the last words Freddie spoke to him that night. Maybe he ought to be more outraged by Freddie's stubbornness, but he could hardly justify lecturing his brother about propriety and respect when Alasdair's thoughts kept turning, willfully, almost obsessively, toward Violet Arden.

We are imprisoned in the same hell, he wanted to say.

"Why are you staring at the back of my head?" Freddie grunted.

Alasdair left him, went to his bedchamber, and put the painted table safely in his own sphere of influence; as he did so, he realized it would look perfect beneath Violet's self-portrait, for it even had small clusters of violets chasing up the sides. A letter from Robert Daly was waiting, as Freddie had indicated, and Alasdair's heart thumped wildly as he read it. A Caravaggio had surfaced in London, and Robert had it from a connection that a member of the Tenebris Circle would soon put it up for auction. Robert preferred Saraceni (a quirk Alasdair would never understand or fully believe) and promised not to contest him for the Caravaggio. He'd happily bid for it on Alasdair's behalf but assumed he would want to experience the thrill of the purchase in person, so could he be in London by Tuesday?

He arrived in London on Monday afternoon. There was a card from Robert in the front hall relaying that he had called, and that Alasdair had been invited to an exclusive dinner that evening. Tenebris Circle only. That left him a few hours to consult with his solicitor, Mr. Finny, to make inquiries about the family's storehouses (in good condition) and to approve and arrange the sale of a few higher-quality pieces, justifying (in his own mind) the likely cost of the Caravaggio. Mr. Finny was sharp-tongued, wry, and mean, exactly how every solicitor ought to be. Afterward, Alasdair dressed in accordance with the strict code of dress for the Tenebris Circle—black coat, Titian-blue cravat with a lapis-encrusted circular silver pin, engraved silver watch carried in the fob pocket.

The Tenebris Circle never met as a collective at White's, and never acknowledged they knew one another beyond the expected social bonds among wealthy men of the ton. Alasdair's friendship with Robert had preceded his membership, and so it was considered natural and less suspicious that it should continue. Robert's house had become somehow more garish in just two months.

"It's Lillian," Robert told him by way of excuse, preempting the expected admonishment for allowing so many more gilded eyesores to appear in the hall. "She grew up impoverished, you see, and I cannot stop her from spending my money on anything that takes her eye."

Alasdair laughed softly as they walked together toward the drawing room where the other members were milling and sizing one another up. "Impoverished, Robert? Her family owns Pargan Poole in Somerset."

"Certainly, but that is a rather small castle, it's given her emotional problems. Let the dear thing have her golden frames, it makes my life easier. Ah! There is Jasper, the dog. Do you know he swiped a Constable right out from under my nose last week? Unbelievable. I ought to call for his head! Ha! Look at him, the smirk! Yes, yes, very fine, Jasper, you win this time, chap, but I'll die before I let you lay hands on this Caravaggio."

It was dawning on him that it had been a mistake to come, not only because Robert was unendurable, but because being surrounded by so much art and so many art admirers forced him to think of Violet. He had been trying hard to lock her in a dark, lonely room in his mind, but that was proving impossible. On the wall behind Robert, someone (presumably Lillian Daly) had overpowered a watercolor botanical with a cumbersome filigree frame.

"Who is this?" Alasdair asked, drifting toward the painting.

"It's Bilbury, I don't know if you're aware of her. Wonderful command of shadows."

"I've heard of her. God, Robert, that frame is diabolical."

Robert sighed. "I'm well aware. It's a good thing Lillian is so beautiful, her taste really is shocking. I'll wait until she's forgotten about the whole thing and change the frame. A shame Bilbury is such a wild figure. I wouldn't mind having more from her. Look, look, Jasper is hungry to gloat, I can see it in his beady eyes. We shouldn't keep him waiting—"

"Wild figure?" Alasdair planted himself firmly before the painting, trying to see around the frame.

"Chased out of Paris for setting some lover's abode aflame.

It was hot scandal for a week or so, but that was before anyone wanted her paintings. London wouldn't have her either, though I'm sure she'll try to beg her way back into the Society. Well. I've always believed we should allow painters their crumb of madness. One must suffer from a serious defect to produce a work of genius, n'est-ce pas?"

Alasdair grinned, wondering what Violet Arden's crumb of madness might be. *You already know, for you have it, too.* "Before we go in," he began, "I had a favor to ask."

"No, you can't have the Bilbury. I like it too much."

"It isn't that," Alasdair said with a laugh. "I wanted to send a gift of paints and brushes to an artist in need of them. I thought given how much time you spent getting painted, you might have the right connections. Could you arrange it?"

Robert shrugged. "Is that all? I'll consult Dawe, he will know all about it. And where shall I have these pigments and brushes sent?"

Shifting, Alasdair glanced toward the busy sitting room. He wondered if Violet even remembered being carried into her home, or if she could recall the way he had cradled her to his chest on the ride there. He didn't know what he hoped she would remember. His face prickled with heat; oh, but did she hear him when he bent down and asked her to stay awake, to stay with him . . .

"It's for a young lady in Cray Arches, a budding artist of some promise and potential," Alasdair grunted. "But please, put no name to the gift."

"Oh! A secretive gift! Does Miss Holzer know? My, how splendidly mysterious and romantic! But take it from me, old friend, a lady tends to love one better if she knows she is, in fact, being courted, and by whom."

"Then you should leave it as I have instructed, for I am not courting the lady. Have you never considered the value of a woman's friendship?"

"Friendship? Why would I do that? Lillian provides all the feminine companionship I could desire. And when I tire of looking at her, I console myself with dreams of a mistress. Then, I remember what a bother it is to keep a woman happy enough to maintain a secret, and I come to my senses."

Alasdair squeezed his eyes shut. "Just . . . do as I asked, please. I will provide the address, do not indicate the sender."

"No need to use that tone," said Robert, abruptly sober, perhaps afraid he had conjured the Mute Brute. But Alasdair let himself shrink, no threat to the man. "But what sort of friend would I be if I did not nudge when a nudge was needed?"

No nudge required, thought Alasdair, tired. *I have already toppled well over that cliff.*

In fact, it pained him not to take credit for the gift of the paints. If only he could see the surprise and delight bursting behind Violet's smile as she beheld the package . . . He shook his head and began to walk off toward the sitting room, hand on the back of his neck, then he swung back around toward Robert. "Oh, and she will need canvases, paper, an easel. Buy the very best and send the bill to the house on Wimpole."

Robert Daly shouted with laughter, bounding after him and clapping Alasdair on the shoulder. "For you, my friend, there is no need to reimburse. Just the thought of you agonizing over a secret gift for a young lady will sustain me for months!"

Less than a fortnight later, Alasdair was ready to return to Sampson Park. He had no interest in displaying the Caravaggio there but had it wrapped and ready for transport, already imagining where it would hang in Clafton. Before departing for the country, he had accepted a hasty invitation from Robert to join him for one last visit. He decided he owed Robert for helping him acquire the Caravaggio and for his role in sending Violet new supplies. As the carriage neared the Dalys' home, he further decided the Caravaggio would have a place of honor in Clafton when it was finished, and that the art acquired for his mother over the years (the sum total of which could furnish two estates) must be confined to certain halls and one sitting room; their tastes did not align, and he saw Clafton as much his home as hers. A place to begin again, a memorial to his beloved father, perhaps even where he might raise a family . . .

What family? He tried to imagine the sort of woman Lady Edith would want for him. Once upon a time, she had tried putting an array of eligible ladies before him, and though they were all nice enough, none sparked a feeling stronger than indifference. The most he could say about his mother's selections was that they were tolerably inoffensive, nothing like . . .

What would he choose for himself? He knew it was corrosive to imagine her.

"Is this weather not gloriously fine?" Robert greeted as Alasdair presented himself once more in the lavish jewel box of the Dalys' library. The shelves gleamed, the neat rows of books smelling faintly of leather. Robert himself stood utterly coiffed in a sky-blue cravat near a table displaying several maps. "Lillian will be along shortly," he continued, joining Alasdair near the sofas. "I'm afraid she's just received devastating news about her mother."

"My apologies. Is she unwell?"

Robert waved him off, eyeing the tray of refreshments that had already been brought in. He chose a pink macaron and considered it with a sniff. "Oh, no, she is very well, but unfortunately joining us for Christmas. Lillian is beside herself. You have never met a person more in love with the sound of their own voice."

Smiling, Alasdair coughed lightly into his fist.

"Ha-ha. I am nothing like her, believe me. She is tedious, and I am merely full of information." Robert ate the sweet in one bite and shrugged. "Which leads me to our business."

"Business? I thought this was a social call."

"Dear boy, it is never *just* a social call with me, you should know that by now." Robert gave a self-indulgent little laugh. "Do you know, after you had me arrange that sly gift, I had my man inquire after the occupants of, what was it? Beadle Cottage?" He said the words as if describing something he had stepped in. "The Ardens live there, yes? And then, I had a cheeky think about where I knew that name, and at last I landed upon it: Violet Arden. Now, there's a name *rife* with material."

Robert's pale blue eyes were sparkling, which was rarely a good sign.

Shifting, Alasdair set his gaze on a vague point in the distance. "I don't see why this is important, Robert. I told you; I've no interest in courting her."

"Yet she's reported to be a great beauty!"

"Some say so."

Robert's grin slid into a smirk. "But not you?"

Alasdair set his jaw. "Why does this concern you?"

"*I knew it.*" Robert hissed; he didn't sound at all excited. "Are you aware of her reputation? Her obscurity? It's almost a pity she's so beautiful, for who would have her?"

Who, indeed. Wandering toward the far wall, he pretended to appraise the portrait of Lillian painted by Dawe. Robert came up behind him, hovering. "I don't need her money."

"Splendid, because she hasn't got any."

A footman appeared, hoisting his chin in the air to announce the arrival of two more guests. "Miss Julianna Holzer and Mr. Elias Holzer."

Alasdair's blood froze in his veins. He turned, slowly, to see the woman he had once cherished gliding into the library, as luminous and angelic as an early morning cloud. Turning to Robert, he lowered his voice to a whisper. "Damn you. This is an ambush."

"Nonsense," Robert replied out of one corner of his mouth. "It's a favor, the second I've done you in short order, mm? You could use a reminder of what a lady of good manners and breeding actually looks like. Julianna's reputation is spotless; Miss Arden's may as well be a leopard. Lord above, man, a tryst with a French painter? Do you want to be the laughingstock of London?"

He bristled; he didn't want to be seen at all. If he could have it his way, Alasdair would emerge from the remade Clafton only to swim and travel occasionally to attend exhibitions and auctions. He had no desire to be perceived at all, least of all by a woman who had called him cold and unfeeling, and whom he had not thought of in weeks. And yet he must be seen, his size making it impossible to blend in and diminish, and there was no escaping Julianna as she and her brother came toward them.

Was he courting Violet without meaning to? The structure of it, a thing unseen but crucial to the later image as it became whole . . . An underpainting. Was that what this gift really was? The beginning of something, just a wash of color, but an effort all the same . . .

Alasdair dropped his head. "This is unfair, Robert."

"No, it's what you need. I like you, Alasdair," he went on, still in a swift undertone. "You've always amused me, and I would like to continue calling you my dear friend, but think clearly. You are quick to complain about your brother's behavior, but where is your own better judgment? Lillian would poison my port if I insisted that she invite *Miss Arden* to dine."

He went very still, wanting to be anywhere else and wondering if perhaps Robert Daly was his friend at all. Julianna offered a shy smile as she approached, asking, "Who were we discussing?"

Slowly, Alasdair straightened up. "Nobody of consequence."

13

Loving goes by haps;
Some Cupid kills with arrows, some with traps.
Much Ado About Nothing—Act 3, Scene 1

The package's arrival at Beadle Cottage sent the home into a frenzy of giggling speculation; the eruption could likely be heard by neighbors in every direction.

"It must be from Ann," said Maggie, hands clasped under her chin as she watched more and more items emerge from the crate.

"Miss Bilbury seemed very alarmed when she heard about the loss of your paints at the Florizel," Winny interjected, climbing over Maggie to get a better view. "I'd wager she sent it! Is there truly no note? Not a single indication? How mysterious!"

"Nothing," Violet told them, clawing her way through the extra straw and, quite frankly, making a complete mess. Mrs. Arden sighed from the doorway and summoned a maid to the sitting room.

Behind her, Maggie cackled. "I do love a good intrigue."

"Whoever it was," said Violet, standing back to admire the new easel, "they spent a small fortune. Who would do that?"

Who would spend so much on me?

"Ann would," Maggie answered plainly. "I will call on her this week, and we will have the matter settled. Winny has it partially—Miss Bilbury probably fretted so much that Ann felt she must make a heroic gift. She is always convinced that she can fix the world. I'm sure the ladies didn't want you to feel burdened by the charity of it, and so it is anonymous."

Winny nodded along, convinced. "And it has been so dreary with the clouds and rain, perhaps they knew the game of it all would cheer us!"

That did make a kind of sense; the Richmonds had always been very giving when it came to the Ardens, for though they often disagreed with Mrs. Arden's choices, her sisters Mildred and Eliza never hesitated to help where they must. The rifts that appeared between them were usually closed swiftly, and all returned to the expected grousing between siblings.

And everyone knew Ann had a flair for extravagant gifts.

"It's so much," Violet breathed. "I shouldn't accept it."

"Well, but you must," said Maggie, touching her lightly on the shoulder. "For whom would you return it to?"

Violet stood back and shook out her hands, flustered. The brushes and pigments were better quality even than what Miss Bilbury used on her more serious attempts. The carrying case for the paints was compact yet luxurious, lustrous mahogany, embellished with brass. The interior was lined with leather, and it included porcelain mixing pans and ample storage tins for chalks or charcoals, trays for the new brushes and crayons, and a place for scrapers, blocks of ink, and colors. The brushes, the furred tips of which were velvety-soft sable, were devised specifically for watercolorists, a personal touch that made her chest flutter. And she had never beheld such a handsome easel, far larger than her previous one, which had been small and designed for painting en plein air. "It almost doesn't seem right to spoil it," she murmured. "I'm just a novice."

"Someone thinks you're worthy of it," Maggie encouraged, leaning in closer. "And isn't that permission enough?"

The shock and excitement of the package had only just begun to wane when Emilia Graddock arrived in a sleek Pressmore carriage. Violet had not seen Emilia since that fateful night at the hollow, and judging by the flinching expression on the woman's face, her mind lingered there. Mrs. Arden received Emilia at the door, and from the sitting room amidst the strewn-about straw, the sisters heard Emilia ask if Violet was available to visit Pressmore for the afternoon. Apparently, Miss Bilbury was concerned about Violet's progress and wanted to make her paints and supplies available to her for use.

"I would be glad to join you at Pressmore," said Violet, ushering Emilia into the sitting room and showing her the newly arrived gifts. "But it appears someone has decided to address her concerns."

"But who has been so generous?" Emilia asked, gasping.

"Come now, it was your sister, was it not?" Violet prodded her in a teasing way.

"Ann? Heavens, no, she could never keep a secret so grand from me. But Cristabel will be relieved—she has done nothing but fret about your predicament."

"Well before today, I discovered a solution," said Violet. "There is nothing more invigorating to the artistic spirit than being confined to one's home to heal. Without an outlet, I would have gone mad. I shall gather everything up and take it to Pressmore. We can show Miss Bilbury together."

The servant who had accompanied Emilia to the cottage loaded the gift of paints, paper, and easel into the carriage while Violet fetched her recent paintings, bonnet, and coat. She had not been idle while recovering from her burn, and she was eager to show Cristabel her recent studies. Violet kissed her sisters and mother goodbye and followed Emilia up the wobbly path, hearing Maggie murmur as they went, "I still think it was Ann."

When the ladies were seated in the carriage across from each other, Emilia stuffed her hands into a furred hand warmer and nodded toward the leather tube on the seat beside Violet. "Then, you've been hard at work?"

Violet smiled wanly at the rolled-up papers concealed within the carrier. "I asked Maggie for some of her ink, then diluted it to make different values. I made brushes from bits of fabric, straw, feathers . . . whatever could be found in the scrap bin or the garden. Maggie was very annoyed with me wanting to paint her all the time, but I got my way eventually."

Looking out the window blankly, Emilia raised both brows. "You usually do."

Violet frowned. "I'm not sure I deserved that."

Pursing her lips, Emilia refused to glance at her or respond.

"Right. Let us have it out," Violet said, sighing and leaning back. "If you are cross with me, be cross. If there is blame to be given, give it. I would much rather have you scream and rage than sit here wondering what is behind those eyes."

Her lips scrunched up tighter until it looked like her face might burst. Abruptly, Emilia pressed the hand warmer against her head and shrieked. When she lowered the fur again, she looked calm. "Forgive me, I needed that."

"Do it again if you like."

Emilia gave a dry, coughing laugh and slid down on the

bench, a rare moment of unladylike flopping. "I want to be cross with you. I want to blame you. I want to, but I cannot. This is all my own doing, but when I think of Freddie, I'm not even myself! It's like I'm in a trance, and all I can think of is how good it feels to love and be loved. And yet I know I should be grateful that it was you who found us and no one else. If Colonel Graddock found out, he would send me away just as he did with Ruby."

"That was my thinking also."

The carriage had turned onto the sloped lane leading toward the Pressmore gates, and the rocking tossed Emilia lightly against the door. She clung to it, the cloud-softened sunlight lending her face a blue glow. "My mind turns that night over again relentlessly, like a coin I cannot help but flip day and night. Out of the dream of it, more comes into focus, and I feel the spell of him waning."

Violet sat up, gripping the bench cushion. "You . . . do? But Emilia, that's quite encouraging!"

"No, it isn't," said Emilia, pressing her forehead against the window. "Because what I remember is not good, Violet, and it frightens me." She drew in a shaky breath, closing her eyes. Briefly drawing one hand out of the warmer, she rubbed her thumb and forefinger together. "When I returned to the estate that night, I found stains on my glove. They must have transferred from his coat, for I was holding his sleeve. The next morning, I heard about the terrible fire at the theater, and something . . . something nagged at me. Insisted. I took that pair of gloves and held them near a candle, and they all but burst into flames, Violet."

Her hands were suddenly cold and stiff on the bench. "But you were together the whole evening. When would he have had the time to—"

"We weren't," Emilia replied softly, sadly. "Together, I mean, not the entire time. He left me in the hollow for a while, he said he wanted to gather wildflowers and present me with a bouquet. 'A pretty bride should have a pretty bouquet,' he said. And then he was gone, but for so long that I began to worry. When he returned, he brought a few stalks of monkshood, not a bouquet, not the work of all that time away."

"What do you think stained your gloves?" Violet breathed. Was it possible? Was Mr. Kerr wrong after all, and his brother was capable of starting not one but *two* dangerous fires? And for what reason? Freddie seemed like an impetuous sort of young man but not particularly malicious. What did he stand to gain by burning down the Florizel?

"Oil," said Emilia. "With how it burned, the kind meant for lanterns."

"That is concerning. Is this why you came to fetch me?"

"Cristabel has been asking for you, but yes, this is the true reason."

"But if you had these suspicions, why did you wait so long?"

"Ann wouldn't let me out of her sight! The baby was unwell this morning and her attention is with him, so I was allowed to take the carriage on the condition that I went to Beadle and returned with you at once." Emilia glared over her shoulder, as if Daniels, the driver, would feel her ire through the layers of fabric and wood separating them.

Violet's thoughts were already racing ahead toward solutions. Enmity between the Richmond and Kerr families would deepen if these accusations against Freddie were made public. Emilia's hunch couldn't be ignored, but nor was it absolute proof of guilt. Her stomach twisted at the realization that this would entangle her with Mr. Kerr again.

"After Mr. Kerr returned you to Pressmore that night, how

did you explain your absence?" asked Violet. Even just saying his name aloud made the pit in her belly tighten.

"I told everyone Puck had gotten loose and wandered off again, and I got lost trying to find him. It happens enough that they believed me—"

"And no doubt they were eager for something innocent to believe."

"Yes, and that." Emilia's cheeks darkened. "Last week the silly creature made it almost to Deppers Bridge. It took the driver's boy half a day to find him." There was a pause before she appeared caught by a different memory. "Monkshood," she said quietly, mournfully, blinking at the passing rows of trees and hedges. "All that time gone, and he returned to me with poisonous flowers." She shrugged helplessly, her voice yet softer. "Love's spell has broken, and after there is just regret."

Violet leaned toward her and gripped Emilia's hand through the warmer. "If Freddie is really to blame for these fires, then I swear we will prove it and bring your heart peace. Though I . . . Well. Though I don't know *how* exactly."

"You will though, you will know! I'm sure of it." Emilia's countenance brightened. She slipped one hand out of the muff and clasped it over Violet's. "You and your sisters were such a help during Ann's wedding. Without your courage, your persistence, who knows what might have happened to us?"

The carriage made a severe right turn, paused as the gates of Pressmore were opened, and then continued up the drive. The gardens and hedge maze spread across the window like a thick, wet smear of green paint. Even with the change of the seasons, the estate somehow maintained its verdant alchemy, the red and gold in the overhanging trees making what green remained even livelier. Puck stood near the gap in the hedge maze, watching them arrive with his usual glassy-eyed ambivalence, his mouth and teeth in constant, repetitive motion.

As Daniels helped them down onto the pebbles of the drive, Emilia stared at the goat and shrugged. "At least he is reliably silent. Daniels? Take Miss Arden's supplies to the Sapphire Library, please. Miss Bilbury has preferred the light there this week."

"Very good, ma'am."

She waited until Daniels had walked back toward the carriage to collect Violet's things to add, "You should have seen your aunt's face when Mr. Kerr brought me back that night. I thought she would faint right across his boots. When she thanked him, every word was like the prick of a needle the way she flinched and fretted." She grew solemn and thoughtful, still watching Puck chew his grass. "Do you think he can be trusted? Mr. Kerr, I mean. If he finds out I think Freddie set the fire, he could turn around and tell everyone what he saw at the hollow."

Violet hadn't considered that, which was strange, given how much she was meant to mistrust the Kerrs. He was protective of Freddie, that much she knew, but beyond that, she couldn't predict how he would respond to any accusations. "I want to believe we can trust him."

Emilia nudged her, suddenly close. "Is there something between you? At the hollow, you were almost . . . I don't know the word for it—conspiratorial, perhaps, even friendly."

"It's not a bond I would have chosen, but our desires aligned in that moment," said Violet, tensing.

"Yet to trust him? Despite what you've said about the disagreements between your families—"

"After he lost so much to a fire, he charged into the Florizel after me, and all to save a cat. I couldn't have done it without him. Maybe that isn't proof of goodness, but it should count for something, don't you think?"

They walked toward the house, Emilia slightly ahead of her. "After the way he urged Freddie to break my heart, I try my best not to think of him at all."

Violet was too preoccupied with thoughts of the fire to become agitated. She felt as if she existed in two bodies now, one that must walk and talk as usual, and one that could only circle round and round Emilia's accusation. As she spoke, she simultaneously walked through every moment of that fateful evening, trying to recall any small, seemingly insignificant detail that might lead to better understanding. Mr. Kerr might remember more. That would mean seeing him again, spending time with him. It ought to be a more unpleasant notion. Distracted, she murmured, "Even if I wanted such a thing, it would never happen. People might not whisper so much about me here, but the same cannot be said of London. I made a spectacle of myself there, and I am not sitting on the sort of dowry that makes impropriety a pardonable quirk."

As soon as they stepped inside, Aunt Mildred and Ann were there to greet them. Elsewhere in the house, Lane could be heard negotiating frantically with a crying baby.

"Violet!" Aunt Mildred gasped as soon as Violet had removed her gloves. "Your hand! How awful, you look like a tradesman with all that scarring . . ."

"And here is my aunt, always ready to remind me of my deficiencies," said Violet.

"I should have offered you my hand warmer," Emilia said with a sigh.

Pleasantries were exchanged, each passing moment making Violet more impatient. How could they stand around smiling and discussing the weather when Freddie Kerr might have attempted to burn them all alive in their beds? Ann embraced Violet, plainly relieved that Emilia had collected Violet so efficiently. Almost immediately, Violet was led to the Sapphire Library, a lavishly appointed room not far from the front hall. Miss Bilbury was already there, easel positioned to capture the blue-tinted light falling around a bowl of apples she had placed near the inlaid and mullioned windows. Daniels bustled in with an apology, bringing Violet's new supplies and placing her easel a few feet to the right of Cristabel's.

"Everyone at the cottage is convinced you're to blame for this," said Violet, gesturing toward the gifts, but Ann went to the cushioned bench near the apples and sat, shaking her head. She looked uncharacteristically haggard, no doubt torn from bed at an obscene hour by her ill child.

"Day and night we are consumed with caring for our little darling," said Ann, reaching for an apple and then stopping herself as she remembered they were for painting and not for eating. "The Ann who would have had time for such generosities is gone now . . ." Her voice trailed off sadly. "I do miss her."

Cristabel set down her brush with a grunt. "You've ruined the light, Mrs. Richmond."

"Forget the light," cried Emilia. "Violet's mystery is far more interesting!"

Forget my mystery, I must return to the Florizel and have a look around.

"Then I will solve it, and you will go, and I can return to what matters most—painting," said Cristabel, wiping her hands on her stained smock before approaching the new easel with a bulging, critical eye. Sometimes her abrupt manner was disagreeable, but now Violet was glad for it and hoped Cristabel would have it all solved in a blink so she could come up with an excuse to leave and go to Cray Arches. Cristabel took up the package of paper Daniels had left on top of the handsome mahogany case. "Whatman's wove paper," said the painter, breathing out a soft sound of appreciation. "And in such quantity!" Then she knelt to inspect the mahogany case, running her fingers lightly over the engraved brass plaque on the front. "P.E. Paris and Sons," she read. "I've seen their work before; they keep a storefront on Great Marlborough in London."

"Then perhaps our mystery benefactor was recently in town," Ann suggested. Wincing, she rubbed her temples and turned her head toward the light pouring in from the window behind her. "How I *long* to see town . . ."

"And these," Cristabel began, picking up the leather tube filled with Violet's studies, flicking off the cap and tapping the end until the papers came spiraling out.

"Hm?" Violet had been half listening, the rest of her at the Florizel, reliving the fire but gaining no clarity. "Oh, those are merely an experiment. I had to make do with whatever we had around the cottage; they shouldn't be taken seriously."

"Nonsense!" Reinvigorated, Ann popped up from the couch, stifling a yawn before going to peer over Cristabel's shoulder. "Why, that's Maggie at her desk! You've gotten the thoughtful crease along her brow just right. She always looks like that when she's puzzling over a story."

"Yes, you've captured something here," said Cristabel, holding them at arm's length. She looked at Violet more intently. "A tender world of intimate domesticity, the trust between sisters, the love implicit in comfortable silences." She smiled, finally, and lowered the studies. "Were the paper less irregular and cockled, I might even be able to sell them."

"Don't be silly, it was just something to keep my mind occupied." Violet had drifted toward the door. Would they think her unforgivably rude if she left?

"Come to your senses, girl. I'm telling you these are your finest work, and all you can do is burble at me like a frog?" Cristabel stormed over to her, but Emilia tumbled over her own feet to reach Violet first. She stared imploringly with her big brown eyes.

"Violet . . . is . . . merely . . . distressed, of course? Of course! Naturally!" Emilia said very, very slowly, gesturing with her head on each word as if to lead Violet toward the right words.

"Yes! Distressed! Naturally!" Violet perked up, forcing herself to be in one body and one mind again. "The Florizel. I simply cannot stop thinking about everyone there. I've been meaning to call on Mr. Lavin now that my hand is almost completely healed. He must be devastated."

Ann joined them, poking her finger straight up into the air. "We should all call on him together! A walk would do me a world of good. And I can have Bloom see what's available in the kitchen; a parcel of sweets and a few friendly faces will be a balm for the soul."

Ann decreed it, and so it was done. Even Cristabel put on her shabby gray coat and dowdy bonnet and came along. Emilia carried the basket of gifts for Mr. Lavin. Arm in arm with her, Ann seemed determined to suck down all the fresh air there was to be had in Warwickshire as they ambled down the lane.

"I have not been myself," she cried. "Cooped up in that house! Befuddled with worry! When my calling has always been to bring light and joy to the lives of others? No, it cannot continue! The Ladies' Society for the Lonely, Abandoned, and Infirm was to be an outlet for my greatest works of charity, and so it will be. And so it will be."

"What are you concocting in that clever mind of yours?" asked Violet, watching her.

"You will see quite soon, Violet, I can promise you that."

Everyone's imagination was churning in a different direction, apparently, for Cristabel snugged up to Violet's side and inhaled in a way that told Violet to brace. What kernel of wisdom or shattering critique would she offer this time?

"Most artists I've taught fell on their knees and wept the first time I told them their work was actually worth good English money," said the painter.

"I'm obviously happy about it." It came out all in a single, rushed breath.

"Oh yes, you sound thrilled." Cristabel laughed and, staring down at her, tapped the tip of her own nose. "Don't forget, my little dauber, that I am a great observer of people."

Violet fell silent, fixing her eyes on the road. *Indeed? I doubt you will observe in me the truth: that Emilia has tasked me with answering a terrible question.* An image imposed itself on her, a glimpse of Mr. Kerr's horror-struck face as he learned the truth about his brother. He would blame her, no doubt, when—if—it all came to light. *And why should that bother me? I did not make his rotten brother douse the Florizel in oil and set a candle to it!*

Why should it bother her at all?

I declared it myself not half an hour ago—no man of sense or great fortune will marry me.

"I *am* happy," Violet said through gritted teeth.

Cristabel swung toward her. They were nearing the edge of civilization, coming the tree-lined and sheltered back way down the narrow dirt road that ran from the Pressmore gardens to the western edge of Cray Arches, where the Gull and Knave postal inn presided over the first turn into the village.

"More believably spirited that time, Violet, but not exactly *happy.*"

"We haven't been able to afford beef at the cottage for a month," Violet murmured. "It would be nice to sell something, achieve something, and maybe have beef again."

Cristabel nodded, solemn, then touched her gently on the wrist above the bandage on her hand. "I choose to believe you will have more than beef for all your effort, in the end."

"Beef is a start."

It was not difficult to locate Mr. Lavin, for he was standing outside the charred remains of the Florizel near a wagon, deep in conversation with a tall gentleman. As they came closer, Violet felt her hands grow cold at the sight of Mr. Kerr; of all the people she'd expected to see in the village that day, he was not among them. Before Emilia or Violet could say a word, Ann had loped right up to the two men and greeted them.

"Mrs. Richmond!" Mr. Lavin exclaimed, his bushy eyebrows bobbing with excitement. "It is good to see your face in the square again, it's been too long."

"I've had the exact same thought," said Ann, gracious. Violet could hide at the back of the group for only so long. Eventually, propriety dictated that she make herself known and curtsy politely to Mr. Kerr. When she stepped out from around Emilia's right side, she watched the gold flecks in his eyes dazzle, his posture suddenly rigid as his lips parted.

"Miss Arden," he said, nearly breathless. It felt like she would be burned all over again by the intensity of his gaze as it roamed over her. God, she had actually *missed* him. She could doubt how reasonable it was to admire him, but there was no mistaking the effect his presence had on her. It felt like the sun was shining on just the two of them as their gazes locked. "Your hand. How is it?"

"Completely healed now, thank you." Anxious flames licked up the sides of her neck, her bonnet immediately too tight. He was just a man, practically a stranger; why did he have this power over her? Violet held her head high, trying not to collapse under the surge of heat trickling down from her head. "You . . . are here."

Behind her, Cristabel snorted. "Artfully perceived."

"Yes!" boomed Mr. Kerr, too loud. He scrunched his brow and adjusted his spectacles, looking at each of the ladies in turn, though his attention came to rest finally on Violet and stayed. "I have returned from London just this morning."

"London?" Both of Ann's dark brows bounced to the edge of her bonnet. "How interesting."

"Is it?" Mr. Kerr huffed a nervous laugh and rubbed the back of his neck. "I think it is a very ordinary thing to do."

"Incredibly ordinary; so ordinary I can't imagine there is anything else to say about it," Violet added for him. He frowned again.

Ann apparently couldn't help herself. "Any destinations of note while you were in town?" she asked coyly. "St. James's, I would warrant? Piccadilly?" Her smile widened. "Great Marlborough, perhaps?"

And, like Ann, Violet couldn't help herself, peering at Mr. Kerr as he floundered for a response, his face reddening to the tips of his well-formed ears. He looked like he might explode and die before ever landing on a satisfying response, and Violet, compassionate before she was mischievous, felt it her duty to rescue him, shouting, "But here is a wagon!"

"Indeed." Mr. Kerr bowed his head, smiling, visibly grateful for the change of subject. "The stoneworks in Anstey sent us too much material, and I thought Mr. Lavin might require the excess for whatever he has planned at the theater."

"How generous," Ann cooed, beaming at him. "There must be a spirit of charity in the air today, and it has dusted its fairy magic over the whole of the county, for here, Mr. Lavin, we have come down from Pressmore with a basket of delightful sweets, and all to cheer you."

Mr. Lavin's red cheeks shone like summer apples, and he pinched his lips together. "Cheer, my God, cheer! It has been in short supply. But there are unexpected angels, aren't there? Thank you, Mrs. Richmond, and you, ladies, for the kindness."

"The Florizel has been a steady source of joy," said Ann. "It is only fitting we return some to you in your time of need. Which brings me to another matter of charity—I have recently established a society for just such alleviations, and it is fitting that the Florizel should be our first beneficiary."

In Violet's mind, it seemed as if Ann were swooping in on Mr. Kerr's valiant effort, but he didn't react to the announcement. In fact, he was preoccupied with glancing at something over Violet's shoulder, always just over her shoulder whenever she got up the courage to look his way. It was a strange kind of game, frustrating, though Violet feared what would happen if their eyes actually did meet again.

London. He was just in London. Great Marlborough, by any chance, Mr. Kerr?

"We will hold a benefit for the Florizel at Pressmore," Ann went on, balling up her fists and shaking them like rattles with excitement. "Miss Bilbury can auction off a portrait sitting, and the players from the theater must come and perform scenes from your *Romeo and Juliet*, for their hard work should still be seen and celebrated. Perhaps Violet can even paint a few scenic pieces for you! Oh! It will be perfectly enchanting, and all the money can go toward furnishing the new theater." Everyone was too stunned to say no. Mr. Lavin turned in a half circle, flapping his mouth and blubbering in surprise. Smoothly, Ann turned to Mr. Kerr, the dancing lights in her eyes alerting Violet too late that there was more than just charity afoot. "And you, Mr. Kerr, you must join us for the benefit. For undoubtedly, with this display of generosity today, you understand that art and artists must be passionately cherished." The demure fluttering of Ann's lashes was the coup de grâce. "What say you, Mr. Kerr? Will you join us?"

14

This bud of love, by summer's ripening breath,
May prove a beauteous flower when next we meet.
Romeo and Juliet—Act 2, Scene 2

Alasdair was once more at a loss for words. The ladies were all staring up at him as if he had the answers to the wild and percolating questions of the universe. An answer was required of him, but he knew what must be done.

Robert's harsh admonishment echoed in the darkening cavern of his mind.

Are you aware of her reputation? Her obscurity? It's almost a pity she's so beautiful, for who would have her?

And she was beautiful. So, so beautiful. Without fail, it made his chest ache. He had hoped to avoid seeing her altogether, for now it was too cold for swimming and he would not be tempted to wander down to the stream that separated his property from the Richmonds'. There were otherwise few reasons for him to visit Cray Arches, and so little chance of their paths crossing.

"I . . . could not please you with a response, madam, when you have not even named a date," he replied. That would settle it, he thought, for this was the fancy of a moment, not a real invitation. But Mrs. Ann Richmond was not to be denied; she threw back her head and laughed merrily.

"That is a small thing." She turned to the theater owner with a shimmering smile. "Mr. Lavin, why don't you choose the date? What would please you most? Whatever you decide, I will accommodate."

Violet Arden was growing fidgety; she kept staring off toward the burned building, her jaw forward, set with determination.

"I'm afraid Miss Thorpe and the others won't stay much longer if there's no work to be had," said Mr. Lavin with a sigh. "No performances, no money. I can't expect to keep them past Christmas—"

"What a lovely idea," the formidable Mrs. Richmond exclaimed, clapping with delight. "The Society can host you all for Christmas! St. Stephen's Day may be more customary for charity, but how I love the thought of celebrating you all in the warm glow of Pressmore on Christmas Day."

"I—well—indeed, Mrs. Richmond, that is a generous proposition, but I couldn't possibly impose—"

"Nonsense, Mr. Lavin. I will hear no talk of imposition." She turned back to Alasdair, still grinning, though now it held a more pressing edge, as if her teeth had all sharpened at once. "There you have it, Mr. Kerr, a date has been given. Won't you consider joining our benefit on Christmas?"

He almost laughed with relief. "I fear the day is quite special to my mother, and I couldn't possibly be away from her. My apologies, Mrs. Richmond, though I'm sure you will all have Mr. Lavin's interests well in hand when . . ."

His words trailed away. His refusal to attend had acted as some sort of permission or provocation, for Miss Arden strode swiftly away. Puzzled, he watched her hurry off toward the Florizel, leaving everyone quietly stunned for a moment.

Patching over the awkward silence, Mrs. Richmond continued in her breezy manner. "Your presence will be missed, Mr. Kerr, but perhaps you will consider making your contribution at some other time."

"Mm," he grunted, distracted. "If you will excuse me . . ."

Once more he found his words trickling and unfinished, and he bowed half-heartedly and followed Violet Arden toward the theater. When he reached her, she was peering into the half-cocked front doors, her shockingly blue eyes huge and darting, as if she were assessing whether the whole building might come down around her ears if she stepped inside. Given the seriousness of the fire that night, it just might.

"Have I given offense?" he asked, perhaps harshly.

"What? No, not at all." She swung around to face him briefly, then did exactly as he feared and ducked inside. "Or, rather, no new offense that I can think of."

Alasdair reached for her hand to pull her back, grazing her fingertips. With black dust dancing in the air between them, Violet looked over her shoulder toward him, hesitating.

"And if I insisted that you are putting yourself in harm's way?"

"How well did that work last time?" she asked, vanishing inside.

"At least be careful," he grumbled. She wasn't going to go in alone, not when many of the blackened crossbeams overhead looked ready to collapse. He produced a handkerchief and pressed it into her grasp. "And cover your mouth. Your paints will not be salvageable, if that is your aim here."

They were standing in the front hall, Mr. Lavin's gutted office to their left, the cupboard where the orange cat had been cowering to their right. Ahead, the ceiling bowed, bubbled pockets of wall bulging out toward them.

"Isn't it strange that someone tried to start a fire at Pressmore, the culprit was never discovered, then soon after the Florizel goes up in flames?" Violet asked, her voice muffled by the cloth held over her nose and mouth. She tiptoed carefully over the debris that had been pulled from the office and strewn across the floor.

"You believe the fire was set intentionally? For what purpose?"

"I don't know yet," Violet replied, forging ahead. "But I intend to find out. Mind your head, there's a dip in the ceiling here."

Alasdair did as she instructed, breathing into the crook of his elbow to keep from inhaling the dust. Every step crunched as if they walked across a bed of leaves, the cracked, burned debris dislodging puffs of dry black powder. They reached the end of the central hall that emptied out onto the auditorium. The flames had eaten away the ceiling, exposing the attic space above, barren and spare as a skeleton. The deeper they went into the theater, the worse the damage, though if Violet noticed the increasing peril, she did not comment on it nor let it slow her down. She started down the carpeted aisle that split the lower auditorium into two sections.

"Help me up?" she asked, indicating the stage with a nod.

He nearly refused, then realized she would simply crawl up with her own power and likely hurt herself. "What do you hope to discover, Miss Arden? The materials that spread fire tend to . . . well, burn."

Alasdair bolstered Miss Arden as she took a bold leap up

onto the stage. He followed, hoisting himself easily, as the lip of the stage was no taller than his waist. The lady drifted toward the set—destroyed, of course, and reduced to sifted piles of ash and charred timbers. Fabric peeled away from one false wall; the oil paint that had been splashed across ran down its face like springtime tears, green and blue and buttercup yellow.

"Better to look and know than refuse and wonder," said Violet. She paused to frown at the spoiled sets, then sidestepped them to search the back of the stage. Red curtains hung in tatters, drooping from the warped, half-melted railings. The stench was terrible, the dust kicked up by their movement clinging to the frail fabric of her pale purple dress. The back of the theater had gotten the worst of it. Most of the far wall was missing completely, providing a macabre, scorched window onto the path of cobbles beyond. There was a space there for wagons to load and unload, then a few meters of untended yard, and finally a thin slice of wooded area. The trees there bent away from the theater, as if blown back by the horror of it.

Miss Arden waited again with her hand extended, and Alasdair joined her but decided it would be easier to help her from below. He jumped down, then turned and offered both hands. Carefully, she put her weight into her palms on his shoulders and bent, and Alasdair took hold of her waist. Gently. When he grasped her that way, her coat and gown conformed to the elegant shape of her waist, exaggerating the yet more pleasant flare of her hips. He felt the strong push of her midsection against his thumbs, then the give of those same muscles as she exhaled, and trusted him, and went briefly into the air. Alasdair lowered her carefully to the ground, closing his eyes as their bodies met briefly on her descent, her breasts, God help him, grazing his chest. In that short suspension, that half a moment between her being above him and then on the cobbles, he held his breath. When she was standing again on her own two feet, looking anywhere but at him, he wondered if she had become as painfully aware of him as he had been of her.

I held you; I felt your breath go in and out, the sweet proof of your life.

Alasdair tore himself away, pretending to find something worthy of his attention in the brush at the edge of the wood. There could be no tender feelings for her—civility, certainly, but no more than that. Even if the world cinched tight around them when she was in his arms, even if that one sweep of contact felt more significant than all the letters and glances he had ever exchanged with the women who came before.

Her gaze swept along the ground and then up the ruined posterior of the Florizel while Alasdair performed his indifference beneath the aghast bend of the watchful trees. Violet drifted past him, kicking idly at the ground, turning over charred roof tiles and bunches of leaves.

The silence felt like needles in his ears. He had to be away from her, or they had to speak, but he could not endure the quiet. "You're looking for something in particular."

"I don't know," she murmured, but it held none of her usual lively conviction.

A few paces away, beneath the first earnest shade of the wood, Violet stopped abruptly. She gasped, then took a few stuttering steps toward what looked like nothing more than a cluster of weeds. Kneeling, she pushed aside the longer, dying gray grass to bring forward a few stalks of faded blue flowers. Picking one stem, she stood and stared at it, the fateful blossom suspended between them.

"This . . ." he began slowly, reading her expression, ". . . is significant?"

Violet Arden's gaze flew to his, an unmistakable shine of fear in her very blue eyes, blue that put the flower she held to shame. There were perhaps many objectionable things about her, but her propensity for plain honesty was not one of those things.

"You know something," Alasdair whispered, lowering his head.

She shied and curled away from him with the same diffident posture as the trees. That shift only made him more certain.

"Miss Arden," he added, checking in every direction to confirm they were alone. There was no one, just the distant, muted sounds of town life and the bare breeze shimmering against the last clinging leaves of autumn. "Violet."

Her eyes raked up his chest to his chin, then higher, and her mouth quivered exactly once. "I fear we must be bound by yet another secret," she said, holding up the flower. "Monkshood. Some of the stalks were shorter, clipped as if recently picked. These are the flowers your brother chose to bring Miss Graddock the night we found them in the hollow. The glove she touched him with was stained with oil, and when she held it near flame, it swiftly caught."

Alasdair felt the world tilt.

"Do not faint, Mr. Kerr," Violet said in an urgent whisper. "I fear I cannot catch you if you fall."

15

The man that hath no music in himself,
Nor is not moved with concord of sweet sounds,
Is fit for treasons, stratagems, and spoils.
The Merchant of Venice—Act 5, Scene 1

"I ask that you allow me time to put this right." Mr. Kerr extended his open palm, silently asking for the flowers. Violet hesitated. "If it was him, if he confesses, I will see to it that Mr. Lavin is compensated and pay personally for the Florizel to be repaired. Any amends that should justly be made will be. Please, Miss Arden, it is not in my nature to beg, but I will if I must—he is my brother."

"He's your brother, and he tried to burn down Pressmore," she hissed, clutching the flower stems to her chest.

"You don't know what your forbearance would mean to my family," he continued, his golden-brown eyes dimmed behind his spectacles. *His family.* As if she had any interest in protecting the reputation of the Kerrs! He seemed almost to reach for her, then thought better of it. "What it would mean to me."

Violet stilled. That was harder to understand, harder to

disregard. She looked down at the faded monkshood blossoms, their purplish-blue cowls shriveled from the dry cold. They were so fragile, so frail. He took the smallest step toward her, his hand still hovering between them.

"I swear it on the stones of Clafton, I will not let anything happen to you," he whispered, then tightened his lips together and corrected himself. "I will not let anything happen to y-your family, of course."

What would she do if their positions were reversed? If Maggie or Winny were in danger of being taken before the justice of the peace, how would she respond? A handful of wildflowers and an oil stain did not exactly place the lit torch in Freddie's hand, but it certainly smacked powerfully of guilt. She tried to imagine Winny languishing in a jail; her heart crumbled, and she slowly handed Mr. Kerr the monkshood stems.

He didn't take them. "No. No. I misspoke just now, Miss Arden. *Violet.* I will not let anything happen to you."

She pulled up her courage and met his eye squarely. "If there are more fires, Mr. Kerr, I will know you have failed me."

"I will not fail you," he assured her. Violet expected that to be that, but Mr. Kerr let the flowers linger between them. He was so close now, she couldn't escape his scent, his warmth, the intoxicating power of his presence, all the things she tried so desperately to banish from her mind when they were apart. "It would skin me to the marrow to fail you, I think. Do you understand?"

Violet froze, then slowly nodded.

"Do you?" Alasdair asked again, his hand brushing her wrist.

"Our thoughts are one."

With a great exhalation of relief, he took the flowers,

touched his hat, and bowed, then strode away quickly, before Violet could react or even wrap her mind around what had transpired between them. The moment he was gone, she wanted him back. *Our thoughts are one.* What an absurd thing to say! Yet it had felt like the truth. It was the truth. Nobody and nothing occupied as much space in her thoughts as he did. As she returned to her friends near the wagon, she noticed the preacher, Mr. Danforth, hurrying down the lane and away from the square, headed in the direction of the church. She liked the doddering old vicar there, Mr. Corner, and hoped he was not subject to Danforth's corrupting influence. While Ann finished her conversation with Mr. Lavin, Violet watched Danforth's shape diminishing; down by her waist, where no one could see, she made a rude gesture.

"Odious little man," she muttered.

Emilia sidled closer to her. "Did you find anything in the theater?"

"Nothing definitive," Violet replied, sidestepping. For once, she decided to keep her mouth shut. If Mr. Kerr was a man of his word, Freddie would never have the chance to set another fire.

Emilia frowned. "There must be something . . ."

Violet did not respond, terrified she would let something slip.

"Did you see the way Mr. Kerr blushed when I asked about his activities in London?" Ann was upon them, laughing with glee. "Oh, but we must find a way to corner him again and dig for more information. Now I am convinced he is the mystery benefactor!"

It was Violet's turn to blush and stammer. "That's ridiculous."

"He probably fell in love with you after carrying you across the fields!" Ann sighed. "It's unbearably romantic, like something from one of those novels you're always reading, Emilia."

Emilia didn't seem as delighted and curled her lip. "But why would he do it?"

"He wouldn't. He thinks my paintings are—"

"*Derivative and silly, and for no one,*" Emilia, Ann, and Cristabel finished for her in unison.

Violet stared blankly, wishing she could sink beneath the road. Her cheeks roared with hot embarrassment. Was her fixation on him so obvious? She remembered the way he had gazed down at her and touched her wrist, and her knees nearly buckled. "I haven't . . . I haven't complained about it *that* much."

"And why should you encourage them together when you despised Freddie?" Emilia asked, thankfully missing Violet's blushing cheeks. "You told me his rejection was a gift!"

"Your prospects are rather grander than Violet's, dearest, you know that," Ann said in a strained undertone. "And the two brothers could not be more different . . ."

"It isn't fair," Emilia said with a sigh. "My dowry should mean I can do whatever I like."

"It does and it doesn't," Ann told her, wrapping her arm around Emilia's shoulders and squeezing. "What sort of sister would I be if I did not look out for your interests? Never mind what our father would have to say about it!"

"I'm sure Mr. Kerr would never marry me," said Violet, for Emilia's benefit; even to her own ears it sounded like a lie.

When they returned to Pressmore, Cristabel urged her back into the cool cerulean splendor of the Sapphire Library, where Violet's new pigments awaited. A letter arrived shortly after for Cristabel, and, grunting with annoyance, the painter began reading it—first just over Violet's shoulder, but the content must have upset or alarmed her, for soon Miss Bilbury quit the library. Violet did not see her for the rest of the afternoon. Nor did she paint, for when she looked down at the neat row of cake colors, ready to be mixed and applied to the prepared paper, it seemed a shame to even touch them. They were like royal jewels glimmering in a velvet box, precious and perfect. And when Violet lifted one of the brushes, tipped with softest Russian sable, her mind went blank except for a single image.

Alasdair Kerr.

She closed her eyes, but he was there, too. Common sense would dictate that she paint him, then, but she had vowed not to, and besides, how could she pursue him when Emilia had been denied her chance at love? She couldn't imagine tossing aside the regard of her friends and family. When Maggie was hopelessly besotted with Mr. Darrow, she had acted much the same—distractible and lost, as if the only world that interested her was the one in her mind where she and Bridger were already together.

The canvas remained empty. The paints went untouched.

Alasdair's fury had stoked itself into an inferno by the time he reached Sampson Park.

Ordinarily, the steady drumming of hammers at Clafton would raise his spirits, for the workmen had enjoyed a stretch of good weather while Alasdair was away in London, and the manor was taking shape. Gordon had requested more builders, and Alasdair obliged, reminding him that expense was of little concern when the goal of restoration was now plainly in sight. But even that, even the walls rising on the hill—jagged but decidedly *there*—did not penetrate his bleak mood.

The house was persuasively silent, nothing required his urgent attention; there was nothing before him but the horrible task of confronting Freddie. His steps grew heavier as he went up the stairs, dread settling on his chest, weighty as the earth piled high on a man buried alive. And as with that oppressive fate, the fear came, too, and the panic.

We have already lost Father. How could we lose you, too?

His mind offered a thousand improbable but tempting alternatives. They had the money; they could hurry him out of the country, send him to a new life in America. Justices of the peace were men like any other, weak in the way all men were weak, easily swayed by power, by bribes, or . . . Or!

No. Their father's portrait hung in a dozen places around Sampson, and each of them seemed to turn and watch him now, casting judgment over Alasdair's next decision.

My great duty is to make you a man of quality, Cub. We have given you an easy life, and easy lives make soft men, so I must impose what the walls of Clafton repel.

Alasdair had tried, in his way, to do the same for Freddie. Had he not made him go to Miss Graddock and refuse her in person? Had he not decreed that his brother would find a profession and better himself?

"Too little, too late," he muttered, reaching the landing.

As he did most days now, Freddie sat at his desk poring over correspondence for Mr. Danforth. The chancellor had written, agreeing to provide a recommendation for Freddie's turn toward an ecclesiastical life. Subsequently, he had become Danforth's top man, shadowing him almost night and day. Alasdair did not announce himself, but rather marched to the desk in the low-lit room and tossed the monkshood flowers onto the letter Freddie was reviewing.

His brother yelped in surprise, then twisted and sprang to his feet, splattering his own shirt with ink.

"You will explain to me how you came to be behind the Florizel on the night it burned."

Freddie stopped moving, perhaps stopped breathing, a torturously long silence stretching between them. With his eyes wide as saucers, he at last stammered, "But I . . . I didn't do it."

"Not a promising start." Alasdair pointed at the flowers. "Explain. Now. Your coat was stained with oil, you were picking monkshood behind the theater, what other conclusions shall I draw? That you are the victim of inexplicable coincidences? By God, Freddie, my one solace is that you have no compelling motivation to do this cowardly act."

"Because I didn't!" Freddie wiped frantically at his shirt, succeeding only in spreading the stain around. He swore and gave up, retreating behind the chair he had just vacated. "Well, yes, very well, I was picking flowers for Emilia behind the theater—"

Alasdair fought the urge to sink down into the chair, shaking his head with despair.

"Which . . . I know, that sounds bad, but I don't know where the oil came from." Freddie grabbed his hair with both hands, yanking. Bent double, he let out a strangled sound of frustration. "Unless . . . unless . . ."

"This had better be convincing, Freddie, or I will have no choice but to drag you before the—"

"N-no! Listen, please, brother, just listen to me. The only reason I was at the Florizel to begin with was because Danforth sent me there. He wanted to deliver a crate of his bloody pamphlets for distribution the next morning, and of course, he couldn't do it his bloody self because Mother's physician diagnosed him with 'weak hands,' whatever that is. Probably got it from writing all of his stupid pamphlets!" Freddie paused in his diatribe to slam his fist down on the desk, sending more ink flying. "There was some sort of grease on the crate, and there were jars rattling around with the pamphlets, which I did think was odd—"

"And yet you didn't consider telling anyone?" Alasdair didn't know whether to be enraged or relieved that his brother was apparently this bird-witted. "Why would Danforth need those jars?"

"I don't know! Sometimes he gives out jams and vegetables to the poor," said Freddie, defending himself breathlessly. "Maybe . . . maybe he's resorted to bribing people to take his literature!"

Alasdair closed the gap between them, laying a careful, gentle hand on Freddie's shoulder. He had to know. He had to be sure. "Swear it to me, Freddie. Swear on my life, on Mother's, on Emilia's, swear that you did not set the fires at Pressmore and the Florizel."

"I swear!" Freddie cried. "I swear . . . I was only doing what Danforth asked of me."

"And he has far more cause to destroy the theater," said Alasdair. "His vendetta against their so-called vulgarity got him nowhere, the play was still going to happen. And you . . ." His words trailed off as a knot of thoughts unraveled before him. "And you are in position to take the living from him. He would have to move to another parish, lose his influence here, and his hold over Mother. Come, he's not here at present, we should search his room." They left Freddie's chamber, retracing Alasdair's route outside and to the east pavilion, stopping to alert Eades, the butler, that they would need keys for Danforth's accommodation. Besides his living at Anselm, Danforth had access to the spacious guest housing that he currently shared with Gordon. Each man had his own suite of rooms, Gordon occupying the downstairs and Danforth above.

The winter gloom of early twilight darkened the skies. Lights twinkled merrily in Gordon's rooms, the pavilion chimney smoking. Once inside Danforth's apartment, Alasdair ushered Eades forward with his lantern. He expected to find everything in good order, tidy and faultless, but nothing could prepare him for the chaotic mess overtaking every nook and corner. Even the butler couldn't suppress his gasp of revulsion.

"The state of it," Freddie breathed. "Mother would be furious if she knew."

"She doesn't," said Alasdair. "She doesn't know anything about Danforth, not really. None of us do, and that's how he preferred it."

He took the lantern from the butler and pushed deeper into the disorder. Crates of empty jars were stacked near the door. The vessels had recently been sealed with wax. Alasdair lifted one of them, smelling.

"Lantern oil," he murmured.

"Do you think he meant to start fires elsewhere?" Freddie asked, taking his own sniff and recoiling.

"Maybe, or he didn't like that most of the Florizel is still standing." A darker idea bloomed like spilled ink, and he wondered if this demonstrated a readiness to punish those who helped anyone affected by the blaze. The Richmonds. Himself.

Violet and her sisters.

Alasdair turned away from the crates, shuffling over the papers that littered the floor until he found the small office off the main sitting room. It was partially a library, and all the likely books were present, including those Alasdair had warned him not to keep on his little painted table. The desk was piled high with correspondence and drafts of his pamphlets. Alasdair picked up the topmost paper, squinting down at it in the grim lantern light.

"He means to attack Miss Bilbury next," said Alasdair. When Freddie did not respond, he pivoted and glared at his brother. The evidence was written on his face in a pale grimace. "You knew about this."

"He had me write to some of his fellow clergymen in London," Freddie replied, hoarse. "And yes, he was searching for any hint of scandal around her. There was some, I'm afraid."

"She's an artist, of course there was," Alasdair grunted. "What did he find?"

"A squabble with a jilted lover," Freddie began in a croak. "That . . . ended in a fire."

So that's what Robert had been on about. Alasdair sifted through the other papers, searching for anything relevant. His eyes flashed across Freddie's name. He snatched up the letter while Freddie huddled close, reading over his shoulder.

"Cambridge? He— Why! The rotten weasel, he was trying to get the chancellor to admonish me." Freddie's mouth dropped open as he yanked the letter out of Alasdair's grasp. "He blames me for the fire! He set me up!"

"You would have taken the living at Anselm from him," Alasdair pointed out.

"It's only a draft. Do you think he sent it?"

"Looks unfinished to me, but we have to assume he's been plotting against you and this family for some time now. This pamphlet about Miss Bilbury seems to be complete. Did Mother already fund the printing?"

"He's been railing about her on Sundays for weeks," said Freddie, downcast. "Her and the Florizel."

"And he no doubt thinks he can blame you and her for the fires at Pressmore and the theater, point the finger anywhere but at himself, the man of God." Alasdair gathered up the relevant letters and drafts, tucking them under one arm. "I'm afraid we have to show these to Mother."

"Oh." Freddie drooped. "Oh, God."

"Yes, exactly. She won't like it, but we cannot let Danforth escape justice for his crimes."

Freddie lifted his head, perking up. "So . . . you believe me, then? You believe that I didn't knowingly help him start that fire?"

"I don't need to believe you; the evidence of Danforth's guilt is here before us."

His brother's expression puddled, his lip quivering. "What if I want you to believe me?"

Alasdair straightened, annoyed. But then he studied Freddie's face a heartbeat longer, and for an instant, he recognized their father's countenance in the young man.

"Yes, Freddie, I believe you, but I wish you had come to me with your concerns about Danforth, about the crate. I would have stood by your side." Alasdair lowered the lantern, clasping him on the shoulder. "If it had been you, I would've stood by your side still, protected you however I could even while punishment arrived. I'd blunt the weapon, Freddie—any weapon—that fell upon you. Father died getting you and Mother out of Clafton. We aren't made of cowardly stuff. We do what is right."

"Well said," Freddie whispered with the faintest smile. "I'll give whatever testimony I must, even if I look stupid, to make sure Danforth is held accountable."

Alasdair nodded. "Good lad."

Through the open library door, they heard muffled voices. Alasdair hoisted the lantern again and stepped out into the sitting room to find Danforth returning to what he assumed was still home. Eades looked to Alasdair. The yellow light in Alasdair's hands bounced along the walls, finding its way to Danforth's churlish smile. His eyes had always been black and piercing, but something intruded now, a darkness that made him uneasy. Alasdair recognized this darkness, knew it somehow.

"Ah. I will gather my things" was all Danforth said. His tone was hollow.

"Eades will stay and make certain that you do." Alasdair passed the lantern to the butler, then gestured for Freddie to follow him.

"She won't believe you," Danforth called as they took the stairs. "I'm more of a son to her than you ever were."

Alasdair ignored him, even if a quick slug to the bastard's jaw was an incredibly enticing and deserved notion. Back in the house, Lady Edith sat in her preferred drawing room by the roaring fire, surrounded by the sculptures and paintings Alasdair had brought her from across Europe, a shawl tucked around her shoulders and a book of sermons in her lap. She wasn't reading, exactly, but looking beyond the spine of the book to the window off to her right, gazing out into the gathering dark, her expression that of a person who had just forgotten something, searching for it on the tip of their tongue. It was an image worth preserving; in that moment, she wasn't his mother, just a woman lost in thought. He stopped across the room from her, struck by the uncomfortable slap of premonition, knowing that what he had to say would likely cause her great harm.

His throat felt like it was being strangled by an invisible hand; that premonitory aura plunged him through time, and as he approached his mother, he wondered who had been the person that had come to tell her of their father's passing in the fire. He felt a kinship with that messenger, the weight of it crushing down on his shoulders.

There would be his mother before this conversation and his mother after; Danforth was damn near like a child to her. And he wasn't wrong; perhaps she had more affection for him than she had for Alasdair or Freddie. Again, that crushing weight, and the sense that this day would haunt him forever.

"At least she's already sitting down," Freddie murmured at his back.

Lady Edith turned toward them. There was fleeting surprise, then a softening of motherly tenderness around her lips that made Alasdair freeze with guilt. Adjusting his spectacles, he took a deep breath and started in. "We need to discuss Mr. Danforth."

"Oh?" She lifted her chin, smiling.

Alasdair flinched. "He's not the man you think he is. He's dangerous, Mother, and never again can he darken our doorstep."

Just as Danforth predicted, Alasdair's loving mother did not believe him.

16

At Christmas I no more desire a rose
Than wish a snow in May's new-fangled shows,
But like of each thing that in season grows.
Love's Labor's Lost—Act 1, Scene 1

December

My Dear Sir,

I received your latest letter in great health, thank you for asking. In fact, I write in good health and in better cheer, for I have such a wily little proposition for you, and I know you will agree to it! Lillian and I will no longer be afflicted with her mother's presence this Christmas, the details of which I couldn't possibly bore you with, and so we find ourselves quite aimless in that regard. Or we did, until clever Lillian began extolling the virtues of Christmas in the countryside. You should have heard her! She was never a poet or even articulate, but it was amusing to us both. "Who has not longed for Christmas but to have it where the snow is crisp, and the trees look like sugared sweets." Something along those lines, though doubtless I have improved it. And I know you are already scoffing, my friend, for snow would very much ruin your building plans at Clafton, but for Lillian's sake, I do hope we are blithely dusted with the stuff.

Or rather, I do hope so if you agree to have us to Sampson Park. And I hear you scoffing again, ha! Yes, it is unforgivably impish of me to impose upon you and your family, but I suffer imagining you in that big house with no one to celebrate with but your brother and Lady Edith. You have never described your mother as a game kind of woman, and pardon me for saying so, but a man should not be dreary at this time of year. Admittedly, I miss you, old friend, for no one here can talk about art the way you do—Jasper tries, but there is something so desperate about him, it's off-putting to say the least. The port has addled his wits, I wager, because he is constantly wrong. I simply cannot abide hearing him mistake Masaccio for Messina again, it might kill me even while the Yule log burns.

Say you will rescue us from this ugly fate! Say you will have us, and we will make such a merry little party that there will be talk of it for years to come. I await your generosity, and who knows? There may even be another Caravaggio—or something better! Ha!—in it for you.

Enduringly your friend,

Robert

If Alasdair was being honest with himself, he did dread the thought of spending Christmas alone with Freddie and his mother. They had each become miserable in their own way. Freddie listlessly continued his pursuit of the ecclesiastical profession, his heart decidedly not in it, and his attention decidedly and increasingly elsewhere, usually a bottle of cherry brandy in the library. He seemed disinterested in Alasdair's speeches and guidance and was often found stone drunk, sleeping in front of their father's portrait. All of his plans had come to nothing, and pursuing the living attached to Sampson Park had inspired Danforth's crimes. He was without a mentor and without Emilia. Alasdair had tried to coax him into meeting the vicar in Cray Arches, Mr. Corner, to which his brother shrugged and made several noncommittal noises.

Lady Edith had subsided into silent protest, so much so that she could be mistaken for one of the marble busts in the drawing room. She had developed a nervous blink and spoke to them in a strained whisper. Dinners were unbearable. As such, Alasdair made certain to stay "late" at Clafton as often as propriety allowed, and truthfully, beyond that point. He almost wished one of them would throw a cup at him, shout, rage—anything but stare into the middle distance in a depressed stupor.

Alasdair read Robert's letter over again. Maybe Robert, boastful and ridiculous, was just the antidote to his creeping poison of silence. Gordon had consulted a number of local farmers who were confident they were in for a relatively dry winter, so Lillian would be disappointed on that score, but that would just give them something to talk about. Alasdair laughed mirthlessly at himself; was he actually *wishing* for idle chitchat?

"Things really are dire," he muttered, and went to his writing desk. To respond, he was forced to brush aside a number of unfinished drafts that gathered in a shameful pile. Alasdair sat down hard, staring at the discarded letters. He really ought to burn them; that he hadn't made the cut of the guilt that much deeper.

~~Dear Miss Arden,~~
~~Dearest Miss Arden,~~
~~My Dear Miss Arden,~~
Miss Arden,

God, he couldn't even begin the damn thing without collapsing into indecision. Recently, at dinner, desperate for a single human sound he himself had not created, he had asked his mother to recall the days of her courtship with their father. The look she gave him could have leveled London. Freddie had made the soup course particularly noisy with slurping after that.

I am writing to inform you of certain events regarding my brother and Mr. Danforth that transpired after our last conversation. Your suspicions regarding my brother were not unfounded; he unknowingly aided the vicar of Anselm, Mr. Danforth, who set the fire at the Florizel and presumably also at Pressmore. He has been transferred to the Anselm jail to await his appearance before the grand jury at Epiphany.

Too cold and unfeeling.

It is my sincerest hope that this letter reaches you while you and your family are in excellent health. ~~That the weather has been so unseasonably merciful exacerbates that wish.~~

The weather? Really? And he hated the word *exacerbates*—it was hideous on the page. Thankfully, the most embarrassing draft languished in infamy at the bottom of the pile. He had gotten into the brandy himself that night and, after staring into the eyes of Caravaggio's lute player for an undisclosable amount of time, gone to his desk with the fervor of a man possessed.

Possessed. I will not say by what.

His hand hadn't even felt like it was his own. Some other creature took control of him.

No, it was me, me stripped to the marrow, just as I told Violet. Me as I see myself in dreams, feeling and thinking while unshackled by the waking, stifling anxieties that stalk me like a pack of wolves. I am vanishing in this house, this prison. When Clafton is finished at last, my body will find a new prison to haunt.

Alasdair stood, angry at himself, and gathered up the pile of unsent attempts, crossed to the hearth, and shoved them behind the grate. Then, possessed again, he knelt, swore, and fetched out the truest one. He shook it, batting down the wisp of flame, and hid it in a desk drawer, where it would taunt him as steadily as the portrait of her beneath his bed.

The cold and unfeeling version would have to suffice. Giving Miss Arden a concise summary of events and promising to write again when Danforth's fate in the courts was better understood. At the bottom, he indulged his true feelings only to the extent that he thanked her for her patience, and for allowing him to clear up the matter himself. Sealing the note, he tried not to imagine her expression as she received it, or the way her hands would smooth out the folded page to read, indirectly touching his own.

Afterward, he dashed off a letter to Robert, agreeing to play host to the Dalys for Christmas. At the bottom, he urged Robert to come with all the mischievous and lively spirit he could muster.

17

Alas that love, so gentle in his view,
Should be so tyrannous and rough in proof!
Romeo and Juliet—Act 1, Scene 1

When Beadle Cottage received a visitor on the first Saturday of December, Violet was elated to discover Cristabel had come. As soon as she beheld the woman's face, however, her joy dissipated.

"But what is the matter?" Violet asked, ferrying the painter inside the cottage where it was warm. Outside, the air was biting, the moss and grass stiff with a frosty crunch.

Cristabel, ever looking with her artist's eye, paused near the sofa in the drawing room beside the front hall and sucked in every detail. She rubbed her hands together and waved Violet away when she tried to guide her toward the fireplace. Just the prior week, Violet had stayed at Pressmore for several days to paint under Cristabel's stern watch, yet between then and now, a brief span, she had grown grayer in the hair, hollower in the cheeks.

"I want you to know that it's been pleasant to teach you," said Cristabel, fixing her gaze out the windows that looked onto the cobbled path and yard. A pair of jays pecked at the dirt and, finding nothing, startled off into the branches hanging over the path. "I can't say that about many or even most of my novices. You listen. Your pride is managed. You do not consider yourself above improvement. You *do* react to criticism with your face, but less and less."

Violet frowned and watched Winny and Maggie peering in at them from the hall. Shooing them away with a gesture did nothing, and they continued their wide-eyed eavesdropping, stacked like owls atop each other.

"Where is this going?"

"You are going nowhere," said Cristabel firmly and with a long, pained exhale. "I, however, will be returning to London. No doubt you have heard the rumors circulating in the village?"

Violet went to take her hand, shaking her head. "It shouldn't matter what that horrid vicar said about you! I've had a letter from Mr. Kerr. Mr. Danforth is responsible for the fires; nobody should believe a word he says about anything."

"What should be and what is are rarely the same, my dear. The whispers have become shouts, and the noise has reached Pressmore. Your aunt no longer believes I'm fit company for her family and can no longer offer me a place to stay and teach."

"But there must be something we can do!" Violet turned to stare at her sisters, who shared her look of despairing outrage. "I won't let you be chased off like this."

Cristabel smiled down at her, calm, and patted the top of her hand. "What sort of artist would I be if I maintained a spotless reputation, mm? You should see what my detractors put in the papers! They were vocal after my most recent withdrawal from the Royal Society. No, no. Your aunt has been generous, and I can embarrass her no longer. This will pass, as all things eventually do, and one day I will return to this place. I fear I have grown fond of it." Cristabel cleared her throat, pulling away from Violet and trundling toward the door. Winny and Maggie scattered, but not before they had been seen. Pausing in the front hall, she quarter-swiveled toward Violet. "If you remember one thing from our acquaintance, let it be this: never turn away from art, Violet. Your expression is more vital than you know. Ah. I hope you don't mind that I packed some of your studies to take with me . . ." She trailed off, and Violet did not protest, for she would have no paintings of any merit if Cristabel had not guided her. "For I have grown fond of you, too."

Here was a woman who could not be persuaded. Violet knew her mind was made up. She smirked and helped Cristabel to the door. "As much as it pains you to say so."

"Indeed. You know how I loathe self-indulgent sentiment." Cristabel took one last look around the small cottage, seeing it, as she did everything, with assessing, fresh eyes. Sweeping up Violet's hands in hers, she squeezed. "Ah, and now that I can no longer offer my commission as a prize at Miss Richmond's benefit, I suggested you as my replacement. Farewell."

"I . . ."

Violet gawked at the door, her jaw to the floor.

"How awful!" Winny and Maggie reappeared, Winny wringing her hands. "I knew Mr. Danforth was a blight on his profession, but to cost Miss Bilbury her position at Pressmore? Oh, but I truly do not like him at all."

"You can hate him," Maggie told her with a snort. "We all do."

"That is such a frightful word. I try not to hate anybody."

"But if anybody deserves it, it's him," Violet muttered. "Poor Cristabel. All those ghastly rumors in the village, I thought it would come to nothing."

"Cristabel has chosen an unusual life for herself. It makes her an easy target," said Maggie, rubbing Winny's shoulder. "I should know."

Violet puffed out her cheeks. "And Aunt Mildred should know better. If one is to be rich and respected, then one should have a backbone stronger than an earthworm and learn to . . . I don't know, stand up for what is right."

Maggie detached from them and went to sit near the fire, her mouth a firm line of frustration. "The way she stood up for Ann when she was accused of misbehavior? The way she stood up for me? Come now, Violet, acts of courage have never been Aunt Mildred's forte, and worms do not have bones."

"And now I shall have to fulfill the commission auctioned at Ann's benefit, which is a disaster waiting to happen! Who will want to pay anything for my work? Cristabel's paintings fetch a lofty price in reputable circles, and I am . . ." Violet clamped her eyes shut and rubbed her face. "Chalk and cheese, that's what it is."

"Chin up, Violet! Ann will make the punch so strong nobody will remember what they bid on anything. Besides, it is all to help the Florizel, so nobody can be cross with you if your painting is an utter failure." Maggie laughed at her from the sofa.

"Which it won't be!" Winny assured them both, offering Maggie her sternest pout. "Cristabel clearly believes in your skill, dear, and so do I."

"Ugh!" Violet tossed up her hands and stormed away, nowhere in particular at first, and then toward her and Winny's shared bedroom. "That is easy for you to say, Maggie!" she shouted as she went. "You're brilliant!"

There was hardly any time to prepare; Christmas was nearly upon them! How could she be expected to take on this responsibility with so little warning? Violet hurled herself onto her bed and shrieked into a pillow, which summoned their mother. Mrs. Arden was a once-soft woman hardened by life's unfairness. Losing Mr. Arden had changed all their lives, but hers the most, for theirs had been a strong, abiding love, and after he was gone, Mrs. Arden almost didn't seem to know how to continue living. She was gaining strength again now that they were all together at Beadle, but Violet wasn't naïve enough to think they would ever really get her back.

Her mother rubbed her back. It didn't help.

"There now, my darling, what will make it better?"

Violet kept her face stuffed into the pillow. What would make it better? She huffed out a wretched sound.

"It isn't the benefit, is it?"

Stifled, Violet shook her head. Tears were gathering, pressurized behind her tightly closed eyes. Cristabel was gone. Emilia had grown sullen and distant. Maggie had her novels and her husband. And what did Violet have of her own? So little. *So* little. Just her mind, she decided, and the gifted paints, brushes, and easel, which more and more she suspected had come from Mr. Kerr.

Mr. Kerr.

Damn him. Damn him! How could he touch her hand and gesture at courtship and then leave?

Heaving in a huge breath, she lifted her head just enough to hover it above the pillow. "Last week Aunt Mildred said I shouldn't even bother going to London next summer; the Burtons don't want me in their house, and none of the bachelors will take interest either. She said if I promise to be polite, she will try to find me a nice farmer to marry! *Maybe a nice farmer will have you* were her words."

"My sister is always saying such things. It's never bothered you before."

Violet let her head fall back down.

And why would he lower himself to have me?

"You know Margaret will never make you leave, Violet. You have a safe harbor here for as long as you wish it," her mother continued. "My sisters are always saying it, and sometimes I worry that they are right—your father and I were too permissive with you girls. But you were so happy and carefree when you were little, singing your songs and putting on your plays, and I fooled myself into thinking the world would never intrude on our little haven."

"'Are you sure that we are awake? It seems to me that yet we sleep, we dream,'" Violet mumbled into the pillow.

"Your ridiculous father and that play," Mrs. Arden said with a sigh, but affectionately. "We must live in the waking world, darling, and sometimes in that waking world we must bend, lest it break us."

Her mother stayed awhile and trailed her hand lightly up and down Violet's back. She pretended to fall asleep, and when she was alone, she reached for the top drawer on her nightstand. It was a small room with a slanted ceiling, dried flowers and herbs hanging from the rafter scenting the space with lavender. The colorful, merry quilt on the bed had been lovingly sewed by Winny. There was a single triangular window with the rocking chair in front of it. The curtains were open, the sunlight illuminating the chair and easel where Violet had been painting. An unfinished watercolor of Winny bent over her needlework was secured to the board. With the room being so cramped, the sisters had a serious pact that they would never disturb each other's dresser drawers, the one narrow slice of privacy in an otherwise overcrowded home.

Violet fetched the letter Mr. Kerr had sent and turned onto her back, unfolding it to read. She knew it by heart, even though there was nothing romantic about it. He may as well have been writing to a complete stranger. None of it made any damn sense. She was sure he had provided the expensive, anonymous gift, had very nearly confessed love or something like it to her, but then why write to her like this? Where was the warmth?

She clasped the letter to her breast and let the tears that had been building roll silently down her cheeks. To him, she was no better than a secret mistress, someone to spoil when nobody was looking, a thing to be enjoyed in the darkness. After all the suitors she had offended in London, after her public scandal with the Frenchman, no man of Mr. Kerr's status and wealth would risk openly admiring her.

Violet turned and shoved his letter back into the drawer, slamming it shut. Let the world break her, she decided. It was better than giving in to its injustices.

The next day, Maggie's husband returned from London. Beadle Cottage was once more overflowing, and Violet confined herself to her bedroom to paint. She had nothing against Bridger Darrow. In fact, she liked him, and especially liked how radiant Maggie became in his doting presence, but she was painfully aware of the thundercloud hanging over her own head. She seemed to darken whatever room she stepped foot in; it was better that she practice her portraiture for the benefit, and for the life Cristabel had warned her was imminent.

She yearned to paint him, to see his face again, even if lifeless and made by her own hand. But she refused to do it; she would not be mastered by her feelings for him if he was intent on only teasing her! The chilly indifference of his letter lingered like the last hard frost of winter.

Downstairs, they discussed the garlands for Christmas Eve, listened to Bridger's stories of London, laughed, sang songs, lit candles, and prepared for the holiday with the boisterous spirit it normally engendered. Maggie had finished her novel and kept Winny company in the drawing room while Winny embellished their old gowns for Ann's Christmas Day benefit. There was no beef, and nobody seemed to mind, while upstairs Violet painted until her hands cramped.

If she wanted a life outside of Beadle Cottage, she would have to scratch it together herself.

18

This above all: to thine own self be true,
And it must follow, as the night the day,
Thou canst not then be false to any man.
Hamlet—Act 1, Scene 3

"It's fine work, Gordon, incredibly fine work." Alasdair ran the flat of his hand along the ashlar wall, admiring the perfect seam where the cornice protruded. Standing back, squinting beneath his hat against the bright, pale gray sky, he recognized Clafton Hall. It was the place of memory itself, right down to the pieces kept from a fifteenth-century Norman castle.

"This hill looks complete now," said Gordon. "Nearly. Close, Mr. Kerr! Very close!"

Unfinished or not, it was inevitable now. Clafton Hall rose to preside over the slopes and pond and streams again. Another month or two of work and he could start filling it with art from their storehouses in London. The limestone gleamed. Each of the three wings on the five-bay, three-story building was finished with a slate tile roof and rendered chimney stack;

the entry and windows faced south toward the pond and stream that cut the border between the Richmond property and his.

Voices, low with disagreement, arrived from the other side of the build site. Just as Alasdair began assigning them to Robert and Lillian Daly, the first fat, spinning snowflakes began to fall. He stepped back from the wall, held out his hand, and watched a flake land on his glove, comically perfect, a many-pointed star with sparkling bridges and designs that soon became no more than a tiny puddle.

"I say, this is quite the climb, and I did not dress for it!" Robert exclaimed, huffing with effort as he appeared along the right wing of the house. He stabbed his cane into the ground with annoyance, resting one knuckle on his hip as he came to a stop.

"It's refreshing to take in the air after that long carriage journey—"

"Be quiet, Lillian. I'm rumpled and without a brandy. It's clearly your fault. Ah! There you are, old friend! We've quite scaled the Matterhorn to find you!" Robert crowed with laughter beneath the narrow brim of his black hat, gesturing his wife forward as they came to join Alasdair and Gordon beneath the swirling dance of snowflakes.

Alasdair took a moment to introduce Robert and Lillian to Gordon, who didn't seem at all impressed by their London fashions and manners.

"Work to do," Gordon said, excusing himself. "Get what we can covered before the snow gathers and send the lads home for Christmas Eve."

"You're just in time to see our luck run out," said Alasdair, glowering up at the sky. "I was convinced we would finish before the first snow."

"You must be disappointed, Mr. Kerr, how awful," Lillian consoled him quietly. She had been considered a magnificent beauty in her debut season, though years of marriage to Robert had tarnished her like a well-worn necklace. Still, behind that influence one could detect the sweetness of a young lady who had spent most of her youth smiling. A sharp, feline cleverness hid behind the English roses blooming in her cheeks. It appeared in flashes when she glanced at Robert and a suggestion of something more wild, more stalwart emerged.

"Awful? Don't be silly, wife. This is precisely what you wanted—your sugared treat forest for Christmas." Robert took a single glance at Clafton, Alasdair's most prized achievement, and started back toward Sampson.

"I didn't want it at the expense of your dreams, sir," Lillian said in an undertone. Alasdair walked beside her as they returned to Sampson. "And I said I hoped we might enjoy a forest dusted with winter sugar. He never remembers a thing I say."

"I only recall things worth remembering!" Robert called grumpily from up ahead.

"Clafton Hall is sure to be *the* feature of the county when it is finished," said Lillian, staring at the back of her husband's head.

"Thank you, Mrs. Daly. And may I welcome you to Sampson Park?"

"You may."

"And may I also suggest that, while you warm yourself and settle into your accommodations, I take Robert to the forest to look for our Yule log? You must be exhausted after—" Robert interrupted him, swearing as a branch swiped his cheek. "You must be exhausted."

Lillian beamed up at him. "Sir, there is no need for further gifts. That singular one will do."

Indeed, once Lillian was escorted to the house and pleasantries were exchanged with his mother and brother, Alasdair forced Robert right back out into the snow.

"Come," Alasdair barked at him, swinging the axe to rest on his shoulder. "It will be the most heroic thing you've done in ages."

"I don't need to be heroic," said Robert. "I pay someone to do that."

Yet it was supremely amusing to take Robert into the steepest climb of the woods as the snow came down and began, hour by hour, to stick. He made his friend hold his hat and coat while he swung the axe at a big, obliging log, chips of bark and wood flesh flying after each meaty *thunk*. The exercise heated him through, and with the churn of hot blood came the churn of other things—the familiar buzz in his head of mingled guilt and desire. He had declared himself to Violet, and now he was building to a confession. To himself. To her. Most unpleasant of all, to his family.

"You have the strangest look on your face," said Robert, laughing nervously.

"I'm merely thinking . . ."

"I wouldn't suggest it. I'm always at my worst when I pay too much attention to myself. Better to just do and live with the consequences. One can get lost in the forest of thoughts and never emerge." As if reminded that they were in a very real forest, Robert glanced around, shrinking.

"Soon," Alasdair muttered to himself, lowering the axe and leaning against it, breathing hard. "It can't go on like this."

"I won't pretend to understand you. And don't expect me to

drag that log through the forest." Robert sniffed, dodging debris. "These Hessians are new."

The log was wrapped in hazel twigs and brought back to Sampson Park. The groundskeeper met them at the edge of the wood and helped them carry the load to the great hearth in the main drawing room, where Lady Edith was already swaddled in her shawls, presiding over a book of sermons. The house was filled with greenery, every mantel, corner, and pillar hung with fragrant boughs, snow-crisped holly shining beside wreaths of ivy and rosemary, though per Lady Edith's instructions, no mistletoe was allowed. Robert and Alasdair retired to the library to refresh themselves after their Yule adventure, sipping port while Robert perused the books on offer and decried the lack of novels.

"Lady Edith is not fond of the secular," Alasdair explained.

"I gathered that from the décor," said Robert, shuddering. "And how the devil do you go on living with all these martyrs staring at you while they bleed out?"

"Without sin, or so my mother hopes."

"Is it working?" Robert barked with laughter, leaning against one well-stocked bookcase, several volumes of Fordyce's work lined up near the rake's head. "How fares your brother?"

"Poorly. He's floundering." Alasdair drained his port.

"Send him to London. I'll take him 'round. You know we dine with a bishop every month; I'm certain your brother will warm to the profession once he sees the size of that man's rings."

Freddie did seem more himself when they sat down to dine that evening, and as much as Alasdair found fault with Robert, his friend did seem invested in Freddie's good cheer. He engaged him in animated conversation, picking his subjects deftly and delighting both Freddie and Lady Edith with stories of hosting the bishop and going to Pargan Poole in previous years for Christmas, as well as listing out all the recent paintings he had acquired. Lillian sat largely silent, though she seemed content to let Robert hold court while she ate the succulent roast goose and received compliments on her stately bearing from Lady Edith.

In fact, by Christmas morning, Alasdair was feeling proud of himself; he had accurately assessed that all Sampson Park needed was a dose of new faces to feel lively for the holiday. Lady Edith insisted that they go to the church at Anselm for the service, Mr. Danforth's replacement giving the overlong sermon. His mother repeatedly swiveled in her seat, gazing off toward the door as if expecting Mr. Danforth to return at any moment.

For the rest of the afternoon and into the early evening, Alasdair felt a building sense of unease. His stomach was in knots as he dressed to go down for Christmas dinner; what if he had too much wine and blurted out that he wanted to marry Miss Arden? Maybe he ought to. He couldn't contain the secret much longer. Freddie and his mother would be enraged for very different reasons. Glancing out the window, he watched the snow continue to fall and mound into higher and higher satin-white pillows. The trees drooped, their branches not so much lightly sugared, as Lillian hoped, but weighted until their tips brushed the drifts rising to meet them. That was it, he decided, that was the source of his unease.

What if Robert is trapped here for a fortnight? How will I survive it?

The house was more quiet than usual, the snow blocking them in muting every sound until it threatened to drive one mad. He thought of Mrs. Richmond's generous invitation to attend her benefit, and he imagined Pressmore wearing its elegant emerald Christmas finery, musicians tuning their instruments, actors practicing their scenes, cooks mixing the wassail bowl, guests choosing their feathers and jewels for the event of the season, and among them . . .

Alasdair dismissed his valet and went to the window, gazing with hard eyes out at the snow. *You fool, you shouldn't have said anything to Violet about your feelings. Did you think somehow you would end up there and not here? In what world would that be possible? Certainly not this one.*

He was stupid to hope but doomed to anyway. He wondered what Violet might be wearing for the benefit. She would look best in silver and white, he thought, or maybe a rich blue to bring out her striking eyes. He almost caved and went to steal a look at her self-portrait, but he tore himself away from the window and went downstairs, where Robert and Lillian were waiting.

"Lord, the mood in here is dire," Robert muttered, his mouth pulling down at the corners until his neck wrinkled. "Lady Edith has read to us from *Sermons to Young Women* for the last hour. I thought Lillian was going to hurl herself at the Yule log!"

"Lady Edith is very shy, I think," Lillian added gently. "I wonder if conversing comes easy to her."

They sat down to white soup bright with parsley and thyme, venison with wine and mushrooms, trays bending beneath the weight of vegetable pies, piccalilli piquant with long peppers and vinegar, lemon cheesecakes sharp enough to sting the inner cheek, and the traditional pudding crowned with holly. The food, served amidst sunset-colored hills of oranges studded with cloves, never seemed to lessen in quantity, despite their best efforts.

"Mr. Danforth would take this in hampers to church tomorrow," said Lady Edith, looking right, as if speaking to a person only she could see. "Maybe Eades can do it, though the snow will be harrowing."

At the mention of Danforth, Robert choked awkwardly on a throatful of pudding.

Everyone moved into the drawing room afterward, to be judged by the ever-present and abundant bleeding martyrs Robert found so perplexing. They were not just in the library, but all over the house.

"At least they feel right for Christmas," Robert commented, shrinking away from the laborious gaze of St. Paul, upside down and reaching toward the viewer of the painting. "Shall we play a game? Cards? Perhaps Eades could be persuaded to fill a bucket with water for bobbing apples."

Lillian positioned herself at the ancient pianoforte and played for them. Nobody in the house used it, and it was slightly out of tune. It jangled everyone's nerves for half an hour, until Robert mercifully proposed a game of riddles, but Freddie began guessing too many shocking answers, upsetting Lady Edith.

"Perhaps you will answer a riddle for me," said Freddie, taking himself to a wrapped rectangle near the open doors leading to the front hall. The package had been there all evening, tipped against the wall, coyly in the shadows. "What have you brought with you, Robert?"

It was perhaps rude to ask, but Freddie had nipped indulgently into the wassail.

Robert had joined him. Swinging his empty cup around, Robert paraded to the package and gazed down at it lovingly. "I promised your brother a surprise, and I never fall short of a promise. Ha! Do I, dear? Do I?"

Lillian, on a chaise near Lady Edith and the Yule blazing in the hearth, shook her head and smiled in a far-off way.

"It isn't Twelfth Night, but we shan't be here until then . . ."

Thank God for that.

". . . so, we may as well present Alasdair with his gift now. Don't you think so, dear?"

Lillian nodded sleepily.

The usual "too kinds" and "you shouldn't haves" were expressed and waved away, and Alasdair carefully removed the brown paper, knowing from the shape and weight that he was bound to find a painting within. Sure enough, when he righted the thing, he was looking at the watercolor he had admired in Robert's hall.

"Don't be shy," Freddie said with a laugh. "Show us!"

Alasdair did, and everyone clapped for Robert's generosity.

"I've spared you the frame," Robert teased, winking at Lillian.

"Who is the painter?" Lady Edith asked politely, stirring from her dense nest of sermons and shawls.

"Cristabel Bilbury," said Robert, standing beside Alasdair to admire the work. "Not widely known, but your brother here was taken by it when he was last with us in London."

"But we know her!" Freddie snapped his fingers a few times, standing and pacing in a tight circle. "She's that steely-haired one who's always with the Richmonds. The one Danforth had it out for. She was run out of town, but before that she was teaching one of the Arden girls."

"Oh?" Robert smiled, the glint off the fire turning it feral. "Arden, is it? I've heard there was a lady by the name of *Violet Arden* with promising talent."

The drawing room walls collapsed in on him, squeezing. Alasdair's spectacles itched on the bridge of his nose, his gaze fixed on the painting but not seeing it as he tried to concoct a way out of this conversation.

"Violet Arden?" Lillian spoke up from the chaise, decidedly less sleepy now that the scent of fresh-meat gossip was in the air. "Isn't she the young lady who was entangled with a Frenchman? It was all anyone could talk about at Vauxhall in August. I had no idea she fancied herself an artist."

"A reported beauty, or so it's been said," Robert added. Alasdair could feel the man's eyes upon him, pointed and searching.

"Oh, a pity," said Lillian with a sigh. "But I suppose it makes sense; having ruined her prospects for an advantageous marriage, she may be seeking acceptance among the eccentric set."

Freddie belched and retreated to the wassail, disappearing into the shadowy nook beyond their mother and near the archway to the dining room.

"Whatever promise she may have possessed, whatever qualities of innocence and gentility existed in her as a youth were corrupted by her proximity to the Richmonds," Lady Edith stated. This was not an attempt at gossip, but information given as fact. She sat up, suddenly brighter-eyed. "No moral person would join with that family. They are sin manifest. They poison everything they touch."

An ominous silence descended. Robert and Lillian shared a look, no doubt realizing their dreams of a merry, simple country Christmas were crumbling before their eyes. Eventually, Robert cleared his throat, gesturing to the painting still in Alasdair's grasp.

"Yes. Well! I'm sure we can all safely forget Miss Arden. Really, I doubt she is worth spoiling the joy we might have this evening. Where is Eades? Alasdair, would you be so kind as to inquire about that apple bucket?"

Robert's ghoulish, spearing smile pricked the right spot. The boughs and the candles and the roar of the burning Yule log fell away. A verse came to mind, perhaps a different sort of gift from the multitude of biblical figures pinned to the walls all around him.

And immediately there fell from his eyes as it had been scales: and he received sight forthwith . . .

They didn't know her. By God, they didn't know the first thing about her.

Alasdair saw his chance and took it. He handed Robert the painting and swiftly left the drawing room and took the stairs three at a time. In his bedchamber, he watched the snow falling for a time, trying to summon the courage to do what he had already decided upon. Just being alone was a relief; he hadn't realized how hot and panicked he had become. But if one more unfair, unfeeling thing was said about Violet Arden, he might have put Robert's head through that painting.

Returning to the front hall, he called for Eades, but not to find Robert's infernal bucket. Instead, he asked for his horse to be made ready and for his gloves, overcoat, and hat. Good gloves, sturdy ones for the weather, and boots that could withstand the snow. By and by, the others in the house trickled into the front hall to see where he had gone. They had all of them gathered—Lady Edith with help from Freddie—when he grabbed his cane and ducked out the front doors.

"Alasdair! What's come over you, old friend?" Robert called, laughing.

He paused just long enough to tell them the truth. "It's horrid here, and I'm afraid I can't stay. Happy Christmas to you all, but I really must go."

Robert's nervous laughter followed him out into the white swirl of snow blowing in playful bursts across the drive. Perhaps a foot or so of accumulation piled around the edges of the house and obscured the finer points of the garden and road. It was no matter; Alasdair knew the way.

He mounted his horse and trotted off into the snow. His family called after him, but he didn't care; he had somewhere far more pressing to be.

19

Good pilgrim, you do wrong your hand too much,
Which mannerly devotion shows in this;
For saints have hands that pilgrims' hands do touch,
And palm to palm is holy palmers' kiss.
Romeo and Juliet—Act 1, Scene 5

"Please, I'm begging you, Maggie. Go look."

"For the last time: no! I promised Bridger the next dance. Have Winny do it for you."

Violet wrung her hands until it hurt, peering into the gallery running alongside the north wall of Pressmore. Behind them, the dancing was in full swing, partners skipping up to each other, skimming hands, sharing glances, then parting once more. The quartet and their insistence on reels, vigorous and soaring, was beginning to give her a headache. The gallery, ordinarily a place for calm reflection or an amiable conversation, had become the very nexus of fear.

"Winny is too tender, I would never make her deliver bad news," said Violet, pleading. She clung to Maggie, who was already trying to escape from her.

"I haven't been paying attention to the auction at all, and why would I? I've no money to spend on anything, and my book isn't popular enough to even be a prize." Maggie relented and took Violet by both hands, squeezing her fingers through the damp silk of her gloves. Maggie was resplendent in her red gown; the new gold braid Winny had added along the neckline dazzled under the chandeliers. "Someone will place a bid, Violet, even if it must be me. I hope you are prepared to paint me for a shilling." Maggie lifted Violet's head with a light push under her chin.

Violet forced a smile for her sister. "It would be the most I've ever made." Just as quickly, she subsided into despair. "But it would be such a waste! I've been so diligent this month, and for what? For a pity shilling?"

"What are we bickering about, ladies? No matter the subject, I must offer an opinion."

Miss Regina Applethwaite materialized as if blown in on a whisper of billowy snow. Icy as the storm battering the estate, she was a wealthy, delicate beauty and once rival to Maggie. They had set aside their misgivings for each other when Regina helped publish Maggie's novel. Regina herself was a novelist of growing renown.

"Violet is going to pieces because nobody is bidding on her portrait sitting," said Maggie.

"I knew it! You did look at the auction."

"I would be more than willing to place a bid, Violet," Regina offered, graciously lowering her eyelashes. "It will be sensational! You can paint Lucia and I together."

Regina had arrived at Pressmore with a mysterious Spanish companion, an heiress who spoke little but communicated plenty with her penetrating eyes. Miss Lucia Ramos had been immediately enchanted by the playacted vignettes dotted around the property and was likely off watching one while Regina made her rounds.

"This is a far better solution," said Maggie, visibly relieved. "Regina can offer the sort of sum your skill deserves, and I will not have to part with a hard-earned shilling. Now, if you'll both excuse me, I should like to dance with my husband."

Maggie twisted away from them, bounding back into the ballroom, where another song was about to begin. The estate hadn't hosted a crowd nearly this large since Ann and Lane's lavish masquerade wedding. Many of those in attendance were barely acquaintances to Violet, but Ann and Lane maintained a robust social calendar; it was no surprise that so many guests had leapt at the chance to spend Christmas with the Richmonds. Like at all of Ann's parties, there would be dancing and merriment until dawn.

"Come along," said Regina, processing into the gallery and weaving among the tables and plinths showing the various prizes on offer. Violet was beginning to wish she hadn't worn white with shining accents, for Regina had donned the same and made it look undeniably more fashionable. Regina was a woman of five and twenty, tall and slender, with the upright bearing and sky-high chin of a person confident in their good looks. Her very straight white-blond hair was swept beneath a festive silver turban. A few of the white feathers tucked into that headdress tickled Violet's ear as Regina led her along. They passed a display with a first edition of Regina's wildly popular book, *Sable Falls*, along with a personalized letter from her. The card laid out in front of the prize already showed a number of interested bidders. Regina sighed with satisfaction at the sight of it.

"Now, where is your table, dear? Point the way. Shall we decide together on a sum that feels right? What would be suitably philanthropic without embarrassing you? Five pounds? Ten? You shouldn't take the empty card personally, Violet, for everyone expected a portrait by Bilbury, and you are not yet a known quantity." Here, Regina paused and swept her fingertip across Violet's nose. Violet had once found Regina's natural condescension irritating, but it amused her now, for she knew that above all else, Regina cared about solidarity with others of her sex, and Violet admired that. Regina herself had put forward most of the funding for Maggie's first novel. "You will appreciate, of course, that I said *yet.* A shame nobody in this homespun backwater could appreciate her presence, which would have been elevating if they had the patience to see it."

"It's a disgrace how she was treated," Violet muttered.

"Her paintings will endure," said Regina, lifting the pen. "History will be the final judge."

Maybe that was true. Maybe Cristabel's time in Cray Arches was no more than a footnote in her life. She hadn't written, and Violet felt silly suddenly for missing her. Perhaps Cristabel had already forgotten them. Could anyone blame her?

"A woman starts one measly fire and society throws a fit," Regina said under her breath, still puzzling over what to bid. "If a male artist had done it, we'd be tying ourselves in knots making it part of his grand mythology rather than a career-ending scandal. God in heaven, Caravaggio killed a man in a brawl, and you don't hear anyone whining about it."

Before Regina could touch pen to paper, her companion, Miss Ramos, melted out from the shadows of the gallery. She was out of breath and clutching a black fan to her throat as she hurried toward them and took Regina's hand. "There is the most delicious commotion in the front hall." Her accent provided a slight purr on the Rs and a lisp on the sibilants in her sentences. There existed an air of the Old World about her, as though she ought to be painted with pigment and egg yolk on vellum, her exquisitely delicate, narrow face Van Eyck saintly.

"What sort of commotion?" Regina demanded.

"An unwelcome visitor," said her companion. Her dark brown eyes sought Violet. "Your aunt does not want to let him in."

Violet didn't wait to hear more. Nobody except Miss Ramos seemed to care about the drama unfolding in the entry, so Violet weaved through clusters of bidders or those just standing in the gallery watching the snow gradually rise around them. The gallery ran the length of the posterior of the house, connecting to the smaller drawing room where Violet often had breakfast when she stayed. From there, it was a sharp right through the open doors leading to the front hall. There, a small number of people had gathered beneath the woodsy profusion of holly, ivy, and spruce hanging from pillar to pillar. Her aunt was present, out in front like a damask sentinel. Ann, Cousin Lane, Winny, Emilia, and several staff fanned out behind the elder Mrs. Richmond.

The grand doors were open onto the night. Violet hugged herself against the bracing cold that burst into the house with swirls of snow.

"You should have never invited him!" Mrs. Richmond was saying in a furious whisper to Ann. "Now I am forced to look ungracious before our guests. But he cannot cross this threshold! I will not allow it. Bloom, keep everyone away from here until the man is gone."

The butler turned away to do her bidding, gently shooing guests back into the deeper rooms of the house.

Ann, arms crossed, did not seem to be backing down. "If this evening is to benefit the Florizel, then he is most welcome. It is he who provided the materials for the theater to be repaired. Mr. Lavin tells me more and more supplies arrive daily."

"And so what? That is very kind of him, I suppose, but it has nothing to do with me," Aunt Mildred replied.

"There must be something I can offer that would change your mind," said Ann. She smiled her most persuasive smile, inching closer to Aunt Mildred. It was known among the family that the two women did not often see eye to eye; Mrs. Richmond considered Ann too flamboyant, too immodest, too foreign, and Ann knew her mother-in-law to be stringent, judgmental, and traditional. "Why don't you redecorate the ballrooms this year? You can do whatever you like with them, and I will applaud all of your choices."

Aunt Mildred's mouth fell open in shock. Violet didn't stay to hear her answer or entertain more bickering; she sidestepped the group and marched out into the freezing cold.

Nobody had come to assist Mr. Kerr, certainly by Aunt Mildred's decree, and so he remained on horseback, turning in a circle while the beast grew impatient. It was almost midnight, and in the glow of that soft hour and the steadiness of the snow, he made a moving picture. Aunt Mildred called after her, insisting she return, that she would catch her death, et cetera, but Violet ignored her. It didn't seem possible that Mr. Kerr had come. They had met like this in the early autumn, when all the natural world was beginning its change, but then she had been startled by him and frightened; now she wanted nothing more than to believe it was really him and that he had come for her, despite it all.

Violet shouted for a groom. Aunt Mildred must have been pulled back into negotiations, for she did not protest, and a boy shot out from the dancing curtain of snowflakes obscuring the drive. Mr. Kerr reined his horse around and gazed down at her, a fine sparkle of melting white flashing off of his spectacles, which were fogged.

"I can hardly see you," he said, pulling down the heavy cowl covering his mouth.

"You can join us inside now," she said, relieved that the groom had come and Mr. Kerr could leap down from his horse, his boots leaving immense ruts in the snow. "How long did they keep you out here?"

"Long enough," he said with a laugh, dusting a shelf of snow from each of his shoulders.

Violet led him to the doors, where Aunt Mildred guarded the way with a tight-lipped scowl. Mr. Kerr presented himself politely, and Bloom and two servants waited in the eaves to swoop in for gloves and hat, if directed.

"My daughter-in-law seems determined to have you in our home tonight," announced Mrs. Richmond. Violet heard the wobble where she had nearly said "my home." "Never let it be stated that I turned a Kerr away on Christmas."

You tried hard to do exactly that.

Nobody pointed out the hypocrisy, and, led by Ann, a cheer went up for Aunt Mildred's heroic sacrifice. The servants came forward to collect Mr. Kerr's things, the seas parted—or, rather, everyone returned to their dancing, drinking, and game playing—and for a strange, suspended moment, Violet was more or less alone with him in the front hall.

"I thought you would be with your family this evening," Violet began, picking at the ends of her gloves.

Both of his thick, dark eyebrows lifted in worry. "Should I have stayed away?"

"N-no!" Violet stumbled toward him, acutely aware of his size, his scent, the smell of leather and open sky clinging to his dark red coat. There was a subtle pattern of ivy leaves woven into his yellow waistcoat; her eyes lingered there as she tried to think of what to say. "Only . . . You gave no indication that your mind had changed when you wrote."

Mr. Kerr—Alasdair—flinched and shook his head, the curled ends of his hair damp from melted snow. "I regret that letter. Could we talk of more pleasant things?"

Regret? Then perhaps it had not been naïve to hope. Violet gestured vaguely toward the inner rooms of the house. "Of course, Mr. Kerr. There are many pleasant things here tonight."

Luckily, she didn't turn away too swiftly, for she caught his smile—private, sweet, just for her. "Believe me, Miss Arden, that is already evident."

They wandered first to the largest ballroom, where the dancing showed no signs of slowing. The musicians were sweaty and disheveled but attacked their instruments with admirable endurance. Alasdair remained close to the wall and did not seem enticed by the clapping and whooping or the rustling of skirts and the soft tapping of feet. The wassail bowl had been refilled, and he joined Violet in scooping up a tiny cup of the strong mulled punch. He leaned down to say something to her, but the noise was too great, and Violet touched her ear and led him back out into the gallery. It would be mortifying for him to see her empty auction card, and so she smoothly slid around the corner and hurried to a darkened nook toward the eastern end of the house. Along the walls, there were many accomplished paintings to admire, but Alasdair seemed to have eyes only for her.

"I said this is quite a departure from the party at Sampson," he said, leaning down again.

"It must have been dreadful to have driven you off," she replied, laughing and drinking her punch. She went to the window to her right and pointed off into the distance. "On a clear day, one can see Clafton from here. I've watched it rise on the horizon bit by bit."

"And what do you make of it?" he asked, shifting defensively toward her, keeping a drunk from careening into her and spilling his drink.

"It's just how I remember it. Sometimes it feels like I'm looking back through time at a memory of my childhood, when we were still friends of a summer and rolling down hills."

Alasdair craned his neck back, frowning. "Are we not friends now, Miss Arden?"

Her lips swished to the side. "I have not forgotten that you insulted my paintings in London."

"Shall I mindlessly puff you up, even when it is not deserved? From our short acquaintance, Miss Arden, that is not the woman I know you to be. The woman I know is resilient, bold, and would easily shake off criticism from a man if she did not want to hear it. The woman I know is far beyond the constant pity that vanity requires."

Violet snorted and covered her mouth. The punch was going to her head. "That is painfully astute, Mr. Kerr. Bravo."

He was not finished, however, and seemed mildly offended at being reminded of his comments again. Sniffing, he added, "I know as certainty that you have potential. Why else would I . . ." His brows drew down as he cut himself off.

"Why else would you send me expensive paints, an easel, and a custom case?" she finished for him. The most darling, strangled noise came out of him, and the tips of his ears burned bright red. "Miss Bilbury put it together, lightning quick, too. My, but you are full of surprises, Mr. Kerr."

"Hm. Nobody else says that about me."

Violet shrugged and continued through the gallery, toward

the tableau prepared by the actors from the Florizel. "Then they don't know you well at all."

She dared to look at him, and he was already watching her. The heat in his gaze made her want to burst. *Our thoughts are one.* Violet had never been so aware of her body, of how his eyes lingering here or there was as meaningful and effective as a touch. She found herself breathing deeper, trying to lure his attention to her neckline and the way her breasts mounded subtly over the fabric. Judging by his strained expression, he noticed.

Every half hour or so, the players performed their scenes in various hidden, delicious nooks around the estate. A crescent of guests arced before this tableau, chatting amiably while they waited for the next performance to begin. Violet had seen this one three times already, but it never lost its charm.

"Did you paint those archways?" he asked, bringing his lips close to her ear once more. Carefully, she tilted her head just so, enough to aim his warm breath down the shoulder seam of her gown. She closed her eyes and made a quiet sound of enjoyment.

"I did, yes."

"They're rather good. The shadows of the vines are uncommonly well observed."

Her eyes opened swiftly, and she pivoted to gaze up at him through her lashes. "Was that praise for my painting, Mr. Kerr?"

"I am more than capable of showering you with compliments," he replied, standing so close that the warm swell of his thigh touched her hip through the thin fabric of her gown. "An ability I intend to prove to you tonight, if you will allow it, and most nights after."

Her breath snagged in her throat. Then it was real. He had

come charging through the drowning snow for her and only her. She would have to prostrate herself at Ann's feet for convincing Aunt Mildred to let him in. The night's festivities had been wonderful, but now it felt like pure magic was falling from the sky, enclosing them in drifts.

"Only most?" she asked, unable to resist pushing back.

Alasdair drained his punch and cleared his throat, straightening up to give the players his attention. "When your portraits are in great demand across the continent, shall I follow from city to city?"

"Follow me? Absolutely not." She grinned at his wounded expression. "We make them come to us."

Beneath Violet's painted arches, Ginny Thorpe stepped into a puddle of chandelier light, twisting to and fro listlessly. Another member of the company strummed a lute from somewhere in the darkness. Winny had painstakingly sewed pearls along the neck of Ginny's frothy pink dress. A few steps away, the forty-year-old Romeo fell to his knees and tucked his hands against his heart.

"But soft, what light through yonder window breaks? It is the east, and Juliet is the sun!" he cried. His lines were smoothly rehearsed, and he drew a few claps from the onlookers for his feeling and diction. Juliet sighed, and Romeo continued his speeches, and with each moment that passed, Violet felt Mr. Kerr draw toward her. Was anyone noticing? Did she care? His eyes never left the players, but Violet knew where he really was—there with her, the two of them part of the party yet utterly alone.

At last, Ginny, the superior actor, flung her arms out toward the audience and began her lines. "O Romeo, Romeo, wherefore art thou Romeo? Deny thy father and refuse thy name, or, if thou wilt not, be but sworn my love, and I'll no longer be a Capulet."

They stood side by side and watched, and as Juliet cast off the yoke of her family name, Alasdair's pinkie finger touched hers, a graze, and then steady pressure. Alignment. Her body recalled the feeling of riding with Alasdair to the hollow, her lap over his, the fine strength of his body surrounding her, the power of it making her feel safe and alive. His finger slipped along the underside of hers, pad to pad, and he held his hand there, perhaps waiting for Violet to yank hers away. She couldn't. Wouldn't. Her breathing deepened until she was sure everyone could hear her and see the hammer pounding in her chest. Just that little touch thrilled her like nothing else could. Yet she yearned for more. How could she not? There was so much of him to discover.

She almost glanced up at him but stilled herself. How much better to keep her gaze ahead, to preserve that delicate contact—just one more secret kept between them, and this the sweetest of all.

20

They are in the very wrath of love, and they will together. Clubs cannot part them.

As You Like It—Act 5, Scene 2

When the scene ended and the crowd began to lose interest and depart, Violet expected Alasdair to remove his hand, yet he must have been lost in thought or otherwise distracted, for he remained frozen there. She grinned and looked up at him, waiting for him to notice they were alone.

"Do you dance, Mr. Kerr?" she asked.

He blinked once, hard, and jerked his hand away from hers. "No," he said. "Partners find my height troublesome." Something at the other end of the gallery drew his attention, and he abruptly bowed, then strode away. "If you will excuse me briefly, Miss Arden."

Violet didn't have a chance to respond. The cold just on the other side of the gallery wall intruded, and she drew inside herself, wondering what had perturbed him so suddenly. She felt silly just standing and waiting for him to return, but she also feared that any movement whatsoever would break the fragile spell of the night.

"Who was that gentleman?" Regina asked, slinking out of the shadows and to her side. Miss Ramos appeared at her other arm. Violet stared down at her shoes, nervous.

"Was he not the source of all the commotion?" Miss Ramos asked.

"Mr. Kerr's family occupies the estate just north of here," said Violet, trying to will the blood out of her cheeks and ears, for she knew the blushing gave her away. "There is some old enmity between his family and my aunt's."

"And he is to inherit?" Regina pressed.

"He already has."

"And that inheritance was substantial?"

"It was."

"Este, how stimulating," Miss Ramos whispered, wiggling.

"How delicious," added Regina. She tapped her pointed chin with one finger, then dug that same finger into Violet's shoulder. "Who doesn't adore a forbidden love?"

Violet rolled her eyes. "We aren't in love, Regina."

The two ladies shared a look over Violet's head, then erupted with laughter, falling all over her and squishing her between them.

"Just have a care where your heart is concerned, dove, mm?" Regina prodded her again. "Protect it. When one has much and the other has little, it's rarely a smooth path to happiness."

As immediately as they had come, the two ladies were gone, linking arms and floating away into the growing swell of guests gathering near the auction tables. Ann was among those assembled there, glittering in jade-green silk, scattered jewels falling from the headband damming her thick black tresses. Violet took a nervous gulp, realizing they would end the bidding at any moment. Noticing her all alone in the corner, Ann waved her over.

Violet went to her on numb feet.

"Congratulations, Violet," said Ann, showing her a folded card. She thumbed it open just enough for Violet to see what had been written inside. It was the bidding card for her portrait sitting. "You've drawn the highest bid of the evening."

"But how is that possible?" Violet snatched the card out of her hands, holding it up to her own eyes. Lane had given the first number, a kind gesture, but he was outdone by Alasdair Kerr. Another sum was proposed by Lane, but Alasdair had clearly grown impatient with the game and finished with a definitive fifty-pound bid.

"I might have urged my husband to move things along and keep them interesting," Ann said lightly. "All for the good of the Florizel, of course."

Violet laughed and flopped the card down to her side. "Of course."

Somewhere in the crowd around them, Mr. Lavin could be heard weeping drunkenly with joy and relief. Ann's golden eyes flashed at someone over Violet's shoulder. "Ah! Mr. Kerr! May I commend you on your inspiring generosity this evening, sir? I daresay you have won yourself standing invitations to any events given by the Ladies' Society for the Lonely, Abandoned, and Infirm. With men like you in attendance, we may solve all the ills in the county!"

Turning slowly to face him, Violet met his eye with great difficulty. How many lectures had she endured from her aunts warning that she would end up a sad, lonely spinster? Worst of all, she had allowed herself to believe them. Her heart felt fit to burst with pride; Violet Arden, beautiful, exuberant, and strange, might amount to something after all. It would be in bad taste to take the card and wave it under Aunt Mildred's nose; just knowing she had not embarrassed herself completely would have to be enough.

"I will leave you two to decide the finer details of your sitting," said Ann, spinning away behind Alasdair, but not before giving Violet a wink.

"Well, Mr. Kerr, I suppose that somewhat lessens the sting of what you said about my work," Violet said, clearing the husk out of her voice with an awkward cough. "Thank you. I'm . . . surprised and flattered and humbled, which is a lot of things to be all at once."

She could kiss him for his gallantry. She *would* kiss him, she decided, for more reasons than that.

Not long after the auction concluded, it became evident to the staff at Pressmore, and then the guests, that the roads had become quite impossible. Indeed, impassable. Several feet of snow had fallen, and until the deluge stopped, or something could be done about it, it was unsafe for anyone to chance their journeys home. Accommodations would be made, naturally, and everyone comfortably housed for the night.

Many of the guests took that as permission to continue the drinking and dancing until dawn, for now that they were all hostages of the snow—musicians included—what could be done? Violet and her sisters accepted this unspoken invitation to excess, dancing themselves to the point of exhaustion, roses shining in their cheeks as the rules of partnership broke down, tipsy precepts taking precedent. With no desire to dance, Alasdair watched the ladies from the edge of the ballroom, glad to help finish off the last of the punch while Margaret Darrow's husband walked him through the ins and outs of their publishing ventures.

Darrow was an all-right fellow, if a bit long-winded, but Alasdair was content to sip and listen, though his eye wandered often to the left, where Violet swung arm in arm with her sisters and friends. Even Emilia allowed herself to be taken by the spirit of the holiday. Looking around, at the guests slumped sleepy and satisfied in chairs, at Ann still soliciting donations even as dawn approached, at Mr. Lavin shaking every available hand, at Mrs. Richmond, who had resigned herself to ignoring him (fair enough), and at Violet—the unexpected toast of the night with her triumphant auction—he was filled with . . . sadness. Sadness that he had been lied to about these people. Sadness that he had been kept from this place, a font of warmth and hospitality.

Sadness that his mother had taken their boat away one summer's day, long ago, and deprived Alasdair of what might have been the defining friendship of his life.

At last, Violet noticed him watching her. She detached from her sisters and hurried over, her skin glowing from the exercise.

"Now, now, Bridger. You mustn't talk Mr. Kerr's ears off until I have a chance to paint them," said Violet, beaming at them. "I've left her without a partner, you should go to her rescue."

Bridger Darrow ran both hands through his thick, dark hair, squared his shoulders, and marched off to do just that.

The quality of the music was deteriorating as the musicians tired themselves out, and Alasdair wished to be elsewhere. Somewhere quiet. Private. He left his punch cup on a table and moved to Violet's side, casting his gaze around the ballroom. "I thought you might show me your favorite painting in the house."

"Absolutely I would!" she cried, sounding genuinely as if nothing in the world would make her happier.

"You . . . already have one in mind?"

"Of course I do." Turning on her heel, she led him back out to the front hall, then toward a set of doors that presided over a library. The interior was every imaginable shade of blue; even the sconces pulsed like witch fire, the cool, serene embrace of all that blue giving the impression one was somehow underwater, in a mermaid's hidden den filled with books, globes, and art. Ahead, a curved bay pushed out toward the lawn, the designs in the window glass throwing the crisp moonlight across the rug in unpredictable shards.

Violet went to stand beside a tall, worn cupboard, the space between it and a bookcase to the left occupied by a small framed sketch. The paper was yellowed and the figure drawn upon it inexpertly rendered. Yet it appealed in its simplicity and in the love for the subject.

"It's me in the hedge maze as a girl," Violet explained. "My father drew it and gave it to Mr. Richmond before he died. Well, before they both died. Obviously. Maybe it's vain that I love it so much. Papa wasn't much of an artist, but I could look at it for hours. I must seem sentimental, to choose this over the portraits and landscapes by far more accomplished artists, but none of them touch my heart the way this does."

"His affection for you is obvious," Alasdair replied, not finding it overly sentimental at all. She could be so headstrong; to see the softness beneath her bold exterior was a welcome change. Reaching over her head, he pointed to a curling line swooshing over her ear. "This mark, the way the curve of the hair accentuates your cheek . . . perhaps he was not a studied artist, but that demonstrates an instinctual skill."

Violet nodded along to his words. "I often wonder if he would be proud of us. Our lives were thrown into disarray when he died. I hope he would understand we've all done the best we can. I . . . I think he would, I don't know." She turned toward him, still in that gently wondering aspect, her eyes bright as she tilted her head to the side. "What was Sir Jonathan like?"

"I once heard him described as a circus bear who got into the port." Alasdair chuckled fondly. "He could make even the most miserable devil crack a smile. He filled every room he walked into, always drawing an audience for his stories. Yet I know there were sides to him we never saw. He was knighted for his services during the war, and a man can't walk away from something like that without incurring a few scars."

"He would be proud, Alasdair. You're everything a gentleman should be."

He smiled faintly. "That may be so, but it takes a toll to wear a mask, to never show your true self to anyone. Until lately, of course."

"Lately?" She pressed her hand to her throat. "Me?"

Taking her by the waist, Alasdair led her to the sofa curved along the bend of the windows. When she was sitting, he reached down and carefully cupped the elegant line of her jaw. "Who else?"

Alasdair nestled beside her, drawing her into him, stroking his thumb along her lower lip before raising her face to meet his kiss. Her breath fogged his spectacles, and they both laughed before Violet's eyes snapped wide open.

"Oh no," she whispered, wrenching her head from his grasp.

"Violet? Was that . . . Have I misjudged—"

"No! No. I just realized I can't paint you!" she groaned.

"Why not?"

"I promised myself I wouldn't do exactly that, or paint any man, really, but that does make this auction business very awkward." She sighed and shook her head. "I didn't consider I might one day come to like your company."

He leaned back on the sofa and scrubbed his face with one hand. "That is grave, indeed."

"I know."

"How will we resolve it?" he asked, watching her, enjoying her playful distress. He took one of her dark curls with his forefinger and wound it around his knuckle, letting it bounce back and sway in the blue light.

"We are doomed, I think, to never see you on canvas. Not by my hand, anyway. Perhaps I could paint your horse instead, or your dog. Do you have a dog?"

"I had one, yes, a faithful lad called Barry, but he died two winters ago. I shall have to get another to give you something to paint."

Violet snorted, viewing him askance. "Maggie will want this for her book—the woman who painted dogs and never a man."

"Mr. Lavin will still get my fifty pounds, but I will be disappointed."

She shrugged, leaning toward his touch as he caressed another curl of her hair. "Mm. And I am sorry for that, but one must never break a promise to oneself; those are the most sacred of all."

"I agree. What if you made another promise to yourself? Something like: I shall only paint a man if he proves himself worthy of the honor."

The lady considered it for a long moment, bobbing side to

side. "That is a promise I would make myself, but I fear it would not solve our current dilemma."

Alasdair joined in with her sudden laughter, surprising her by leaning forward and taking her in his arms. Smoothly, he pulled her down to the back of the sofa until they were reclining, the cold of the windows a bracing shield against the tops of their heads. When he brought her face to his this time, she did not resist with any outbursts, and he was grateful for it. He kissed her, softly at first, searching for permission she gave with a swift little bite to his lip. He nipped her back and deepened the embrace, crushing her against his body until he felt the sweet pressure of her leg sliding over his, holding him to her.

Violet leaned back, pausing just to remove his spectacles and set them aside. One metal rim had left an impression on her cheek, and Alasdair tried to smooth it away with his thumb.

"I promise," she murmured, half against his lips as they returned greedily for more. "I promise I shall only paint a man worthy of me."

Whatever quip he might have returned with was forgotten in his urgency to have her. Grabbing her outer thighs, he pulled until she was completely on top of him, straddling his thighs. They both heard a tear in the fabric of her skirts, but neither of them paused to inspect the damage. He would buy her a hundred dresses, whatever her heart desired, when they were married. His hands sought the tempting curves of her legs and hips and waist, drawing the most irresistible sounds from her as he did so, his lips similarly seeking down her neck and along her collarbone. She seemed to like it best when he swept his nose into the hollow of her lightly perspiring throat; he smelled the touches of perfume rising from behind her ear—linden blossom, elderflower, primrose. Her fingernails clawed into his hair and down his neck, shoving his head into her until he was certain the scratch of his regrown whiskers would leave a passionate red trail.

He groaned at that thought, of marking her, having her, keeping her with him always, carrying her back to Clafton to be flung down on every obliging surface and ravished until they were both too exhausted to go on.

Someone stumbled against the door, whooping with laughter, their companions shushing them before they all went on their way. Violet froze above him, rigid.

"The doors, my God," she mumbled, tumbling off of his lap and grabbing her head with both hands. "Anyone could have seen us!"

Alasdair cleared his throat and sat up, fetching his spectacles and putting them back on before adjusting the neckline of her gown, restoring her modesty. "Forgive me, Violet. Hardly gallant, as you earlier accused me of being."

She stood on shaky legs, rotating slowly to face him. Her cheeks, throat, and the tops of her breasts were a heavenly shade of rosy pink. "You *are* gallant," she assured him, taking a step back to curtsy. "Shall we meet again in the afternoon, to begin your portrait?"

He stood and took her hand, pressing a firm kiss to the back of it as he bowed. "Worthy, then, Miss Arden?"

"Undeniably so."

21

Her passions are made of
nothing but the finest part of pure love.
Antony and Cleopatra—Act 1, Scene 2

The merrymakers of Pressmore woke to a blazing, sunny St. Stephen's Day; the light blasted off the newly fallen snow, bathing the world in white fire. Violet pulled the pillow over her head and ignored the stirring noises of the house and her sisters until Maggie hauled her out of bed by one foot, dragging her onto the carpet with a triumphant little wheeze.

"Good morning, sleepyhead. Did you go to bed in the punch bowl? I've never known you to doze this late." Maggie herself yawned and went to the window, ripping open the curtains as the final death blow to Violet's rest. Her sister turned Violet over onto her back, prodding with her toes, then stood over her, knuckles on hips. "Or did you fall asleep outside? What happened to your neck, dearest? It looks like you danced the night away with one of the spruce boughs."

Violet became horribly awake. She covered her neck with

both hands, feeling for herself the tiny bumps of irritation that had jumped up from Alasdair rubbing his face all over her.

Above her, Maggie's smile turned smug. "*Or* did you already begin your portrait sitting with the solicitous Mr. Kerr? Tsk, tsk, Violet, you really shouldn't try to paint someone in the dark."

"Leave me be," Violet moaned, turning back onto her stomach and shielding her face from the windows. More footsteps shuffled across the carpet. Winny.

"Look at her," Maggie said with a laugh. "She went to sleep in her party dress."

"And tore it," Winny added with a gasp.

"How did that happen, Miss Arden?" her older sister asked, prodding her with stockinged toes.

"I . . . tripped," Violet said into the carpet.

"Onto Mr. Kerr?"

Violet kicked randomly, hoping to land a blow on Maggie but merely succeeding in slamming her foot into the bedpost.

"Maggie, have mercy on her." Sweet Winny, always the mediator, came to her aid, gently draping a shawl over Violet's head until she could adjust to the bright light in the room. "There, there, dearest, we all had a late night."

"Some of us later than others," Maggie added from somewhere near the door. "I will go down to breakfast and fetch you a tonic, Violet, and see if that sets you to rights."

It did not. After the tonic, Violet changed out of her gown and into a nightdress, slept two more hours burrowed beneath the blankets away from the seeking, wretched sun, then emerged when she felt a shade less like death warmed over a candle. She fretted at the mirror for ages, rearranging her hair into different piles, and poked at her tired cheeks until she was forced to accept what the mirror reflected back. Summoning a servant, she requested that her easel and paints be moved to the north gallery and Mr. Kerr found and informed that she would meet him there shortly to begin their portrait sitting. She borrowed a frock from Ann, a day dress in a pale blue so faint it was almost white, gathered a warm shawl around her elbows, and went down to the gallery. Ann had almost forced the dress into Violet's possession several times, insisting it was perfect to bring out Violet's cornflower-blue eyes.

Pressmore was surprisingly vacant; Lane had apparently roused several guests for a stroll outside now that the weather had warmed and the sun was out; Winny and a few other ladies occupied the west drawing room to sew and chat; still others remained abed, having fallen afoul of their late-night dancing and too much mulled punch. Violet therefore encountered only a wandering soul here and there as she traveled the house, growing more and more nervous by the step. As she wound her way through the sitting room beside the Sapphire Library, she noticed Emilia standing at the door open onto the gallery. It was impossible to avoid her, though judging by the prim, tight expression on Emilia's face, it was not going to be a pleasant exchange.

"Good afternoon, Emilia," Violet greeted her, offering a questioning smile.

"I knew it" was all Emilia said, brushing by her and striding swiftly away.

Violet flinched and peered around the corner, finding Mr. Kerr waiting for her at the far end of the airy gallery hallway. What could she say to Emilia that would be comforting or fair? She didn't have the heart to point out that Freddie had, indirectly, helped Danforth start the fire at the Florizel. It was only his proximity to Mr. Kerr and the wealth of his family that insulated him from consequences. He was no prize. Besides, their circumstances were not the same; they did not love the same man, and Emilia ought to have the pick of any gentleman she wanted. That she had fallen in love with a wayward Merry-Andrew was not Violet's problem, but that didn't stop her from feeling choked with regret.

"Emilia!" she called out, deciding Mr. Kerr could wait a bit longer.

Her friend kept walking but slowed just enough to let Violet easily catch up.

"Please," said Violet, pressing her palms together. "I know this must seem strange—"

"What's strange is that you never had the courage to be honest with me," Emilia replied, sagging against the open doorway. "You are my friend, Violet; we are meant to keep secrets together, not from each other."

"I know," Violet said with a sigh. "This was a secret I was keeping even from myself. I didn't know until last night what my heart wanted."

"After how I was treated, how could your heart be so foolish?"

Violet shook her head, withdrawing. "It isn't that simple. Mr. Kerr isn't like his brother. You know it was more than the old family grudges—you with your beauty and your dowry and your connections, you could have anyone."

"Yes! And I wanted him!" she cried. "Now we are both women with stained honor, but at least you will have the man you desire." The lady's expression cooled until she looked no longer angry, but sad. "Love turns the twistiest path into a straight and narrow road, doesn't it? I worry for you, Violet, I worry that you will lose the love of your aunt only to discover Mr. Kerr is exactly like his brother."

"But would I lose you?"

Emilia turned away from her, drifting through the doorway. "I don't know, Violet. I don't know if we could ever be as we once were."

Violet stood alone in the empty drawing room for a long moment. It was her turn to think the feud ridiculous and overblown. All the advice she had given to Emilia, all the consolations and soothing words returned to haunt her. But she was sure of two things—her heart was not lying about her feelings for Alasdair, nor was he untrustworthy. He had left his own family home on Christmas to come to her; what further proof of his love could she require?

As Violet entered the golden patch of light Mr. Kerr had discovered at the far end of the gallery, he stifled a yawn, then he caught sight of her and bowed.

"You, too?" she asked, aware of the twin sleepless smudges beneath their eyes.

"Rest was fleeting and scarce," Alasdair admitted, ducking his head. "We can do this another day if you—"

"N-no! No, I would like to get started."

He smiled, and it tugged at the deepest part of her. His eyes were questioning and patient. "I would like that, too. There is no telling when your aunt will allow me back; perhaps we should take advantage of the snow." Gesturing to the wicker chair behind him and then the walls, he added, "How would you like me?"

Going to her easel, Violet coughed lightly into her fist, hiding her delighted smirk.

"You know what I meant," he called, suddenly appearing around the easel. It was like they were back in the library, smeared across each other on the sofa, his strong hands cupping the backs of her thighs, his lips searing across her throat . . . Violet looked down at the small table holding her porcelain dishes and paints. He glanced over his shoulder to verify that they were alone, then grazed the small of her back with his fingertips. "Though I might have phrased it better."

"You will please stand over there," Violet murmured, hoarse. "Or we will accomplish nothing at all."

Deliciously obstinate, he stayed long enough to lean down and brush his lips across the edge of her left ear. "Would you call last night nothing?"

"No," she replied, turning somewhat toward him, wishing she could meld completely into his side. There was a pronounced chill in the gallery, and his warmth would remain a temptation. "I would call it the happiest night of my life. Now, if you please, Mr. Kerr, go and pose for your portrait before my concentration evaporates altogether."

He wound his finger lightly through a ringlet dangling over her ear and let it spring away. "This place, being trapped here, it feels like a moment out of time; it makes me forget myself."

"Forget yourself?"

"There are . . . considerations to be had. Lady Edith would naturally prefer that I find someone who isn't related to the Richmonds," he said. Violet's heart began to sink. "And Freddie will see this as a slight, I'm sure, given your proximity to Miss Graddock."

"And when you leave here, those voices will be louder."

Alasdair flinched. "I am here now. That is what matters."

As he left her, Violet felt a pang of sadness; he was right that this chance for them to spend time together, nearly unchaperoned, unnoticed, blissfully alone, would melt as surely as the snow had begun to outside. Panic rose in her, a sense that she must squeeze and hold and burn into memory every minute of this day. If the snow did not start again or this warm upshot continued, he would be gone as soon as the next morning.

She busied herself with laying out her brushes and pigments how she liked them—the cake of red farthest from her, then yellow closer, then blue, and burnt sienna at the top of the next column. The orderliness somewhat calmed the chaos in her heart; she knew how to do this, and the routine of it would get her through.

"Shall I stand?" he asked, near the wall again and to the left of her easel.

"If you can tolerate it, yes," she said, closing one eye to study him and decide on her composition. "A little to your right, perfect! That fern is agreeable where it is, and the boughs behind your head will tell the story of this . . . rather unusual Christmas. Have you been painted before?"

"As a child, yes, with my family," he said, adopting a three-quarter profile stance, head comfortably neutral, one hand on his hip to flare out the waist of his coat. "Strange, I suppose, that loving art as I do, it never occurred to me to commission someone."

"And where shall this masterpiece hang in the magnificently refurbished Clafton Hall?" asked Violet, putting on a booming, serious voice that made his smile widen. He did have such a blazing smile when he was at ease, though it was terrible to paint teeth, and she would not consider attempting it.

"In the hall with the best light, right beside your self-portrait. After you finish it, I mean."

Violet nearly dropped the paper she was stretching over the easel board. "My . . . But it survived the rain that night? Why did you never tell me?"

"To savor your look of surprise now?" He shifted and shuffled his feet back and forth. "Do not ask me to explain it, Violet. My urge to take and keep it is as befuddling as what lies between us now."

"And what lies between us?" she asked, raising a brow. It was her turn to glance here and there to make certain they were still alone. This was a conversation for hushed whispers, not a wide-open gallery in a house full of nosy guests.

"You know," he said. Then, lowering his head, and softer, "You know."

"Our thoughts are one."

Alasdair nodded.

She smirked and disappeared behind the easel again. *Say it,* she pleaded with him silently. *Say it, and I will do the same.* But Alasdair had fallen silently into thought, staring out the window, across the piled, snowy fields to the very home they had just mentioned. Clafton loomed in the distance, a dark shadow, unfinished and waiting.

"How long until your home is restored?" she asked, stalling.

"A month, perhaps two," he replied. "The snow is a considerable setback, but progress will be swift after the thaw."

She looked between him and the blank canvas. "It's a formidable structure."

He raised a brow. "I'm glad you think so. The master builder and I endeavored to re-create it as faithfully as we could. The ruins it was originally built upon were largely untouched by the fire, so the castle foundation endures. We even repaired the tunnels that run underneath. Freddie and I played in them as children, which irritated our father. Local legend insists the lord who built the castle was a nervous lunatic, and his ghost is said to wander those tunnels still, though I never saw him. I don't know if they will ever serve for a daring escape, probably more useful as a wine cellar."

You had better start painting, little fool; before you know it, he will depart.

"And so too will the light," she muttered.

"Hm?"

"Nothing important," Violet assured him, picking up her pencil. Her mind went blank. That practice she had just decided to rely upon for comfort fled. All at once, she had never drawn or painted a day in her life, did not know which colors to mix to match the lightest hues of his skin, or which color to apply for a subtle shadow. The pressure to get it right—to recreate the full height and grandeur and weight of him, to properly commute observation to paper—was too much.

"Good lord," she murmured, loud enough for him to hear. "I'm petrified."

"Frightened? The woman who risked burning up to rescue a cat?"

"I . . . can't explain it," she said with a sigh. But she could. "I'm afraid. Afraid everyone will find out something about me when they see this, suddenly know what I feel when I look at you. It's . . . terribly exposing."

Alasdair watched her steadily, the light flashing off his spectacles obscuring his eyes. "And what is it that you see? What are you afraid they will know?"

That even this short distance between us is agonizing. That I would give anything to be back in the library, thrown over your lap, sealed to you in passion, with no obligation but to chase whatever fancy takes us.

Without answering, she tied on her smock and reached for the pencil again. Then, pulling in a deep breath, she aimed it toward the yawning stretch of blank canvas.

"Your hand is trembling."

Violet bit down on her lip, hesitated, closed her eyes. "I want to get it right."

"You will," Alasdair gently assured her. "No one sees me as you do."

They fell silent while Violet completed the drawing then set about mixing her paints. The wobbles never left, but she found greater confidence with every stroke. As the hours evaporated and the honeyed light faded, that fear she had given voice to came true—there was more than just Alasdair in the painting, but some of her, too, the affection she felt for him shining through in the heroic tilt of his head, in the noble space he occupied, imposing but not overpowering, in the special attention she had paid to capturing the slanted shadow his spectacles cast across his cheek.

Everyone will know I'm falling in love with him.

How could I possibly care?

"It isn't finished," she warned, putting her brushes down for the day and working the creaks out of her fingers. Alasdair drew his shoulders back, forcing an audible pop from his sternum as he unfroze from the pose he had held admirably for so long. "Lord, what if you hate it? Remember, there's far more to do. You don't even have both legs yet . . ."

"I won't look if you don't want me to."

"No, no, it's fine," she said, sighing, scrunching her eyes shut while she awaited the verdict. "Just please don't call it silly."

Alasdair approached the easel as if it were a feral, cornered beast. When at last he had the courage to behold it, she saw the breath catch in his chest. His eyes softened, and for an agonizing spell he was speechless.

"Is this truly how you see me?" he asked in a whisper.

"I . . . didn't want to include any birds or symbols," she said. "Just you as you are. There's no need for anything else when the subject is dear."

He was reaching for her again, closing the narrow gap between them, when someone loudly banged the gallery door open behind them. They flinched and jumped apart. It was a maidservant going room to room, announcing that dinner would soon be served.

Violet wiped her hands down her smock, smoothing the fabric against her stomach. She could sense him sliding behind the genteel wall of manners that ought to dictate his every thought and deed.

"We will have to arrange another sitting, Miss Arden. The piece already shows promise," he said, bowing and turning on his heel to walk toward the doors that had just been opened. Violet stayed in the dying embers of the sunset, watching the wetter areas of the canvas dry. The edges crisped, the colors settled into themselves, and the watery sheen dulled down to a satisfying matte. It was good, she thought, perhaps her best work yet, but something about it made Violet turn away in terror. She wondered if he sensed what she did, that time was slipping away from them. Once he left Pressmore, the world would impede, and she could do nothing but hope and pray that he held firm.

To what? There is no formal understanding between you, just kisses and implications.

She felt sick all through dinner. Alasdair must have noticed, for she caught him staring with concern after the soup was taken away. A jovial mood pervaded the table despite Violet's sulking, and with great excitement, Lane reported that the road conditions had improved markedly. Violet slumped lower in her chair.

Later, in bed, that sickness blossomed into a fever. Maggie and Winny swore she did not feel warm to the touch, but Violet had convinced herself of her grave illness. She shivered under the blankets, willing the sky to unleash another storm and hold them all hostage for a few more days. Preferably months. When sleep came, it did so like spilled ink bleeding across a page. In her nightmare, she wandered a barren field of waist-deep snow, following distant shouts, sometimes from Alasdair, sometimes from what she knew to be wolves.

She tore awake dripping with sweat.

Anything was better than the nightmare, so she wriggled under the warmest shawl she could find and left Winny and Maggie snoring peacefully. A house in winter, dressed in moonlight and haunted by unseen breathing bodies, was hardly better than a nightmare, but Violet refused to go back to bed. She wandered, her cold ankles sliding together for the wisps of warmth each time they rubbed. And she didn't know where to go but felt called to retrace her steps back to the gallery, now empty and dark as a tunnel straight to hell.

The portraits on the wall followed her with their flat and painted eyes. She found her easel, marking her progress by the slats of silver moonlight slicing lines across the marble floor. Her careful footsteps sounded like hard slaps to her own ears. Stopping in front of the painting she had begun that day, she sank into herself, seeing only the unfinished, cloudy areas, the flaws. Something moved in the shadows then drew near; something brushed her shoulder, and she stifled a scream, flying out of her skin.

"Softly," said a familiar voice. She turned and found herself drawn into an embrace so encompassing it instantly banished the chill. Alasdair. "What are you doing out of bed?"

"I couldn't sleep," she said, tucking her hands against the

hot plane of his body. His shirt was rumpled and undone, open far enough to reveal a broad swath of bare, furred chest. She had seen him naked standing at the water's edge, something from myth, Hector bathing in a crystal stream, and the remembrance of it made her swoon into his grasp.

Her reputation was already tarnished, and if he meant to be hers forever, truly forever, then what was the harm? They had always been headed toward this; from the moment he took her into his arms by that stream and held her to his wet body, they had been careening headlong to this deeper embrace. Violet expected him to resist her, to reject the openness of the gallery and the inherent danger, but instead he pulled her closer, locked her to his chest, and pressed her down against the wicker sofa along the wall. The paintings above them clattered with the force of it, and Violet felt all the air rush out of her. No resistance. No objections. He was hers at last, or they were each other's, or they were already one mingled thing.

The pale moonlight in the long corridor made his skin glow. This would come out in her painting of him, too, she knew, this powerful beauty that pulsed within him. She pushed Alasdair's shirt open, freeing more of him to her eyes and to her hands.

Touching him was confirmation. Running her hands up the firm, roped cords of his arms to his shoulders, digging her fingers into the sloped pyramids of muscle along his neck made him real, banished a deep fear. It was a fear she had prowled around but never named, never given it the power to linger in daylight, only to visit in the loneliness of a sleepless night. Alasdair's hands explored her back, and she wondered if he was experiencing the same cleansing—it was a scouring by fire, for she felt feverish all over, more so as he parted her legs and fit himself between them. She didn't know what it was to be touched like that, with curiosity and heated intent, as if his fingers—first skimming up her inner thighs and then seeking along the outer folds of her slicked sex—were ever searching. He found the core of her, and Violet's head fell limp against the wicker back of the sofa, her right leg kicking out uncontrollably from the sudden shock of sensation. His teeth worried along the ridge of her right collarbone, the warm gusts of his breath billowing into her nightdress, rhythmically bathing her breast in a heat she arched to meet each time.

The house had never been so silent or Violet so aware of her own noise. Not that she would, or could, stop any of it. His body pressing against her, smothering her into the couch, testing the limits of what weight she could support, was the proof. Banishment. Truth. *He needs me as much as I need him.* When she glanced down to look at Alasdair, she saw the glaze that must have been across her own eyes; she could go into a similar state when lost in her art, swept up in the consuming act of creation, emerging hours later hungry and wide-eyed and a little dazed. Violet closed her eyes again and submerged back into the moment, telling herself it didn't matter what gasps came out of her mouth or how stupid she might look—they were together in their need, bound by it, and how could she put an end to it?

She didn't want to come to her senses. She wanted *him.*

Alasdair's fingers pushed deeper into her, and Violet dug her nails into his shoulders, pressing her hips forward in passionate encouragement. There was no hesitation on his part to accept such an invitation, though he lifted his head, guiding her legs around his waist and holding them there securely while their lips met, their kiss deepened, and Violet felt the first exquisite pressure of his body meeting hers. That single touch jolted him backward, breaking the kiss. He let go of her, bracing his hands on either side of her against the sofa. Blinking, he shook his head as if jarring himself awake.

"Are you quite certain?" he asked, his voice rasped with desire.

She could feel the tension running through him, the restraint keeping him from doing what they both wanted. Violet reached for him, pushing the damp curls off his forehead. He leaned into her touch, growling softly, seemingly soothed and further spurred by the action.

"I was certain in the library," Violet assured him in a whisper. "I was certain when our hands met at the party. I have never been more certain of anything, Alasdair; for you make me feel so utterly myself."

"Violet," he said quietly, head cocked to the side. His smile might have lit up the night, though it would expose them both. He leaned toward her, holding her tightly, repositioning their bodies and returning steel to velvet; she hadn't expected such a profound ache, a feeling as if her entire body were turning inside out toward him. Her mind might have sparked first in desire, but now it was her body that craved and craved and would have satisfaction.

It wasn't effortless, she knew it wouldn't be—he was a large man in every respect—but she had never felt so flooded and eager, and the early difficult pressure gave way to pleasure, her body stretching to accommodate, learning him, and Violet was sure again of the sense that he was seeking something as surely as she was. They were getting close. He thrust into her once, twice, but it wasn't quite what Violet sought, for no matter how hard she squirmed or arched toward him, there was an awkward gap between their hips. Alasdair read between her frustrated huffs, leaning back, pulling her with him, and standing just long enough to rearrange them.

"Better?" he asked, smirking at her brief distress.

Their bodies had never parted, and as soon as they were settled again, Violet on her knees, straddling his waist, she knew he had addressed the problem. More of him. She needed more, not less, not to flop around beneath him like a fish.

"You know it is better," she replied, nuzzling into his cheek. His right arm pushed lightly against her waist, guiding him deeper inside until it stole her breath away. She stayed there for a moment, just soaking in the knowledge that someone could even *be* there.

"I know you are beautiful," he said, sifting his hand through her dark waves of hair, then combing them behind her shoulder. "And I know I want whatever you are about to do to me."

Violet laughed against his cheek. "Yet again, I find myself atop you, sir."

"It's a habit I hope you never break, Miss Arden."

Alasdair took hold of her hands, placing them on his broad chest; now she used that leverage to raise herself up and down, then back and forth, finding a rhythm and angle that let her chase the just-out-of-reach completion she sensed was nearing. His shifting expressions of concentration and wonder were enthralling, doubly so because she knew she caused them. Her hips moved of their own accord; she couldn't control herself, couldn't call back the storm. Alasdair embraced her, crushing her against his chest, kissing her, groaning into her mouth as his whole body bunched with strain. The end she had been chasing crashed down before she was ready—Violet cried out, tearing herself from their shared kiss, flinging her arms around his neck and shaking as she came undone. She had given herself pleasure before, but this was different—Alasdair was there inside of her, and inside of the relief with her, all of it headier. She could smell their sweat and passion mingling, taste the salt of his skin still on her palate, absorb the thunder of his heart as it slammed against his chest and transferred to hers.

She throbbed and she floated, and gradually, she touched her forehead to his, restful. A turbulence inside her quieted; how could she doubt his desire for her after that? His quivering little smile was precious, and she wondered if she looked just as wobbly and amazed.

Her lips parted, she needed to tell him about all the honest love welling up in her heart, but there was a muted yelp and a scuffling sound from down the corridor. Violet flattened herself against Alasdair and the sofa, terrified.

"Did you hear that?" she whispered, shivering.

Alasdair raised his head, listening. "We shouldn't stay here." Carefully, he helped Violet to her unsteady feet. She hugged herself, immediately cold without him. He leaned into her quickly and pressed a kiss to her forehead. "Go now," he said. "Before we are discovered; I couldn't bear to share this secret you with anyone."

The storm Violet so desperately wished for did not materialize, though the light tingle across her lips from where Alasdair had left his urgent kisses was strong consolation. As she went to dress, she did so slowly, gingerly, feeling as if she had been dragged several miles by a mule cart. The evidence of their lovemaking was pressed into her from every angle, the soreness sort of pleasant once she got used to it. And it made her smile privately to recall the sounds he had made; how wonderful it was to be the player of an instrument that powerful.

He was not at breakfast, and just as Violet worried, he was found afterward preparing to take his leave. Mrs. Richmond had made snide comments all through the morning, indicating that her patience had run out for hosting "the Kerr man." Violet and her sisters went out into the frosted sunshine to say goodbyes to those departing. She trailed behind Winny and Maggie, wishing to squeeze every last moment dry of its meaning before Alasdair was gone.

Standing by his horse, the groom nearby at attention, Alasdair wished her sisters a good morning and asked them to extend his gratitude to Mrs. Richmond, who had mysteriously made herself unavailable to him. Violet waited for her turn to speak to him, rosy to the ears with nervousness. How was it that the more she saw and felt of him, the harder conversation became?

"I trust you slept well," he said, rigid in a way that told her he was trying his best not to lean in too far or sidle too near.

Violet nodded, pressing her lips together. "You won't be away for long, will you? I will need at least one more sitting to complete your portrait."

Maggie and Winny, bless them, drifted away.

Alasdair gave her a forlorn smile and swung up into the saddle, dismissed the groom, and tipped his hat to her. He beckoned her closer, and Violet rested her hands on the saddle just beside his knee. "I promise to return for you, Violet, a promise I make to you and to myself, and one must never break a promise to oneself; those are the most sacred of all."

22

Him have I lost; thou hast both him and me.
He pays the whole, and yet am I not free.
Sonnet 134

Robert and Lillian's things were being loaded into the carriage when Alasdair charged up the drive to Sampson. There were plenty of staff to attend him as he leapt down from his horse and watched the last of their luggage being stowed away. It was a crisp, clear day and growing warmer, and the ride had left him breathing heavily. Those breaths curled away on white streamers, scattering as Robert and Lillian appeared from within the house.

"Leaving so soon?" he asked, not without surprise.

"That's hilarious. Truly. What sort of buffoon invites his friends for Christmas and then leaves them that very same day!" Robert's gaunt face burned with outrage as he bumped his chest against Alasdair's stomach.

"Dr. Fornwell said you mustn't get so upset, dear," Lillian begged at his side.

"Oh, to hell with Dr. Fornwell! My *upset* is very much deserved! I am a man insulted," Robert raged on. He had the good sense to lower his voice for the next bit of complaining. "By God! Where were you, man? How could you leave me with the two most depressing souls in England? How many sermons can a man stomach before he is sick with boredom? Take a guess! No, do not, for I will tell you the answer. Seventeen. Seventeen sermons. I came to heroically rescue you from that exact fate! I feel swindled, Alasdair, *swindled.* I can be very unpleasant when I feel swindled."

Alasdair rocked back on his heels. "Indeed. I feel confident that if you think long and hard, you will hit upon why I left that evening."

"Over . . . over . . . that woman?" Robert stammered, not even willing to use her name. "Incomprehensible. You have always been an odd one, Alasdair, but this is a degree of inscrutability I cannot unravel, and believe me, I have had ample time to do so while listening to seventeen sermons!"

"Thank you for your hospitality," Lillian added softly, trying to pry her husband away. "It was charming to meet your family."

"I do apologize for any confusion or discomfort you suffered, Mrs. Daly," said Alasdair.

"Apologizing to Lillian? Of all people! Apologize to *me*, you scoundrel, at once."

"No," said Alasdair, stepping away.

"Here!" Robert yanked a folded letter from his coat pocket and shoved it with both hands against Alasdair's chest. "This was the surprise I spoke of in my letter. I don't even feel like giving it to you now, but I am a gentleman. Do you remember what that's like? Being a gentleman?"

Alasdair stared down at the note, unblinking, recognizing

Julianna's handwriting. With two more exasperated huffs, Robert stormed into the carriage, bumping his head, swearing, then dropping down onto the bench hard enough to rock the whole apparatus. Lillian offered a helpless shrug and followed her husband.

He watched the carriage roll down the drive, realizing he had given little thought to what he would say and do once he was back at Sampson. There had been a vague urgency to remove himself from Pressmore, a rising awareness that his presence was no longer to be tolerated after the benefit had concluded. Standing alone in the cold, he found himself missing Violet already. Her scent was all over him, like a dream persisting into waking hours.

And he was awake now, painfully so.

Inside, Sampson was roaring with heat. The Yule log still burned dutifully away; he could hear the snapping and cracking from the front hall. Nobody in the family appeared to greet him, and he did not pretend to be disappointed. Instead, he dispensed with his gloves and hat and bounded up the stairs, knowing he could do with a wash and a shave.

With creeping guilt, he stood at the window of his bedchamber and slid out of his boots, stretching his toes and working a cramp out of his calf. He opened Julianna's letter and read it, surprised at the indifference it inspired. Something in him had shifted, a new stubbornness unfurling—he knew it, but how long until the world caught up?

My dear Mr. Kerr,

It will be Christmas when you receive this, and I will be thinking of you fondly. Do you remember last winter in Vienna, when we strolled the Innere Stadt and I took you to my favorite fountain? There was a man with the funniest little dog, and he fell right into the waters of the Donnerbrunnen chasing it away from the edge. Nobody at dinner understood why it was so ridiculous. That was the day with me you laughed the most; I keep that day close to my heart.

Perhaps it is folly to continue this. You were not yourself when we last met. I know the man who laughed at that dog and the fountain is still there somewhere. How do I reach him? What is the right thing to say? I think you loved me once, but you have never spoken freely about your feelings. You are a man enclosed. Still, it is not altogether unpleasant to be with a person so self-possessed. Something tells me to return to the memories of us, again and again. It's maddening. Come to see me in London; I will be there until 7 January.

If you do not come, I will consider you lost to me forever.

Yours still,

Julianna

Behind the indifference was a brief surge of sympathy. He would not go to her, but she should know that his heart belonged to another. It was strange to see himself described like a stranger—he was not a man enclosed, or rather, he had found a way to give himself over, it had simply required a like-minded soul.

Julianna was kind and clever; life had been easy for her. She was elegant, she moved elegantly, her manners were elegant. The refinement never seemed to restrain her, and it seemed like she could laugh at anything. Knowing that, he hoped she could laugh at the rejection he must send. Someone better suited would swoop in to love her, he was sure of it.

He tossed the letter onto his desk and remembered needing

a shave. Yet he was reluctant to wash Violet off of his skin. Well. The sooner he made their engagement real, the sooner he could have her again. He wanted to do it the proper way, nothing sloppy; she deserved to be treated as honorably as any woman of quality.

Still. What was the harm in reminding himself of her brash beauty? He knelt to retrieve the painting from beneath his bed; he found nothing but empty space, a faint impression in the dust where a rectangle had once been. Alarmed, Alasdair righted himself and dusted off his breeches, then caught sight of someone watching him from the open doorway. Lady Edith.

"You shouldn't take the stairs without assistance," Alasdair chided gently, moving toward her.

"It was worth the effort," she replied, gnarled and still beneath her fluttering cap of white lace. Her mouth trembled, pinched. "By now you have noticed its absence."

Heat rushed up from under his collar. "Where have you put Violet's painting?"

She flinched at his casual use of her given name. "It's gone. I told you to be rid of it, and you disobeyed me. I will tolerate many things, and I have, but not that. Not her. Not a Richmond."

"She is hardly a Richmond," he shot back, furious.

"The relation is enough!" Lady Edith cried. "Do not go searching for the painting. It is beyond your reach, we—I—have made certain of that."

"Danforth," he muttered. "I should have thrown him from this house long ago. He has worked every kind of sinister sortilege on your mind."

"There you are wrong," she said, nearly toppling over from the force of it. Alasdair hurried to her side, guiding his mother into his bedchamber and to a bountifully stuffed chair near the window. She accepted his help but seemed to withdraw at his touch. "Thank you. I will try to remember that kindness; you are unlikely to repeat it."

Alasdair watched her from across the room, leaning against the mantel. *Violet's painting ought to be here.*

"I will forgive quickly if you tell me what happened to that painting," he replied.

"No, no . . ." She waved him away, tossing her head in a strange, distracted way. "I know you left this house and went to Pressmore. There is an air of betrayal about you."

Alasdair didn't deny it.

"And it has quite broken me. You left, dearest. You left on Christmas. You had to know what it would mean, what it would do! There is only so much a woman can bear. There is only so much pain one can carry before the cracks appear, before all the secrets come spilling out!" Her voice rose to a near shriek. A pit widened in his stomach. Secrets? "You must understand; he was the only one who stayed. The only one who listened."

His hands curled into fists. "Danforth is at the jail; his trial will commence at Epiphany. Tell me you have not intervened on his behalf. Tell me that degenerate filth does not roam free."

Lady Edith pulled her head back, statue-still. "I maintain some influence. Our family is respected, and your father was well-liked."

Alasdair yanked off his spectacles and wiped at his eyes in frustration. "How dare you invoke Father in this—"

"I will invoke him whenever I please," she interrupted, suddenly calm. "Do you remember when John Danforth arrived at Clafton?"

"I suppose. It was not long before I left for Cambridge. He was well-spoken but unsure of himself, determined to impress.

We were similar in age, though he seemed much older somehow. Why? Am I to pity the criminal once I hear his sad story?"

"He is not merely a criminal, Alasdair," she replied, shrinking. "He is your brother."

Impossible. Deranged. He sliced his hand through the air as if he could ward off the revelation. They did resemble each other in certain ways. More than that, if he considered it, Danforth did favor his father from certain angles. "This cannot be true."

"I did not know the truth at first," she said, hardening again as she sat hunched in the chair. "I was made to welcome him to the parish, the new young vicar for the living! He was eager and devoted, a blessing." She coughed out a dark laugh and shook her head. "Here I should stop. Here I *could* stop. You will never regard me the same way again. But no, the secrets are out now, let them come. Clafton burned the night your father told me that the young clergyman I had grown so fond of was his blood, his son. He had gotten a serving girl from Pressmore with child. I don't remember her name, why would I? Creatures like her deserve to be forgotten."

The blood drained from his body. Sir Jonathan, the man he admired, worshipped, had foolishly let his passion lead him astray, then brought the fruit of that mistake into their home.

"My God," he breathed. "You must have been furious."

"He hid the child in London for a time, with a family of lamplighters," she continued. The shawl fell back from her, and she seemed lighter somehow, as if releasing the secret had pulled back a stifling veil. "That night, that horrible night, we quarreled; suddenly the flames were everywhere. I don't think I started it, but how could I be sure? I was just so angry, angry as I had never been before. He had made a mockery of the life we built together, made a mockery of the love I bore him. And I couldn't punish John. John hadn't asked to ruin everything, had he? He simply was, and when he learned that he had issued from sin, he was contrite. All his life, contrite, interested in nothing but this family and earning my forgiveness."

Alasdair pushed away from the mantel, sickness roiling in his gut. "Danforth knew?"

"Yes, he put the pieces together himself," said Lady Edith. "He devoted himself to me, the child of sin bringing me ever closer to God, and perhaps to one day finding my own forgiveness. I have often failed. The last time Mildred Richmond and I were in the same room, she laughed and asked me to keep your father away from her maids."

"Where is he now?" Alasdair asked, afraid.

"London, I would think," Lady Edith replied, smiling faintly at something across the room. "That's where I told him to go. I gave him a letter with our family seal. The letter instructs our solicitor to give him access to the storehouses." She sniffed and raised her shoulders. "To the art."

Alasdair spun and slammed his fist down on the mantel, upsetting a candlestick and several vases. "It has taken me years to collect those pieces! They were meant to fill Clafton, not to furnish this . . . this damned altar to your shame! Why must we suffer now for Father's mistake?"

Lady Edith retreated behind a blank mask. "We must all suffer together. That is the way of families."

"Is that what you told Cousin Muriel when she was sent away to be forgotten?"

A muscle fluttered under Lady Edith's left cheek. "I did not think you would remember her."

"How could I not, when I see now that I am so like her? Yet of the two of us, she is the less cowardly, refusing to comfort you all with a mask of civility, becoming the victim of your judgment and discomfort."

Alasdair refused to accept it. He hurried to his desk, ripping the paper in his panicked haste to begin a letter to Violet. His mind began to work quickly, spinning, spinning, spinning, churning toward the narrow margin for success he hoped existed. The most important thing was to stop Danforth, make sure Mr. Finny hadn't given him the keys to the kingdom in London, then return him to jail. Afterward, he could make the arrangements for his marriage to Violet. His eyes filled with hot tears; all those works of art he had loved and curated, all the beautiful things he had expected to show her . . .

"What are you doing?" Lady Edith asked from her cold throne.

"Fixing this," Alasdair hissed, scribbling furiously.

"He has had weeks to make his arrangements."

"Then I will undo them in a day if I must!" Alasdair shouted, throwing the pen across the room as he finished the letter. It was short and insane, but it would have to suffice. He called for his valet—there was still so much to do, and time was unavailingly short. An hour would come later, likely on the road to London, when he could make sense of everything his mother had said. For now there was only the urgency.

As he left his bedchamber behind, he paused in the doorway, sparing a single glance at Lady Edith. "When I return, that painting will be returned. Violet Arden will be my wife, and the name John Danforth will never be spoken in this house again."

23

Our doubts are traitors
And makes us lose the good we oft might win
By fearing to attempt.
Measure for Measure—Act 1, Scene 4

Miss Arden,

Regretfully, there is urgent business in London that requires my attention. I must ask for your patience until I return, though I do not know when that might be. Please forgive the haste and brevity of this note.

I remain yours,
A. Kerr

The letter trembled in Violet's grasp. She read it several times before the man who had brought it from Sampson Park was at the end of the drive. It felt like Alasdair had been there mere hours ago, yet in truth a day had passed since his departure. Perhaps thinking of him every moment made him seem closer.

Someone had come up silently behind her and read the note

over her shoulder. Emilia. Violet turned and dropped the letter down to her waist. She expected smugness, maybe, or anger, but Emilia's head drooped as she gestured to the note.

"Time passes and I become convinced you and Aunt Mildred were right," she said. What sparkle remained in her brown eyes was sharp with fury. "Well, you were until you disregarded your own advice. I told you to be careful."

"Mr. Kerr and his brother are nothing alike."

"Are they not?" Emilia huffed a bitter laugh. Her black hair was swept efficiently back from her forehead, contained by a thick red velvet ribbon, her knit gray shawl as protective and concealing as a chain-mail cowl. A foreboding cold slithered through Violet's stomach. "They make you fall in love with them, take your innocence and call it shared pleasure, then disappear to deceive the next lady."

"Take your—" Violet shivered. She lowered her voice carefully. "Was it you who saw us that night?"

The fury in Emilia's eyes dimmed somewhat. "No, that was Fanny, but she tells me and Ann everything. She won't tattle to anyone else; I warned her not to." She offered her hand, palm up. "Let us be friends again, Violet. We were led astray, but there's strength and comfort in solidarity."

Misery does love company, but I am not miserable yet.

Violet took the proffered hand. "I will always be your friend, Emilia, but I will wait to hear from Mr. Kerr again before seeking that kind of solidarity."

With her other hand, Emilia touched Violet's shoulder, and she held her chin high, that little sweep of her fingers containing the magnanimity and pity of a woman far beyond her years. "Oh, Violet. I wish it could be otherwise, but you will see. It will break my heart to watch it; that's well enough, I'm accustomed to heartbreak now."

A restless day became a week; a week became two. The words *I remain yours* had never bowed or bent so as they did when buttressing Violet's heavy hopes. Nervous to transport the painting and risk damaging it, Violet was allowed to stay at Pressmore, given her usual room, and she was subsequently watched with increasingly condoling eyes as Mr. Kerr did not return or send word. The boughs and wreaths came down on Twelfth Night, and Violet remained awake in bed until very late, reading the whole of the play by the same name.

Journeys end in lovers meeting, she read, cleaving to the phrase.

I remain yours.

In her passion for him, in her impatience, it was becoming harder and harder to believe.

"How hard is it to send one stupid letter?" she shrieked, throwing *Twelfth Night* across the room and going restlessly to put out the candles. Ann had assuaged her with various explanations. The roads were still terrible from the weather, first the snow and then the melting. Perhaps this business he had spoken of required his undivided attention. Maybe he *had* sent word, but the post had been stolen or otherwise destroyed. And Emilia watched it all with the silent, gloating impassivity of an oracle.

The second week of January, a letter arrived for Violet at Pressmore. The exaltation she felt was short-lived, for it was not from Alasdair, but from Cristabel Bilbury.

"At least *she* remembers I exist," Violet muttered, trying to be happy about receiving correspondence. She was surprised to find a few coins jangling in the flaps of the letter as she unfolded it. Ann and Emilia joined her to hear news from Cristabel, the ladies sitting in their usual sunny drawing room where they liked to peruse the post and eat their breakfast.

"Four shillings," Violet said, counting out the money. "She says she found buyers for some of the ink studies I made while my burns were healing."

"How marvelous!" Ann clapped with excitement. "Your first sale as an artist—Violet, you must be so proud! Though not as proud as I am. I knew it would be a stroke of genius to introduce you to Cristabel. And what a result we have achieved!"

"Marvelous, indeed," said Emilia, still resonating with that odd, knowing peace. "It's a sign, isn't it? A sign you can make your own way." Her voice darkened with significance. "Sweep aside that which doesn't gladden your heart."

"Ridiculous, she will never have to," Ann chided. "You have given up on Mr. Kerr too soon, Emilia, and I will not let the flame go out."

Violet sat dumbstruck, feeling the weight of the coins in her hand. It really was incredible.

"Beef," she murmured.

"What, darling?" Ann asked, having taken the letter for herself to read.

Violet didn't answer. That night, Ann organized a bonfire outside to celebrate Lohri, a festival her family had observed when they were still living in Lakhnau. The Ardens took advantage of the warm day and walked up to Pressmore to join in. Ann and Emilia sang songs about the folk hero Dulla Bhatti, and afterward, the bonfire dyeing her hair red and gold, Ann explained his story, how he had rescued girls from slave markets, and that two of those young ladies, Sundri and Mundri, were also part of the legend and the songs.

I remain yours.

Violet's attention climbed above the bonfire to Clafton on the hill, silhouetted there like a sentinel, solemn and empty as they both waited for its master.

I'm not the waiting kind; tomorrow I will get back to painting.

She was sick of feeling pathetic. Cristabel would have choice words for Violet if she knew the young lady was wasting her time pining over a man. He had said he would send word, he had said he would return, and Violet would simply have to believe him and content herself with that belief.

The next morning, she dressed warmly and walked back to Beadle Cottage, presenting her mother with the four shillings. There was a spark of hope in Mrs. Arden's eyes that made Violet's heart clench. Pride. She didn't say what she wanted to, that she had never been a lost cause, even if everyone feared she had become one.

"This is just the start," she promised her mother, asking if they could use it to buy beef. *There will be more than that, much more; Mr. Kerr will marry me, and our lives will change for the better.*

When Violet returned that afternoon to Pressmore, Ann and Lane were waiting to pounce on her. They descended on her almost as soon as she made herself known in the front hall. Ann's hands were crimson from being wrung out so persistently, and she couldn't meet Violet's eye. "Darling, something was delivered in the night. Perhaps it would be better if we just described it, and you did not have to see it yourself."

"I agree," Lane said stiffly. He was almost never this grave. "There's no reason for you to see it."

"See what?" Violet was still handing her bonnet and cloak off to a servant. "What are you talking about? The scarier you make it sound, the more I want to see it."

"I should've considered that," said Lane with a sigh. He gestured for Violet to follow them. They had sequestered the object in an upstairs library where Lane conducted most of his private business for the estate. Amidst bookcases, cabinets, and the odd globe sat a painting tipped against an obliging table leg. Someone had covered it with a cloth as if to make it a grand surprise, or, given how Ann and Lane were behaving, for modesty.

"Here, darling," said Ann, holding her hand while Lane strode forward and whisked the cloth off the painting.

It took Violet a moment to absorb what she was seeing. She recognized her self-portrait, the one she had left behind in the ruins of Clafton, the one Alasdair claimed to have taken and kept safe. But here it was, returned, yet defaced with a broad, garish smear of scarlet paint. Her eyes had been dug into with a blade, and the word *WHORE* was splashed across the piece in that horrible red paint.

"I don't understand," she murmured, frozen.

"Come away from it," Ann whispered, trying to guide Violet by the shoulders back to the door. But Violet wouldn't let her. She went on staring at it, at the painting that had, by her own measure, been one of the finer examples of her skill. It felt like a dream. Her hands and feet went numb.

Alasdair had been the one to have this last. It was like icy water splashing on her face. Violet tore herself out of Ann's grasp and rushed out into the hall.

"There's an explanation for this," Violet declared. "And I will have it."

Ann and Lane tried to stop her a polite number of times, Ann even verging on the hysterical. Carriages, at last, were offered. Violet declined. She couldn't do nothing, just sit and take this kind of insult. If she wasn't the waiting kind, then she wasn't a sit-and-take-it sort either.

"The air will do me good," she told them, and went on her way.

It was a two-mile walk to Sampson Park. Violet was hot

and frothing by the time she made it there. Every part of her revolted at the idea of actually going up to the door. Confrontation on her own behalf was torture; if her sisters or friends were threatened, she would hurl herself at the problem with abandon. But this was different. It was *her* pride on the line.

Her broken heart. The brief surge of pride from that morning was gone; the pain had stolen that, too.

She was met with the unblinking gaze of a deeply unimpressed footman. Violet squirmed in her shoes, which had become wet and clinging from the slushy terrain.

"Is Mr. Kerr at home?" she asked. "Could you tell him Miss Arden is here to see him?"

"Mr. Kerr is not currently receiving callers."

"I see."

"Would you like me to relay any specific message?"

Violet squished from side to side; it was suddenly difficult to breathe. The thick sludge of mucus running down the back of her throat was choking her. She had to sniffle constantly to keep a string of unsightly goop from running out of her nostrils. The footman was coaxed aside, and Violet was saved from answering. An older woman with a fluffy white lace cap and a burgundy-colored velvet shawl shuffled into view. The house behind her was dark and oppressively hot. The warmth called seductively to Violet, whose teeth had begun to chatter.

"You must be the Arden girl," said the woman, presumably Lady Edith. In that tone, the word *girl* sounded like an accusation.

With a curtsy, Violet forced herself to remember that she could one day be related to this person. First impressions mattered. *And here I am, teeth rattling, covered in my own snot, sweating a river beneath this woolen cloak.* "How do you do?"

"Poorly, child, very poorly. You have the pleasure of standing before Lady Edith Kerr, though of course you know that." She heaved a tremendous sigh rich with noble exasperation and withdrew a folded note from her shawl. Presenting it to Violet, she continued, "I know why you are here. My son will not see you. His feelings, I hope, have been made abundantly clear."

"He didn't ruin my painting like that," Violet replied, lifting her chin. "He wouldn't."

Lady Edith's left brow twitched. "Be as stubborn as you please; it will not change the truth."

"I *know* the truth."

"Do you?" Lady Edith gave a short, cold laugh. "This letter should cast aside any remaining hopes you might have. Read it now."

Violet trembled under her cloak, taking the letter and reading it with watery, freezing eyes.

My dear Mr. Kerr,

It will be Christmas when you receive this, and I will be thinking of you fondly. Do you remember last winter in Vienna, when we strolled the Innere Stadt and I took you to my favorite fountain? There was a man with the funniest little dog, and he fell right into the waters of the Donnerbrunnen chasing it away from the edge . . .

Sickness surged up her throat. Her vision blurred as the tears came. The woman's hand was unbelievably elegant, the penmanship of an angel. She finished reading. Julianna. Even her name was like delicate music.

"This could . . . this could mean anything," Violet murmured. *I know the truth.*

"You will note the date writ down there," said Lady Edith, satisfied. "What day is it today, child?"

"The thirteenth of January," Violet whispered.

"He was sure to be in London before the seventh," Lady Edith said with a smile. "Do not let it come as a great blow. I hear you have some skill with painting, and that should be a consolation. Hope is dangerous, child; hope will not serve where practicality is needed." She waited for Violet to return the letter. Violet almost dropped it, her mind moving so fast it used up what little vigor she had left. Lady Edith tilted her head to the side, regarding Violet as if she were an urchin that had come begging for twelvepence. "You are an Arden, in my mind as good as a Richmond, a comparison I make with no respect. Forget him, as he is certain to forget you."

The butler returned, and, without warning, the door was slammed in Violet's face.

It was dark by the time she neared Pressmore. Her feet felt like chunks of ice in her shoes, but she couldn't make herself move quickly. The realizations came in waves. He saw this Julianna person when he was in London buying Violet her gift of paints and the easel. With the one hand, he courted the refined Miss Julianna, and with the other, he spoiled the woman of no real reputation. The message was clear, as clear as the word slashed in red paint across her ruined self-portrait.

When she was greeted in the front hall, Ann felt her cheeks and exclaimed in fear. They needed to warm her up, and fast. Violet let them fuss; they bustled her here and there, but she was not aware of any of it.

She had lost him, and with that loss came the understanding that her aunts had been right—that a man like Mr. Kerr would never see Violet as an equal, or a viable companion.

Emilia watched her from the corner while Ann scooted Violet's feet right up to the fire. Something passed between the women then, an understanding, a bond. Violet stared into Emilia's eyes for a long time and let the truth come.

"Could someone please remove the painting from my easel in the gallery?" Violet asked, shocked at the roughness of her own voice. "Shove it in the fire, leave it in the snow, I care not. I just never want to lay eyes on it again."

24

If it will feed nothing else,
it will feed my revenge.
The Merchant of Venice—Act 3, Scene 1

"Upon my honor, sir, if I had known, if I had any idea—"

"I don't blame you, Finny, please, you really must stop apologizing." Alasdair interrupted the solicitor in his fourth self-flagellation of the day. He did appreciate Mr. Finny's contrition, but it wasn't necessary; the damage was done, and all they could do now was pick up the pieces. Even if Alasdair wanted to dismiss him, he couldn't; no one knew the family warehouse ledgers as well as Mr. Finny.

He would never forget the look of dawning horror on the other man's face as Alasdair explained the situation. Mr. Finny had gone so limp and pale, Alasdair worried he had accidentally killed the man. His journey from Sampson to London had been arduous and slow, the roads in dangerous condition, his mind in an even worse state. Just as he feared, Mr. Danforth had already come and gone, presenting Lady Edith's letter of permission to Mr. Finny, who unwittingly turned over the warehouse keys to a reprobate villain.

Alasdair had dragged himself to East London, preparing to find the warehouses utterly empty. Instead, he discovered they had been looted, certainly, but not liquidated. The theft was enough to concern him, of course; stranger still was determining what exactly Danforth had taken, why, and where it might have gone.

Presently, he was reviewing correspondence from the other members of the Tenebris Circle, who had been alerted to the theft. If any of the artworks wound up at strange auctions or at shady markets, his fellow Circle members would stumble across them first. Robert had not been asked, given the recent nastiness between them.

"Just tell me you've managed to cross-check the items from warehouse three," said Alasdair, straightening the pile of letters on his desk.

"Here is the list, sir," said Mr. Finny, pushing the ledger page toward Alasdair.

He tore himself away from Jasper's mind-numbingly boring letter (no, he had not noticed any of Alasdair's stolen artworks up for sale, but would he instead enjoy a blow-by-blow account of his most recent evening at White's? Who was wearing what and who spoke to whom?). Squinting at the list of thefts, Alasdair felt—for the third time in as many hours—his chest tighten with alarm.

"The Vernet, two studies by Bruegel, the Huys, the Bronzino . . ." He trailed off, frustrated. "Something is strange," he muttered, rubbing his forehead. "Well. All of it is strange, but I can't seem to grasp his method. Why not take it all? Why these pieces specifically?"

"Maybe there isn't any method," Mr. Finny suggested. He

poured them each a measure of brandy and went to stand at the window. "He's just a criminal, you mustn't try too hard to understand it."

Alasdair's townhouse in London was yet another storehouse, in a sense, the walls packed with any paintings he couldn't fit in the Wapping warehouses or Sampson. Most of the pieces were of little monetary value, most of them from his early days of collecting, when he could be moved by any amateur's sentimental scribble. A handful of the paintings had real charm. One sketch framed and hung above his office desk reminded him of the drawing Violet had shown him at Pressmore. That unease in his chest redoubled; God, he wanted to be with her again. He thought of the unfinished portrait languishing in the halls of Pressmore, a man incomplete, a man who would stay incomplete until artist and subject reunited.

I will never forget the pressure of your hand against mine, the kiss of our palms as the players gave voice to my feelings. "O, she doth teach the torches to burn bright." My world is in shadow without you, and I eagerly await the moment when you are with me again to quench the darkness. I will come to you soon and make final in matrimony what my lips against yours silently promised. He had written it to Violet just the day before, as well as a more complete explanation of his absence. Without giving too much detail, he assured her that this matter had nothing to do with her and was of a delicate familial nature. Miss Bilbury had done an extraordinary job refining Violet's painting skill, and the two of them had solved the mystery of his gift; perhaps their wits would help him now. But it would take time to track down Bilbury in the city, and Alasdair was afraid Danforth already had a worrying head start on whatever he planned to do next. There was an ironic poetry to needing Bilbury's expertise to catch the man who had run her out of Cray Arches . . .

"Wait." Alasdair snapped forward in his chair. "The other ledgers, from one and two, give them to me."

"Of course, but what have you discovered?"

"Irony. Poetry. Something Miss Arden said, the symbols . . ."

I didn't want to include any birds or symbols. Just you as you are. There's no need for anything else when the subject is dear.

Alasdair revisited the lists of stolen art from the other warehouses. He leapt to his feet, shuffling from ledger to ledger, reading the names of the artists as if they were a song, a litany. Closing his eyes, he conjured an empty wall and, bit by bit, filled it with the works by the listed painters. The other Tenebris Circle members hadn't noticed an influx of art on the market. Danforth wasn't selling the stuff, so what did he plan to do with it?

He paced in a circle, holding out his hands as if he could hang the pictures on his imagined wall. "Vernet has the *Vue du Port de Rochefort*, and Bruegel . . . that one with all the eyes. *Mad Meg!* Yes, *Mad Meg*. Then . . . then . . . *The Temptation of Saint Anthony*—*no*, yes!—and *Inferno*." Alasdair's eyes opened as he came to a stop. "Inferno. That's the method. All of them painted fires."

Yes, the other ledgers only added merit to his theory. Arcimboldo, Rubens, de Champaigne—all artists that featured fires prominently in their work. Bronzino in particular. There was a man with a tortured soul.

A man with a tortured soul.

Danforth.

"Mr. Finny, I'm afraid I must leave the rest of this in your capable hands," said Alasdair, that strangling sensation in his chest moving to encompass his throat. "I know now what Mr. Danforth intends to do with that art. I return to the country tonight, even this moment."

And now there must be hope, hope that I reach Clafton before it is too late.

25

Heat not a furnace for your foe so hot
That it do singe yourself.
Henry VIII—Act 1, Scene 1

Violet had spent the last half hour trying to get Emilia's eyes just right; an eye was not a flat object in the body, and Cristabel had always stressed that one must imagine the orb itself, the liquid within, and picture where the light would enter, how it would bounce within the luminous jelly, and where shadows would remain. The pupil, the light, the orb, the perfect touch of the white paper peeking through where the reflection ought to go. With the right crescent shape of color, the right balance of deep, deep brown, and finally that dash of white to represent the wetness shining across the eye, an artist could capture the personality and the soul.

"Your eyes have changed since last I painted you," said Violet, lost in the gaze she had rendered.

"This is a more sedate setting than the Clafton ruins," Emilia replied, seated primly on a velvet chaise near the drawing room fire. “But maybe I was wilder then. Maybe we were both too wild.”

“That is certain,” said Violet, trying not to sink into the carpet with despondency. Cristabel had taught her to see the world in colors and shapes, to see not what she wanted to, but what was. A pale hand posed beneath a leaf would gain a green reflection. An artist could discern the true colors in anything. Black was not a color on its own; black was mixed from red, yellow, and blue. The night of passion she had spent with Alasdair had been a dizzying wash of rich purples, of vermilion splashed across a black more red than blue. Now she was noticing gray everywhere—in her own eyes, in her nail beds, in the fading luster of her skin.

“You told me once to be patient, that my heart would mend.” Emilia shifted, working the stiffness out of her neck. “I didn’t want to believe you, but it’s true. Time is a balm like no other. Shall I say: I told you so?”

Violet’s head snapped up. “Is this better? For us both to be miserable?”

“You’re miserable, not me,” said Emilia, still. “My eyes are wide open. Are you ready for that solidarity now?”

“I’m sorry, Emilia, sorry for what we have both endured, but I refuse to believe this new peace of yours! How could I? How could I when I know now how much you must have been burning up night and day from the pain!” Violet slid to the floor, her eyes welling with tears. Emilia stood and came to her, kneeling.

“It’s what I’ve had to tell myself to go on,” Emilia whispered, embracing her.

“Do you love him?” Violet asked in a wail muffled by the other woman’s sleeve.

“I love who I thought he was, who I wish he was.”

Violet nodded, hearing a glimpse of what she now feared was her future. "And if he came to you now?"

"I would pummel him for abandoning me so easily, and I would not trust a word out of his faithless mouth." Emilia sat back, holding her at arm's length. "Well. At least we can be melancholy together."

"Yes, the hurt is lonely," Violet murmured. Melancholy was good for painting, Cristabel always told her. *You can always tell when a gleeful artist painted it, because it doesn't say a damned thing.*

That was encouraging for Violet, who was convinced she would never be happy again.

An hour later, Emilia required a break to stretch and take a turn about the house to get the pins and needles out of her feet. Violet undid her smock and hung it on the edge of the easel, then massaged the soreness out of her fingers and wrists. Whatever tension had settled between Emilia and Violet had eased, and Violet was at least glad for that. Ann and Lane had been preoccupied with the baby, whose frustrated screams punctuated the deep winter silence of the house. She wandered to the windows facing out onto the front drive; they were partially obscured by thick curtains within and draping, snaking vines without. Shifting one curtain edge aside, she watched Puck chasing a messenger toward the front door. It wasn't the postman, for he had no bell or satchel, but she recognized the outfit he wore from the butler she'd encountered at Sampson.

Her gaze sharpened on the folded note in his hand, and Violet was there to meet him at the front doors, outrunning even the Pressmore staff. She and the messenger were both breathless when they came face-to-face.

"This bloody goat!" he shrieked, thrusting the letter into her hands.

"I'll handle him," said Violet, laughing. "You get a head start."

She slipped out into the cold and held Puck by his belled leather collar while the man from Sampson shot back up the drive. The goat nosed against her, curious, trying to bite the message out of her grasp.

"If it's more disappointment, it's all yours," she told him. Violet let go of Puck, and he scampered off to chase the messenger, likely halfway back to Sampson. Back inside where it was warm, Violet raced up to her room to read the note in private. There was every possibility it would be more bad news, and she couldn't stand to crumple in the front hall. Everyone was treating her as if she were made out of glass, and she was tired of it. Violet's breath caught in her throat as she sat on the bed; she recognized Alasdair's handwriting immediately.

Dearest Violet,

I will never forget the pressure of your hand against mine, the kiss of our palms as the players gave voice to my feelings. "O, she doth teach the torches to burn bright." My world is in shadow without you, and I eagerly await you at Clafton Hall. Come there at dusk, and I will make final in matrimony what my lips against yours silently promised.

I remain yours,

A. Kerr

She couldn't hear her own thoughts over the mad pounding of her heart. Drumming, drumming, drumming. To her surprise, she was angry. How dare he! No word for almost a month, clandestine meetings with that Julianna woman, her painting destroyed and defaced—what sort of game was this? Something about the letter was so strange. Not a single mention of the painting, or her horrible conversation with Lady Edith . . . but perhaps he meant to address those things in person. Her mind warred with her heart; she pulled his last letter from the dressing table (yes, she had kept it, though hidden under cards and sketches and bits of ribbon, just on the small chance that he one day came to his senses and begged for forgiveness) and compared one to the other. The penmanship was identical, though she found it strange that he had changed his way of addressing her. Every time before, it had been "Miss Arden."

But perhaps that one day is here and he has come to his senses, and he means to plead and beg and crawl across the floor in weeping contrition.

In the end, it was the reappearance of "I remain yours" that did her in. How could she resist hearing his side of things? More than that, she deserved to express her own disappointment and heartache. He had sorely abused her trust, and he needed to know that, needed to suffer and hurt the way she suffered and hurt.

She made some excuse to Bloom about feeling overtired and not well enough for supper, then waited for the afternoon to wither away into darkness. Just before sunset, she crept down to the gallery, taking advantage of the staff preparing for dinner to slip out of Pressmore the back way, under the portico facing the fields and pond, picking her way across the patches of dry earth between piles of snow. When she was well clear of the house, she paused and looked toward Clafton; indeed, a single light shimmered there. A beacon. Violet jumped forward, startled, cursing as Puck butted into her backside with his stubby horns.

"Back, you horrible imp," she muttered, then stifled a shriek as he chomped down on her skirt and pulled. Violet wrenched herself the opposite way, a piece of blue fabric hanging from his mouth as if he had torn loose a piece of sky. "Enjoy that, I won't let it happen again!"

Puck wasn't finished with her, and Violet was forced to run away down the hillside toward the edge of the water, then follow it to the bridge at the edge of the forest. At last, Puck relented, trotting off with his prize piece of her skirt, his head held arrogantly high. As she took the narrow road north, her thoughts circled the major points she needed to make known to Alasdair. Mr. Kerr. She didn't owe him familiarity. She had rehearsed the speech at night while she tried and failed to sleep. As the days went by, it had taken on a more vicious tone.

In these fantasies she concocted, she always came off incredibly well; Mr. Kerr listened and hung his head and had no rebuttal for her masterful enumeration of his many crimes. Also, her hair looked perfect, her skin unblemished.

Violet had whittled the speech down to a dangerously fine point by the time she took the curved road leading through the trees and up to Clafton. The terrain was too muddy and unknowable to go overland. The building site was abandoned; several carts of materials stood off to the right side, the ground churned and rutted from all the activity. She picked up her skirts (ruined, thanks to Puck) and tiptoed around the divots and puddles until she reached the front entrance. That light she had seen from afar was a single torch lit and stuck into the ground near the front doors. The unfinished mansion was otherwise dark and empty.

One door, however, was ajar, a clear invitation.

Violet plucked up her flagging courage and went inside.

She warned herself to remember her speech—it would be annoyingly difficult to keep her wits about her when Alasdair appeared. *Mr. Kerr.* When Mr. Kerr appeared. She insisted upon hating him, though the thought of his face, his sweet little spectacles, the blade-sharp jut of his jaw, and his quizzical brow made that a challenge. Violet tried to get her bearings in the shadowy house, finding that a trail of candles had been left for her to follow. God, but that was romantic. No! She hated him, she told herself, carefully following the trail. She hated him, and she would not be undone by a wayward brown curl falling over his forehead just so, or—

Just don't let him see the back of your dress; he will want to know why a goat had your skirt for dinner.

"Hello?" she called, finding her way up a curved staircase. As Alasdair had mentioned, the lower level was composed of ancient stone, the repurposed, sturdy base of a Norman castle. Her voice echoed for an eternity. She reached the second floor of the house, following the flickering lights away from the landing and to the left. They disappeared into an open door that led to what she assumed might be a small bedroom.

"Hello?" she called again. "Mr. Kerr, are you here? This is all very strange . . ."

Violet dipped around into the bedroom, finding it better lit and anything but empty. She registered first the profusion of lanterns scattered across the floor, then six dirty barrels lined up against the far wall beneath the window. At the back of the room, someone had haphazardly piled up an immense amount of art. She drifted toward the piles of art, bending down to see them better. Her throat tightened; some of these, if real, were priceless. What were they doing here? She tenderly righted a Bruegel, fearing that even that slight touch would somehow destroy it. "Stranger and stranger," she whispered.

The door slammed with a bang behind her, and Violet startled to her feet. She spun to face whoever had come, finding it was not Mr. Kerr who had arrived but the vicar, Mr. Danforth.

"It is very strange," the vicar agreed. "Strange that you should be treated so poorly by my brother and agree to meet him anyway. But—pardon my saying so—a woman in your situation has few options." He was dressed not in his usual attire, but in a sweat-yellowed shirt, tattered coat, and brown breeches. Attired like this, he might have been any random porter or tradesman.

"Brother?" she asked. "Mr. Kerr is not your brother."

"Is he not?" Danforth smiled and withdrew a pistol from the back of his breeches. He gestured with it toward a chair beneath the windows, just beside the barrels. "He did try to tell you the truth."

Violet backed away from him, staring at the pistol, bumping into the chair with a tiny yelp. Carefully, she lowered herself down, feeling something there on the chair beneath her. She pulled it out, finding a letter. It was in many ways similar to the one she had received at Pressmore, with some significant differences. In it, Alasdair mentioned that there were several delicate family issues he needed to elaborate upon at their next meeting. *Like having a secret brother, perhaps?*

"My God," she whispered. "How did you get this?"

"Everyone trusts a vicar," Danforth said, shrugging, still aiming the weapon at her. He went and picked up one of the lit lanterns, then returned to the door. "I hope you understand, Miss Arden, that I personally have little against you. In fact, I love you in the way we should all be loved. You are one of God's children, even if you are incredibly naïve and irritating. My part in things would never have been discovered if you hadn't gotten involved."

Violet shifted, holding the letter to her stomach. "The barrels, the art . . . What do you intend to do, Mr. Danforth?"

"I think you know, Miss Arden, for you may be naïve and irritating, but you are also clever. Cleansing fire. Cleansing fire to set my family free. Lady Edith has suffered enough."

"Sir Jonathan had you out of wedlock."

"Yes."

"And the mother?"

"A maid at Pressmore."

All the air rushed out of her. The feud. Of course. That was a great deal more serious than hedge maze envy. Now that she looked closer at Danforth, she saw the thin resemblance to Alasdair and Freddie. They had the same brow, the same curl to their hair.

"You defaced my painting," she said, her jaw tightening.

"He did love you, intend to marry you," Danforth replied. "Small consolation, I know. Forgive me. *Forgive me.*"

"I will. I'll forgive you if you set this foolishness aside," Violet lied. "Please. Please don't do this."

"It's time. Lady Edith is not interested in pretending any longer, and I confess—I am tired, too." Mr. Danforth went to the barrels, running his hand across the lids. "I am Sir Jonathan's shame—all my life one man's shame and another woman's living reminder of it. Lady Edith did what she could for us both, but atonement comes in many forms. We tried, *I* tried. She took me in, doted on me; even that love was pain. Pain for us both. This way, the Kerrs will have a chance. Alasdair will marry Julianna, Freddie will take my place at the church, and Lady Edith will have peace. She has done everything for me, so now I must do everything for her, spare her the pain of her eldest son choosing to marry into the family that ruined her spirit."

Violet shook her head, refusing to accept what the vicar proposed.

"This," he said with a sigh, lowering his head and squeezing his eyes shut. "This is for her, to protect her from yet more pain. I always . . . I always removed whatever she didn't like, whatever made her suffer. She deserves better."

Danforth slid the lid on the nearest barrel to the floor, oil sloshing down his front as he did. She flinched as the lantern in his hand skimmed perilously close to it. By heaven, he was really going to do it, kill them both, destroy Clafton again. There had to be an answer. There had to be a way to stop him. *I'm part of this. My defects, the shame I brought to the family, my place in society and in this, all parts of this.*

Lady Edith. Lady Edith was his earthly savior.

"What a waste," she muttered. Then, softer, "You were *chosen*."

Danforth turned abruptly, the dark, slick curls over his forehead ruffling. He took a single step toward her. Violet eyed the lantern in his left hand for just an instant. It was conical glass, frosted with age and grease, open at the top. Pistol. Lantern. She had to manage both if she wanted to survive. If he just came a little closer . . .

"What did you say?"

Violet tossed her head. "Nothing. It isn't important. You're determined not to hear a word I say."

"*Chosen*," he repeated. "What do you mean, *chosen*?"

She gritted her teeth, glaring up at him. *Play the part well, Violet, remember all those summers spent embodying Titania, Ophelia, and your namesake, Viola.* "Alasdair had no intention of marrying me, just like Freddie would never have given himself to Emilia. We were just . . . just playthings to them. Distractions. With the Kerr name and fortune, they could have anyone; why would Alasdair choose me? He didn't. He was always going to pick Julianna in the end, someone demure, someone dainty and discriminating who knows what a Donnerbrunnen is and never raises her voice above the gentle whisper of a summer's breeze. I can delude myself all I like, but we both know I'm too ruined to love."

Danforth studied her, his eyes moving back and forth across her face nervously.

"Lady Edith *chose* you," Violet added quietly. Tears sprang to her eyes. This wasn't the speech she'd intended to give, but it drew upon her broken, aching heart all the same. She said the next part incoherently, forcing Danforth to step even closer. Violet saw her chance.

"And of course she would. Look at what you're prepared to do for her! You would spare her pain, something her sons never bothered to worry about. She chose you above even her own sons," she whispered, holding his gaze, milking every word. "Lady Edith chose *you*."

He wavered; he flinched. His shallow breaths skittered across her forehead. Violet straightened up, aimed a single puff of air at the candle in the lantern, blowing it out, and launched herself forward, screaming. She wrapped both hands around the hand holding the pistol and forced it up into the air. It fired, startling him, but Violet had prepared for the noise. She slammed him into the wall, then darted to the right, threw open the door, and spun into the hall. Darkness would be her friend. She retraced her steps, following the candles but kicking them as she went, hot wax flying in every direction as she tried to find the front door. When she did, she found it unreachable, two heavy barrels of oil in front of it. Bastard. While she'd fretted over the piled art, he had made certain she couldn't get free. She heard a hiss and a click, then the pistol fired again, the shot exploding against the barrel just by her hand. The hole left behind gushed and splattered.

Violet scrambled away from the door in the dark.

"No!" she heard him thunder. "Where are you? WHERE ARE YOU?"

The tunnels. The old medieval tunnels built by the mad

idiot who commissioned the castle. Would Danforth even know of their existence? She dropped low and felt along the wall until she reached an archway. Too fast. She plunged down the steps, falling, losing her balance and tumbling for the latter half. Her knees screamed in pain, ankles bruised, but she stayed on all fours and crawled down the next flight. She squinted into the unforgiving shadows but saw nothing. Still. She could feel the air getting colder, the smell of mossy, wormy soil rising around her. This was the passage, she just had to trust it.

Violet heard the fire burst to life behind and above her. Danforth had thrown one of the lanterns at the barrel in the front hall; she could hear the flames eating and spreading. One of the barrels came bouncing down the passage behind her. Violet covered her head as it slammed into the landing wall just feet behind her, feeling the debris of the shattering wood shower her. Danforth was using the light to find her, plunging into the fire itself as it roared down the passage. Violet got to her feet and ran, taking another curved, tight set of uneven stone stairs to a dirt tunnel that led straight onward. Somewhere outside, she heard raised voices that didn't belong to Danforth. People. Hope.

The pistol fired again, the bullet singing past her shoulder. He was coming. He was close. The cold was soon dispelled by the smoke and heat flooding the house. There was another sound, too, the sound she heard when the bullet found its destination—not the dull thud of stone or the clunk of wood, but a sound almost like a stifled cough. It had hit dirt. The floor raised, the passage now climbing steeply. Then, the most beautiful thing she had ever seen: the suggestion of different light beyond three narrow bars. A door. Violet threw herself toward it, searching with frantic fingers for the handle. She found it, turned, and pushed, but nothing happened. Locked.

"No!" Danforth's hands closed around her shoulders and yanked her back. They tumbled back down the slope together, tangled, kicking, shrieking. "Don't fight this," she heard him hiss in the darkness. "We are lost. The undesirables."

Violet lashed out at him with her foot, turned onto her stomach, and clawed her way back to the door. She pulled herself up by the handle, yanking until her fingernails broke and bled. A shape moved beyond the bars, obscuring the meager light. Then a jangle, a scrape of metal over metal, and a gasp of sobbing relief as the door swung toward her.

Danforth's fingers dug back into her waist just as freedom arrived. Violet swung her arms around the shape in front of her, holding tight. There was a *whoosh* and a wet *crunch*, and then Danforth's grip on her loosened, going slack. Strong hands gathered her up, guided her up the rest of the passage to the clean, crisp night air. Several lanterns circled around her, and she gazed up into Alasdair's face.

"I hoped, I hoped . . ." His voice, thick with panic, trailed off. He crushed her to his chest, pushing his nose into her neck and holding her. "All I could do was hope you remembered. You're safe, Violet, you're safe. By God, you will never leave my side again."

Men called to one another from the other side of the house, where they faced off against the fire. After an age, Violet peeled herself away from Alasdair. He cupped her face and whisked the tears from her cheeks with his thumbs. Breathing hard, she turned and stared at Danforth, clubbed over the head with a shovel and groaning for help. Alasdair scooped Violet into his grasp, carrying her away from the gruesome sight. She rested her head against his shoulder and huffed out a weary laugh. "Somehow I always end up back in your arms."

26

Hear my soul speak:
The very instant that I saw you did
My heart fly to your service.
The Tempest—Act 3, Scene 1

Alasdair closed the door, dampening the sound of his mother weeping and wailing downstairs.

"Danforth will live," he said, watching Violet stir and sit up in the bed. She had been moved to one of the guest chambers at Sampson to recover from her harrowing ordeal. "I suppose I'm grateful for it, he is my blood, but I will never forget what he put you through."

"The fire . . ."

"Clafton will endure." Gently smiling, he went to sit beside her, finding her hand under the blanket and squeezing. "Most of the damage was contained to the tunnels, and those ancient walls are strong. Though perhaps not as strong as you, my darling. You cannot know my regret for arriving too late."

"You were just in time," she assured him, nestled down into six well-earned and overstuffed pillows.

"No, I should have been here. I owe you an apology, and Freddie, too. I forced him to give up Miss Graddock. Perhaps it was for my mother, but I was the one to do it. And you were right, he could have been kinder. And now where am I? Exactly where he was, desperate to marry a Richmond, terrified of all that stands in the way. God, but I have been a consummate fool." Alasdair leaned forward and brushed the errant curls from her temples. "Danforth tried to take everything I cherish, Violet; he tried to take you from me. Without you, I have nothing—am nothing—please say all the madness these past weeks has not put you beyond my reach. Please say you can forgive me."

Her eyes widened. "I had a whole speech prepared, but I seem to have forgotten it."

"I'm certain you will remember when the shock wears down."

"Yes, and harangue you with it when you least expect." She grinned, rolling her head from side to side. Her smile dimmed, and she looked past him at the far wall. Beneath the blanket, her fingers curled against her palm, withdrawing. "Why didn't you tell me about Julianna?"

"I had no idea she still desired a life with me," Alasdair explained. "There was never a formal understanding between us. My friend Robert was intent on pushing us together, and I'm sure that his antics put certain ideas in her head. I regret that; Miss Holzer is a good woman, but she is not *my* woman."

Violet's gaze gradually shifted back to him, and she regarded him for a long, torturous spell, during which he felt sure she would say it was too much. And how could he blame her?

"How did you know to look for me?"

"Lane Richmond arrived at Sampson almost a moment

after I did; he was raving about a goat and torn fabric," he said. "They couldn't find you at Pressmore, and my mother must have come to her senses somewhat, for she blurted out that she witnessed Danforth moving things into Clafton. I don't think she wanted your death or his on her conscience."

"Brave," Violet muttered sarcastically.

"She has much to answer for," he agreed. "So much destruction and despair, and all because of secrets left to fester. My father, her, Danforth . . . if I had known any of it, our lives might have been very different. I would have embraced John as a brother if I knew he and my mother were being twisted by shame." He paused, a small smile growing across his face. "Speaking of real bravery, Lady Edith told me you came to the house. Confronted her."

Violet squeezed her eyes shut, groaning. "I thought I would stride up to Sampson and convince you to see sense. Completely tragic."

He pressed his thumb against the little bony groove beneath her lips. "No. Bold. And it is that boldness that makes me love you so. You don't know Lady Edith like I do. You might not have won her affection, but perhaps some respect. More, in fact, than she would be willing to admit."

"Then there's hope," she told him, hoarse. The smoke and the screaming had roughed her voice. Alasdair tried not to imagine whacking Danforth over the head again, because it had felt alarmingly satisfying. "We can bury this feud for good." She tugged his hand out from under the blanket and laid hers over his, palm to palm. "'For this alliance may so happy prove, to turn your households' rancor to pure love.'"

"Love," he repeated, leaning down to kiss her forehead, then her lips. "I should have told you the last time I had you in my arms, Violet. I love you, and no matter what our families think or say, I will have you as my wife, and ours will be the love that banishes this dark chapter with light."

Her arms looped around his neck, urging him to stay.

"Are you certain?" he asked, his voice thick with concern. "You must be exhausted . . ."

"Do not make your declarations of love and run away, sir!"

"No? Then I will stay, and seal them with a kiss." Alasdair unwound her arms from his neck, letting them drop to her sides just long enough for him to discard his waistcoat, boots, and the remainder of his clothing. He tried to slide right back under the blanket beside her, but Violet grinned lazily and held out her hand. Just knowing she wanted him was enough to make the blood roar in his ears. Even a moment away from her was deprivation. She had unfurled for him so beautifully that night at Pressmore, her eagerness drawing out his already fervent desire. Even so, it was new to be asked to stand naked in the daylight and be closely appraised by an artist's eye. Yet as her gaze roamed from his shoulders to his chest to his waist and the stirring evidence of his need for her, he could see the gradual darkening of her eyes. Her passion gathered in that look like a dangerous storm on the horizon, and before long she was reaching for him again. Her clever hands hooked around the backs of his thighs, and she pulled herself closer, nuzzling her nose into the groove over one hip before glancing upward and indulging in a long, slow kiss to the swelling tip of his arousal. A single flick of her tongue was enough to weaken his stance. He pushed her back onto the bed, reminding himself to be gentle, that she had just survived a harrowing scare, and still . . .

Still, she wanted him. Clamored for him. Violet lay across the pillows, observing, though even her keen eyes were hazy and unfocused. Alasdair leaned down, claiming her mouth with his, sucking her lower lip between his teeth, letting himself groan as loudly and deeply as he wanted. With her, he could be fully himself. It mattered not if she wanted him to stand nude by the window for the whole morning; he would do it, unflinching, trusting in the rare bond between them. He tore off her nightdress and cast it aside, sweeping a hand under her lower back and lifting her hips, his other hand dipping between her thighs to test the slick readiness he knew awaited him.

He had seen passion like this in paintings and statues, in shining white marble carved to be as sleek and lively as Violet beneath him. He had glimpsed, wonderingly, the way a sculptor could turn stone to flesh, rendering strong fingers digging into muscle that repelled and then gave, hands grasping thighs, breasts flattened over the plane of the chest in an urgent arch. And it had stirred him and made him think, longingly, of a time when he would plant his own fingers against a supple leg with that same desperation. Violet raised her legs and clasped them around his waist, and Alasdair felt the robust muscles there, the sinew of a woman who happily walked the hills of their homes, his palms running the length of her outer and inner thighs, memorizing them with touch.

And it was love, he thought, that made this simple act of worshipful touch feel so near to the ecstasy of standing before a masterpiece.

"There have been secrets between us," he whispered against her neck, smiling as she plucked the spectacles from his nose and dropped them onto the bedside cupboard. "But there was more—every kiss we shared, every glance was just such a declaration. Love. There has been love between us, Violet, though I should have given it voice." He lowered her back down to the bed and fit himself between her strong legs, growling his need into her clavicle as she blossomed for him and opened, and took him into her luxurious, wet heat.

"And I should have never left," he added, closing his eyes tightly. "I let the world pull me away. But you were right . . ." Alasdair tilted his head, hunched over her, sinking into her body as he found her gaze and held it. Her mouth dropped open in the most spurring way. "We were together in those fields all along. We are back now, or we never left."

He kissed her again, hungrily, his lips claiming her as steadily and greedily as his body. *Our thoughts are one, we are one.* Violet's fingers tangled in the hair on his nape and stayed there, the urging of her hips and the rising tide of her unwinding cries taking him to the crest of the wave that would soon plunge them back down. It couldn't last; they were too eager.

"Please," Violet begged him, and he knew for what.

"I want to stay," he grunted. "Stay like this—"

"There will be every day after," she promised him, giving a laugh that twisted into a gasp as he sank home once more. Her head fell back, loose, and Alasdair mastered himself long enough to feel her draw up tight before she bit down on her wrist, muffling her final cries of pleasure. Urgency and heat had been building inside of him, loosening at last, his body tensing before the unraveling, and Violet's obvious delight was too much; he followed her off the precipice, cleaving her to his chest as he shivered and spent. He rolled off of her quickly, gathering her to him as he went, sprawling her across the bellow of his chest while the world lost its blur, and the almost overwhelming relief dulled to something more bearable.

Violet was soon asleep on top of him, lulled to peace as he carded his fingers through her hair. Knowing she needed the rest, Alasdair carefully slid her back down among the blankets, righted the pillows, saw to her comfort, and gathered his clothing. He was clearheaded and straight-backed as he put on his spectacles and returned to his chambers, drew a bath, and dressed in clean garments. His gaze lingered on the place where Violet's self-portrait ought to be. As soon as he left his chambers, Freddie was there, waiting for him.

"So," Freddie snorted, crossing his arms. He looked terrible. Sleepless. Waxy. "One of us will marry a Richmond after all."

It was tempting to look away, but Alasdair forced himself not to. "Perhaps there should have been a longer conversation between you and I . . . I . . . Violet—Miss Arden—recounted to me some of the things Danforth said in his madness. All of it was for our mother. His devotion to her was his total undoing. We could have been better sons, but I will never say that his way was the right one. I thought myself better than him, but I put her feelings before yours. I hope you can forgive me, Freddie, I hope you will allow me the time to earn that forgiveness."

Freddie's eyes widened as he guffawed. "You? Apologizing to me? I never thought I would see the day! My God, but that feels incredible."

"Then—"

"No, no, I don't forgive you, not yet. I want to revel in this a while longer." Freddie shook his head and batted something invisible away. "You were not all wrong—I'm not good enough for Emilia. I don't know how to be. I don't . . . Without Father, without you, with Mother giving all of her attention to Danforth, I suppose I just thought I could live like nobody was looking, because nobody was."

"That will change, Freddie, I swear it. I'm here now, I'm looking."

"I'll hold you to that," he said, laughing shortly. He shrugged, making himself yet more rumpled, and wandered away toward his own bedchamber. "And you'll be pleased to hear I've decided against the clergy. It never suited me. No, I'll train to be a solicitor. Someone needs to help Finny protect art!" Alasdair stifled his groan. His brother dashed down the hallway. "And then, I shall win back Emilia!"

His amusement at Freddie's outburst was short-lived. The next conversation to be had would not be so brief or so genial, he knew. Lady Edith was not in her chair when Alasdair found her; instead, she was standing at the back window of the drawing room, staring out onto the wintry trees that reached with their bare and shrunken limbs toward the house.

"There is no need to look maudlin," she told him, not turning away from the cold landscape. She was studying his reflection in the glass. "I know you will marry her. You are the man of this house, and I will be powerless to stop it."

"Violet is not responsible for what my father did, nor should she be blamed for the unkind reactions of her aunt," said Alasdair. Compassion crept into his voice, for her despair was palpable. "Whatever your opinion of her, she discovered Freddie's unwitting involvement in the fires. If she hadn't, Freddie might be the one condemned for the crimes. Would that be better?"

Lady Edith shrank, her forehead skimming the window. The chill of the glass shocked her, and she pushed away from the wall. "John went too far."

Alasdair waited for more, but she remained silent. "Tomorrow, I will order all of the portraits of Sir Jonathan removed to London. If any are to make the transition to Clafton, that discussion can be had later. I will inform Gordon to draw up plans for a small chapel to be erected on the grounds; perhaps you can give him your thoughts on its design, too. Miss Arden has suffered terribly, and our wedding will be delayed until she feels at her best."

Lady Edith turned around at the mention of the chapel, and he was somewhat gratified to see that his mother did not react viscerally to the mention of his wedding to Violet. It would have to be enough.

"I will try, Mother. It will not be easy, but I hope you will join me in the trying."

He returned to Violet and found her drowsy but awake. Supper would be brought to her; she would have whatever she needed. Predictably, the next day, well-wishers from Pressmore and Beadle Cottage swarmed Sampson. They came tentatively, perched a respectable distance up the drive as if terrified to trespass on forbidden ground; even Emilia was there, which struck him as a good portent. Margaret and Winny Arden charged past him with nary a word, though the threat in Margaret's eyes promised retribution if a single precious hair was out of place on Violet's head. They stayed to fuss over their sister for days, refusing to leave, though he dared not suggest otherwise. Margaret in particular warmed to him when he promised, at length and with all due humility, that he would never let harm come to Violet again. The threat in her eyes lingered, as was expected from a loving older sister.

Mrs. Mildred Richmond was not among the well-wishers, though she had sent a very pleasant card expressing her concern for what had transpired and extending a chilly yet polite invitation for the Kerrs to dine at Pressmore the following week. Said card was presented to him as if he were being handed a holy relic.

Violet was stunned into five entire minutes of silence when given the card, so perhaps it really was a miracle of a kind. Once Violet recovered from her surprise, she flung her arms around Alasdair and kissed him and pronounced that they had done the impossible.

EPILOGUE

A heart to love, and in that heart
Courage to make 's love known.
Macbeth—Act 2, Scene 3

Clafton Hall was properly repaired, furnished, and finished by May. Violet Arden was never very good at patience, however, and her wedding quite preceded Clafton's hosting debut. No, she could not wait to marry her Mr. Kerr, who agreed that a swift wedding was the best idea. It was a happy event made better by the profusion of friends who arrived to fête the couple. Violet was particularly moved to discover that Cristabel Bilbury had made the journey from London, bringing with her a surprise that fittingly blessed the union—she revealed to the couple a wrapped frame, and beneath the covering lay Violet's self-portrait, vividly restored. Ann, of course, had conspired to ship the thing to London and have Cristabel rectify the defacement.

A still greater revelation followed, as Ann and Emilia cleverly presented the portrait of Alasdair that Violet had started and abandoned. Though she had bade them to *shove it in the fire, leave it in the snow,* they had safely hidden it in a dark corner of the house. When finished, it would hang side by side with Violet's, positioned just over a small, charming table with a floral design.

The wedding took place on a bracingly cold morning at the small church in Cray Arches. Aunt Mildred held her nose long enough to attend, though Lady Edith swore she would not deign to appear. To everyone's sustained surprise, Lady Edith did march through the wedding breakfast at Sampson Park, tilt her chin low enough to glimpse Violet, and state, "That is a pleasing shade of blue," in regard to the bride's gown. For the moment, it was enough.

A thrill of hope went through Violet, and she squeezed Alasdair's hand beneath the table. Perhaps one day, Lady Edith would stay in the room long enough to see how glowingly happy the young lady made her son. Freddie Kerr announced to anyone who would listen (and those who expressed total disinterest) that he was going to be a solicitor. Mr. Finny, who had come from London, coolly schooled his expression into one of feigned acceptance. He would be seeing much more of Freddie. These professional declarations were not missed by Emilia Graddock, who peered at Freddie occasionally, though any who saw these looks would assume they indicated no more than passing curiosity. Emilia had devoted herself to her sister's charitable society, and while Ann graciously endured the trials of motherhood, Emilia took charge. It was not clear whether she had sworn off love for good, though Maggie confided that Emilia had begged for her next novel to be a romance. The Arden sisters took this as an encouraging sign.

Many at the wedding whispered doubts that Violet Kerr

would continue painting beyond what suited a rich hobbyist. Yet they would all be proved wrong, for Violet had made a promise to Cristabel that she would never turn away from her art, and Alasdair had fallen so madly in love with the woman and the work that he encouraged her to continue. She did, of course, and while she was not being accepted into the Royal Watercolour Society anytime soon, commissions soon poured in from the members of the Tenebris Circle. Perhaps Robert and Lillian Daly refused to lower themselves to dine with Violet, but there were other men with other wives, wives who were hungry for clever conversation and good company.

Violet set aside all of her earnings to pay for their beef and would not hear Alasdair's protestations about it.

When it was time for the family to relocate to Clafton, Alasdair took exactly one portrait of Sir Jonathan from their warehouse and kept it in his private study. By and by, his fury toward the man settled into something more like disappointment. He would live longer than his father and turn around toward the past to cast his gaze disapprovingly on the man's mistakes. Alasdair did not pretend to understand the man but loved him for the fine lessons he had handed down. Some he took, some he left behind.

John Danforth was lost to the prisons, and Lady Edith never spoke of him again.

Clafton was the sort of great house that required dogs, and so Violet chose several from a litter. She painted them frequently, often joking that she had made good on her promise to paint only dogs and never men. This rule was swiftly broken, as she could not resist painting Alasdair, the man, *with* his hounds. And the goat, Puck—for how could we forget him—at last met his match in these very hounds. Often set loose upon the grounds of Pressmore, the pups could be seen giving Puck a merry chase, and when, at last, they were all exhausted, they made a bed of his round, obliging belly.

Their little joke of men and hounds indeed found its way into one of Maggie's books, and Violet provided a small painting that fit the story. Bridger Darrow had it made into a woodcutting for the frontispiece of Maggie's novel, copies of which landed in the Sapphire Library—a place of destiny for both sisters—and others were placed into the new library at Alasdair's vision of Clafton, and it was, at last, enough.

ACKNOWLEDGMENTS

I'd like to extend heartfelt thanks to my agent, Kate McKean, for her continued support and hard work. I'm also grateful to Alicia and Jean, and the whole team at Dell, for bringing this book to life with their feedback, passion, and creativity. Patrick, Tawny, Trevor—thank you for taking an early look at this manuscript and providing feedback, suggestions, and moral support.

I also want to acknowledge the Metropolitan Museum of Art's resources on watercolor painting, the work of Jack Hrkach, PhD, on the history of theater, the Historic UK online magazine for their information on Georgian Christmas traditions, and Liza Picard's book *Dr. Johnson's London* for providing insights into the cost of living at the time.

To my readers, none of this would be possible without you. If you picked up a copy, borrowed it from the library, told a friend, or made a post, it mattered, and I'm sincerely grateful.

ABOUT THE AUTHOR

MADELEINE ROUX is the *New York Times* and *USA Today* bestselling author of the *Asylum* series, which has sold more than a million copies worldwide. She is also the author of the *House of Furies* series and several titles for adults, including *Salvaged* and *Reclaimed.* She has made contributions to Star Wars, World of Warcraft, and Dungeons & Dragons. Roux lives in Seattle, Washington, with her partner and beloved pups.

madeleine-roux.com
Instagram: @authoroux
Bluesky: @authoroux.bsky.social